HARPER FALLS BOOK ONE

If I Loved You

MARY J. WILLIAMS

Dedication

To Noan Brook Williams,
For all your love and support.
I couldn't have done it without you.
Thanks, Mom.

More Books by
Mary J. Williams

Harper Falls Series

If I Loved You
If Tomorrow Never Comes
If You Only Knew

Contents

Prologue

IT WAS SOMETHING out of a fairy tale.

Thousands of flickering lights dazzled her senses, almost as much as the tall, wickedly handsome man who so expertly danced her onto the shadowed balcony. The music that filtered from the nearby ballroom only added to the already magical atmosphere.

Women dreamed their whole lives of a moment like this — a prelude to a happily-ever-after ending. Ever so briefly, she let herself drift into that fantasy as if she was one of those women. For a moment, she let herself pretend that her childhood had been filled with the kind of whimsicality that allowed those fantasies to carry over into adulthood.

But no, she wasn't a romantic, hopeless or otherwise. She didn't want a prince to sweep her into his arms and carry her away on his faithful steed. She was more than capable of rescuing herself. She preferred it that way.

The stars were in the sky, not in her eyes.

"I'm glad you asked me to dance," her partner whispered, pulling her closer.

Suddenly, she was nervous. The champagne she downed earlier had completely worn off. No more floating on a cloud of false courage. If she was going to do this, she was going to have to do it on her own.

"Jack," she said. Damn, it was hard to sound seductive when your voice squeaked. "Jack." That was better, lower, and slightly husky. She'd read somewhere that guys liked husky voices.

"Rose."

"Yes?"

"Nothing, I just thought we were saying each other's names." He put his lips next to her ear. "I like the way you say mine."

"Jack." Good Lord, she had to stop repeating his name. "I need a favor, Jack. A big one." Or should she say, she hoped he *had* a big one. Rose groaned to herself. At least she hadn't said that aloud.

"I'll help if I can."

"You're the only one who *can* help." She took another deep breath. "I need you to take me home and screw my brains out."

Chapter One

ONE WEEK EARLIER

"IT NEEDS TO be dirtier."

"If I had a dollar for every time I heard that, I could retire."

"If I recall, you made your many, many dollars being very, very dirty."

Rose laughed. She could just imagine how that sentence would sound if someone heard it out of context. She knew what Frank meant, and it still sounded much more salacious than it really was.

"Grind is sensual, not dirty," she reminded her long-time friend and writing partner.

Now, Frank Weller was over three hundred miles away in his New York apartment. Modern technology allowed them to work together without traveling or changing out of their pajamas. Well, she was still in her PJs. It was impossible for her to tell what Frank was wearing. For all she knew, he was naked, as his chest was bare. Frank being Frank, he was in all likelihood sitting around without any clothes on. Not that she was complaining; it was a spectacular chest. He might as well show it off. However, the point wasn't to incite any sexual interest. Frank loved to tease. It was just like him to appear to be naked, hoping to get her to acknowledge his state of undress. They had known each other too long for her not to be onto his tricks. Frank provoked; Rose ignored. A dynamic that had worked to great success, both personally *and* professionally.

"Grind," he reminded her, "is raunchy and filthy, and *that's* why it is wildly successful. Don't try to rewrite history at this late date."

Rose considered mounting a token argument, but she knew he was right. Grind was a song that never should have seen the light of day. She'd considered it the therapeutic equivalent of writing in a diary. Fate and a persuasive producer had had other plans. It had turned out to be a multi-platinum, award-winning phenomenon. To this day, everyone asked who or what had inspired her to write a song that was so raw — so primal. In the early days of her career, Rose had dated some very high profile singers and producers. They all assumed one of them had to be the inspiration. Rose had become an expert at evading the questions. She usually just shrugged and gave what she hoped was a mysterious smile. Only her two best friends knew the truth, and Rose meant to keep it that way

"The backstory or lack thereof, is part of why that song has never fallen off the Billboard charts. Two years later and it's still a huge seller."

"I'd *like* to think it has something to do with it being a damn good song," Rose grumbled good-naturedly. She considered all her songs to be her babies and, like any mother, she could be a bit defensive if she thought they were being insulted.

"Absolutely," Frank assured her. "But the mystery never hurts." He leaned closer to the screen. "Now, let's talk about getting you back to civilization. You're too beautiful to let yourself waste away in that backwoods oblivion."

"Are you saying the backwoods are okay for ugly people?"

"Yes," Frank answered with his usual bold honesty. "Oh, don't give me that look. You are super model hot, not that you ever take advantage of it. You could have any man you wanted, but for some unfathomable reason, you always pick fizzle over sizzle."

"I'm not going to have this discussion with you for the umpteenth time, Frank." Rose had her reasons for avoiding high gloss, high maintenance men — reasons that were nobody's business but her own. "And my living in Harper Falls has nothing to do with my looks or who I date."

"You're right. I want you here in New York, down the hall like you used to be because I miss you."

"I miss you too," she admitted, then added slyly, "You could always move here."

Frank's eyes widened in horror. "The people in that little town of yours wouldn't know what to do with me. And I can't imagine what I would do with them."

"You'd be surprised what goes on in Harper Falls, Frank. Small town intrigue tops big city drama every time."

"You mean everyone knows their neighbor's business." Frank shuddered. "I don't even know my neighbor's *name*. I certainly don't need to know what they're getting up to behind closed doors. And I like it that way."

"That's because you're afraid they'll start asking what *you're* getting up to."

"Damn straight." Frank wiggled his eyebrows suggestively. "Or in the case of me and Len, not so straight."

"Two hot guys? You could sell tickets."

"Honey, it would be standing room only. I like to keep my man to myself. And I like the anonymity of the big city."

"Well, I like knowing my neighbors," Rose argued. She wasn't about to admit how right Frank was about small town grapevines. As annoying as it could be, it was also part of the charm. Mostly.

"But are your neighbors worth knowing?"

"Don't be such a snob, Frank."

Many of the people she dealt with in the music business tended to look down their noses at her small town lifestyle. There was no point in arguing, so she ignored them. Since Frank was a good friend *and* a colleague, she wanted him to understand that she didn't find his insults amusing.

"You're right, love," Frank said, genuinely contrite. "Sometimes I can be a real pain in the ass. I appreciate you calling me out on it."

"I know you don't mean any harm, Frank," Rose assured him. "But living here makes me happy. When the need arises, I fly to New York or Los Angeles. Harper Falls is my home. It's where I'm the most creative. That's why I came back, and that's why I stay."

"And I'm selfish enough to keep trying to get you to move back to New York. It's been two years. Haven't you gotten your yen for nature out of your system yet? And where do you go when you want sushi at three in the morning?"

"Sushi is your thing, Frank. I like scrambled eggs. And before you ask, in spite of my lack of culinary skills, scrambled eggs I can make myself." Sometimes they had the texture of rubber, but she was getting better. "Besides, eating anything at three o'clock in the morning is a bit out of favor around here."

"God, don't tell me you've become *Farmer Rose*, all early to bed and early to rise."

Frank was so appalled at the thought that Rose decided to cut him some slack. "I'll admit I'm still more likely to *stay* up for the sunrise than *get* up for it. But clubbing and all night parties are pretty rare."

"Don't you miss it?"

Rose shrugged. "I took advantage of the big city perks when I was there. Now I'm happy with a quieter day lifestyle."

Rose had lived in New York after college. Writing music was her passion, and she had been lucky enough to get some early success. There were so many more people to meet and work with, so many opportunities, that she thought staying there was her best option. When she started to grow tired of the constant hustle and bustle, her thoughts turned to the first home she'd ever known. Harper Falls was where she learned about friendship and the stability that came with having people you could count on no matter what. New York was fun and exciting — an endless party. Harper Falls was more grounded; it provided her with a sense of community. As for career opportunities? She found that other songwriters and artists sought her out no matter where she lived.

Talent and a string of hit songs made her location a minor inconvenience.

"Sorry, Frank. I'm not changing my mind. Besides," she reminded him, "I'll be in New York in a few weeks to meet with Sam Laughton. I promise we'll paint the town."

"So you're going to do the movie?"

Rose shrugged. "Nothing is settled yet. Either way, he wants to meet. It's a lot of work under the best of circumstances, but with the last songwriter not working out, I'd be rushed to finish on time. I don't know if I'm up for it."

"You are perfect for this project and Sam Laughton knows it. That last hack should never have been hired. Besides," he added with a knowing look, "He has been trying to work with you for years. Though, it isn't just your music he's interested in."

"Not my type," Rose dismissed the thought with a wave of her hand.

"Honey," Frank snorted in disbelief. "He's everybody's type. Women, men. We all either lust after him or want to be him. In some cases, both."

Rose didn't need to ask Frank which category he fell into. She'd never known him to envy anyone, professionally or otherwise. Since Frank was unapologetically gay — it had to be lust.

"I didn't know you had a thing for Sam. What does Len think about that?"

"Believe me, Len has nothing to be jealous of," Frank assured her. Len was the love of Frank's life and had been even before he and Rose had met. Rose thought of them as one of the few exceptions that proved the rule when it came to happy romantic relationships. "But we can both look and admire from time to time. In Sam Laughton's case, there is plenty to admire. I think yummy says it all."

"Again," she reiterated, "not my type."

"So, branch out, love. You may think you like middle of the road, cookie-cutter bland. I say a trip to the wild side is just what the doctor ordered."

"Nope." She liked mild-mannered, easy to figure out men. She had seen what high drama relationships did to a person. She enjoyed the company of men, but she would never make one the focus of her life. "The men I date are perfect for me. I don't see any reason to change."

"I read once that change is good for the soul."

"I think that's chicken soup."

"Oh, very clever," Frank said sarcastically. "Though, those books are pretty good. Len got into them a few years ago, and I was surprised by how much they moved me. You know, Rose—"

"And speaking of change," Rose said, bringing the conversation back to where it started. Frank was easily distracted, and she wasn't in the mood for any of his rambling philosophies. "I have a date tonight and I need to start getting ready."

"Let me guess. Average height, average build, average everything. Where do you find this string of unremarkable men?

"There's a website. Only the mediocre need apply." Rose said with a straight face. "Goodbye, Frank."

"Fine," Frank finally conceded. "Since we've almost finished the song, we can wrap it up next week. Oh, and call me with the details on your date. I've been having trouble sleeping lately, and that should work better than a couple of Ambien."

"*Goodbye*, Frank."

Rose closed the laptop with a decisive snap. It didn't help that Frank was right. Her dates were routine, even boring. The men she went out with were nice. So why was that a bad thing? Since when was nice a crime? Moreover, who was to say her dates were the problem? Maybe she was the boring one. Maybe the next day, they regaled their friends with stories about how they could barely stay awake through the appetizer.

Rose scrubbed a hand over her face. Not for the first time she thought about taking a break from dating. The only reason she hadn't done so before now was that it seemed like admitting defeat. People needed other people. Human contact was necessary, right? Going out with friends was great, but now and then, she needed at least to make an effort with the opposite sex. Unfortunately, sex rarely had anything to do with it. It *had* been a while. Longer than she wanted to think about. Damn it, Rose liked sex. And she liked sex with men. That meant now and then, she was required to have some social interaction with one. Too bad the sex was usually as forgettable as the men were. Again, maybe it wasn't the guy's fault.

As Rose put away her guitar, she gave a quick look around her office/music room. Located in the basement of her home, it was professionally soundproofed, partly for the benefit of her neighbors, but mainly because she considered her music intensely personal. What she created here was a part her. Even though most of it would one day be shared with the world, while she was working, and creating, and sweating through every note, she wanted it kept private. Strictly for her ears only.

She closed the door and made her way up the narrow staircase that led to the kitchen. Rose took a glass from the cupboard and opened the nearby refrigerator. Her friends kidded her about using the state of the art stainless steel appliance for storing nothing but bottled water, orange juice, and yogurt. However, she liked knowing the room was a gourmet's delight. She could cook if she put her mind to it. When, on the rare occasions she felt like entertaining, everything she could need was right at her fingertips. When it was just herself, she was content to eat out or buy fresh vegetables for a salad.

Rose took a drink of juice and looked around the room with a sigh of satisfaction. She loved the renovations she had completed right after she'd purchased the four-bedroom fixer-upper. It was a small house located on the corner of Magnolia and Dewey. Harper Falls, Washington wasn't a large town, but it had very distinct neighborhoods. When the town had been founded just after the turn of the twentieth century, there had been two kinds of residents. Those who had money and those who worked for them. Over the years, that had changed, for the most part. Though some of the people who lived in the big mansions on the north side of town disagreed, the change had been a good thing. New businesses opened all the time, and the jobless rate was one of the lowest in the state. Unlike so many small towns that lost their youth because of lack of opportunities, people who grew up in Harper Falls tended to stay. Or eventually moved back.

Rose had come here at the age of nine, left for college at eighteen, and returned seven years later. She had promptly bought the dilapidated house that she used to walk by every day on her way to school. As a girl, she had secretly dreamed of owning the yellow and white cottage. She'd dreamed of having a home of her own. At the time it had seemed impossible. Her mother was dead. Her aunt and her new husband had sent her away to school, and she lived with a family that desperately needed the small amount of money paid to board her. Even though Rose had secretly started writing songs, it had never occurred to her that there would come a day when anyone would pay to hear them. Now, at twenty-seven, she had the home of her dreams, fully renovated to her taste. And she had done it all on her own. If she wanted a man in her life, it was for his company or his body, not his bank account.

Which brought her back to the man she was going out with in a few hours.

Tonight, she was going to make a real effort. She was going on this date without any negative expectations, with no reason it had to end like all the rest. She would make more of an effort. Starting with what she wore. Why was she saving those brand new, pale pink suede Prada pumps for a special occasion? She would make *tonight* special by going all out. She was going to sparkle, inside and out. Crap, what was his name? Calvin? That's right, Calvin. Tomorrow, Calvin would be telling his friends about the best date of his life. Okay, she didn't want to get carried away. Maybe she would shoot for above average and hope for not terrible. Baby steps, baby steps that would be taken in her spectacular pale pink suede Prada pumps.

Chapter Two

JACK WINSTON STRETCHED his arms over his head, wincing when he heard a definite popping in his neck. A glance at his watch told him he had been bent over his computer for hours without a break. Nothing new there. When he was working on an idea, time tended to get away from him. Things were coming together nicely on the new software program, and his body told him it was past time for lunch.

He stood and walked to the wall of windows that dominated one side of his office. It was a killer view. Built on Crossfire Hill, the building that housed H&W Security looked over the town of Harper Falls and the parallel running Columbia River. The valley was long and winding, and Jack could understand why founder Russell Harper had chosen this place to build his town. The falls no longer existed; the building of Grand Coulee Dam had eliminated them back in the nineteen-thirties. However, it was a beautiful valley flanked by pine-covered mountains on one side and a long, flat mesa on the other. The towering bluff on the west side of the river had made the perfect place to build Harper House. Russell Harper had wanted his home to dominate, to make the statement, "I own this town and everyone down below answers to me." For a good part of the last century, everyone had. When his time finally came, at the grand old age of ninety-eight, he did not go with quiet dignity. To this day, the story was still told how the old man cursed and railed to his final breath, a fighter to the end. Jack liked that story though he had it on good authority that it had been greatly embellished over the years. As far as Jack was concerned, all the great stories were part fact, part bullshit. Time blended the two until the truth was whatever remained.

Jack stretched again, this time moving all the parts of his tall, athletic body. Sure hands and a gift for running just a bit faster than the other guys had landed him a full-ride scholarship to pretty much the college of his choice. A keen, inquisitive mind had made him a fortune.

He could have turned pro, the experts had him as a high second round pick, but Jack knew his heart wouldn't have been in it. Football was fun. It had given him a first-class education and all the women even *his* overactive libido could handle. However, computers were his real passion. Therefore, to everyone's surprise, he had walked away from the fame and fortune of professional football and started a security company with his best friend.

He had met Drew Harper the first week on campus. On paper, they seemed like unlikely friends. Jack grew up the youngest of seven children. His parents were flower children who had no problem blending their nineteen-sixties' sensibilities with twenty-first-century technology. When Jack was little, they grew their food and bartered for the rest. Money was always tight, but he couldn't remember ever going without. Whether it was a new pair of shoes or a radiator for the old tractor, his parents always found a way. The household overflowed with laughter and unconditional love. Jack knew his burning ambition for money and success had always been a puzzlement to people who never craved either. But they never said a word. They were proud of him, of all their children. His mother saw no difference between his making his first million or his oldest sister's peach preserves winning first place at the county fair. Jack grinned. They *were* spectacular preserves.

Drew, on the other hand, was an only child. His great-grandfather founded Harper Falls, and his mother never let anyone forget it. Love was not an emotion one showed in the Harper household. Drew once joked, after more than a few beers, that he had been five years old before he realized the nice smelling lady who never smiled was actually his mother. Jack thought it was a drunken exaggeration, until the day he met that *nice smelling* lady. Regina Harper had cold down to a science.

Different backgrounds aside, they had clicked immediately. Jack spent every moment not devoted to football and girls in the computer lab. Drew majored in computer science, so it was inevitable that their paths would cross. Jack was laid back, Drew intense, even brooding, but both were single-minded and unwavering. Four years later, they graduated — best friends with a dream and a solid plan to make it come true.

To say money had been tight was putting it mildly. Drew hadn't taken a cent from his family since the day he left Harper Falls. Jack had never had any to start with. They were young and arrogant; convinced they had the brains and determination to conquer the world. Therefore, they moved to Los Angeles, rented a rattrap apartment, and lived on boxed macaroni and cheese while developing the software that would make them a fortune.

In the meantime, they had rent to pay. Luckily for them they were both tall and muscular, so they had no problem getting jobs doing security around L.A. It didn't hurt that Jack had a bit of lingering celebrity cache from his football days. Rich guys liked the idea of showing off their semi-famous bodyguard. Soon they had reputations as reliable muscle. They looked intimidating and if necessary, could kick ass. Luck and social media soon gave them unexpected success and the means to start their own small but exclusive security firm. They hired a few guys to handle the overflow, sold their first software program for a mind-boggling amount of money, and decided to move the whole operation to Drew's hometown.

Jack had been ready for the move. He liked Los Angeles, but at heart he was a small town boy. Drew's suggestion of Harper Falls had come as a complete surprise. In all the years they'd known each other Drew rarely talked about his childhood, or had any contact with his family. Sometimes he'd make a few random but telling comments, none of which led Jack to imagine Drew would ever visit, let alone move back for good. Yet here they were, one year later, settling firmly into the community. For Jack, it was a happy transition. He wasn't quite sure *how* Drew felt about it.

"Let's get some lunch." Speak of the devil.

"You read my mind." He was more than ready to get out of the office and leave work, and his musings, behind. "I had an early workout and then came straight to the office. If I don't eat soon, my brain will turn to mush."

"Pizza?" Drew held the door as they walked out of the building. There were only three cars in the parking lot: Jack's Explorer, Drew's classic Thunderbird and their assistant Pam's Prius. At the moment, everything was quiet around the compound, but by the end of the week, things would be jumping.

"Have I ever said no to pizza?" They headed for Jack's SUV without debate. Drew thought a lunch run was beneath his baby's dignity. Jack didn't get it. Why own a car that sat in the garage ninety percent of the time? Drew was always adding to his collection. He would drive one of them the five miles to work then park in the covered space built just for him. Then at the end of the day, he would drive it home to be tucked away for the night in his custom-built, climate-controlled garage. The man loved his cars. Jack would never say anything for fear of losing his head, but he thought Drew should use one of those cars to drive down the mountain to claim the *real* love of his life. Except for a drunken night in college, they never talked about the woman his friend had spent the last ten years eating his heart out over. Drew heaped his affection on several tons of metal and ignored the elephant in the room or, in this case, the town.

Jack pulled out of the parking lot and past the obstacle course and outdoor training facilities they had built in the clearing across from H&W headquarters.

"The guys are set for their regular training session," Drew reminded him. Over the years, they had expanded their bodyguard business to almost two dozen men. They had decided to keep the personal security crew even after they started making money from the cyber-security software they developed. Part of it was stupid sentimentality, but mostly it was for the clients who depended on them. Neither of them was very hands-on anymore, but now and then it felt good to workout with the crew, just to prove they hadn't lost their edge to the younger guys.

"I'm starting to worry about Craig," Drew frowned. Craig Lowe was in charge of training the crew and dealt with any day-to-day problems. If anything serious cropped up, Craig would come to one of them, but otherwise he had the authority to run things.

"He's getting more and more erratic. I think it's time we seriously considered getting someone to replace him."

As much as it saddened him, Jack had to agree. There were perks that came with rubbing elbows with the rich and famous, and neither Jack nor Drew begrudged any of the crew their right to indulge a bit. They certainly hadn't been saints when they started out. However, Craig was taking it too far. Late nights and alcohol were starting to affect his physical appearance and his job performance. He was late more often than not, and there were times when they called to find out where he was and they couldn't reach him.

"I talked to Craig yesterday." Jack ran a hand through his dark hair in frustration. He couldn't help but notice that it had gotten longer than he liked. His mother had thought her baby's hair looked so sweet that she never let anyone cut it. He'd been six when that had changed. The first time a stranger mistook him for a girl, Jack grabbed an old knife that his father kept in the barn and hacked at it until the curls littered the floor. What little hair was left stood up in little jagged spikes. His mother had cried — his father laughed his ass off. He tended to forget haircuts when he was in the middle of a project. By the feel of it, he was way past due.

"What excuse did he give you this time?"

"No excuse," Jack said ruefully. "He swears that he quit. Quit the late nights. Quit the drinking. If it's a vice, he's quit it."

"Does he think we're idiots?" Drew scoffed.

"He's not thinking at all. I told him what you and I agreed. He enters a detox program or he's fired."

"It's for the best, Jack," Drew told him. Jack had more sympathy for human failings than he did. Jack's first instinct was to reason first, kick ass if necessary. Drew's patience had a much shorter shelf life.

"Best for him *and* the business. We can't afford to have him screw up and get somebody hurt. Neither of us wants that."

"I agree." No amount of insurance could cover the guilt they would live with if a client or employee was injured on their watch. "I'm driving him to Spokane tomorrow and I promised him a job would be waiting for him when he gets out."

"But you didn't promise him he'd have the *same* job."

"No. He'll be on probation for a while," Jack assured him.

"Good." Drew sighed. "That leaves us with the crew arriving this weekend and no one to handle the training. It's too late to reschedule."

Jack and Drew exchanged resigned looks. "Well, shit. I can't say I'm looking forward to long hours in the hot sun and nights soaking my aching muscles. Didn't we get enough of that when we were poor and stupid? I'm beginning to wonder if we shouldn't rethink our decision to keep the personal security division. We don't need the money or the publicity."

"The crew will only be here for a week," Jack reminded his partner. "Besides, we're getting soft sitting behind our desks all day. It will do us good to mix it up with the guys."

Drew huffed but agreed. They both kept in shape but punching a bag was different than punching another person. He didn't doubt they could still hold their own in a fight, but getting down in the trenches would be good for both of them. Kicking ass was no longer part of their job description. Still, it didn't hurt to keep their skills honed.

"Fine. But we should start looking around for a replacement for Craig. There's no guarantee he'll stick with rehab, or stay on the wagon afterward. We need to move on this soon. It's not just the training. The day-to-day crap is time-consuming. It's time I'd rather be using on developing new software."

"I'm way ahead of you," Jack assured him. "There's someone I have in mind who'd be perfect. You remember I mentioned an old friend from high school who joined the Army right after graduation?

"Right. Alex something."

"Alex Fleming."

Drew frowned. "Didn't you say he was career Army?"

"That was always his plan," Jack said. His blue eyes darkened with concern. "Something changed about a year ago. He didn't give me any details; whatever he was involved with was strictly hush-hush. But it ended with him in the hospital. Six months later, he was out of the Army with an honorable discharge."

Drew could tell that Jack was worried about his friend. Jack tended to let other people's problems become his own. When he cared about that person, he would move heaven and earth to help. He hoped Alex Fleming knew how lucky he was to have a man like Jack Winston on his side. Drew had thanked his lucky stars more than once for a friend like Jack.

"You don't know anything else?"

"Nope," Jack admitted. "In fact, I didn't know that much until a couple of days ago. Apparently, he bought a motorcycle and rode around Europe. Says he wants to see a bit of the world as a civilian for a change. When he called me, it was out of the blue. I told him there was a job waiting for him; all he had to do was show up."

"And do you think he will?" Drew didn't say anything about Jack offering his old friend a job without consulting him first. If Jack believed in Alex Fleming, then that was all Drew needed to know.

"I do." Jack pulled to a stop in front of *Mama Joan's*, the town's best pizza place. "I think that's why he finally got in touch. He's ready to come home. He just needed to hear that he had a place to come."

Drew opened the door to the restaurant, taking a moment to breathe in the spicy aromas that hit them as soon as they walked in. He gave a wave to some familiar faces that were already enjoying their lunch. "Well, let's hope he gets here sooner than later. Back in our younger days, I enjoyed strapping on a gun and playing James Bond, but not anymore."

"We're only twenty-eight," Jack reminded him. "But I know what you mean. I always found those jobs to be a dead bore. The women were amazing, nothing boring about that.

"You act as though your love life has dried up." Women of all ages loved Jack, and it didn't matter if they were in Los Angeles or Harper Falls. Jack never went without for long.

"Nope, I find small town women to be very friendly. In fact," he tilted his head slightly towards the back of the room. "There are two very lovely ladies smiling at us. What do you say we go persuade them to let us share their table?"

Drew hesitated. He glanced around as he always did when he was in town but as usual, she wasn't there. So why not join Jack and eat with a woman who smiled at him, one who didn't cross the street if she saw him coming? Besides, Jack would do all the talking. Pizza and feminine company. Not a bad way to spend the next hour. And if he wasn't interested? Well, it was only lunch.

"Sure, Jack. Why not?"

Chapter Three

ROSE HAD SPENT most of the time since she'd gotten up that morning assessing her mood. She'd begun with mildly depressed, segued into righteously pissed, and had even considered justifiably homicidal. After talking herself down, she'd finally settled on optimistically resigned. Last night might have been a disaster, but she couldn't stay grim when the early May weather was so warm and sunny, with a whiff of lilac in the air. She had come to a decision, and she was happy with it. Now was the hard part — sharing the news with her friends.

Crossing the street toward the coffee shop where her best friends, Tyler Jones and Jordanna Wilde, were waiting, Rose knew what their reaction to her decision would be. Tyler would tell her she was crazy, and Dani would calmly point out all the flaws in the plan. It would be hard to argue with either of them. For now, she was sticking to it. Once they realized how serious she was, they would support her, full-on best friend mode.

Three little girls had formed a bond over a summer. Celebrations, whispered secrets, heartaches, and inevitable separations had proven that bond unbreakable. Not that it had been a smooth beginning.

At nine years of age, Rose had still been reeling from the sudden death of her mother six months earlier. Her mother had never mentioned any family. Her father wasn't just out of the picture; he'd never been in it. Locating a next of kin had taken a few weeks, and then all of a sudden Rose had found herself in the custody of an aunt she hadn't known existed.

It hadn't taken Rose long to learn the woman's chiseled-in-stone rules. First, she was under no circumstances to call her anything but Louise. Calling her Aunt would get her a firm slap across the face. Rose only broke that rule once. Second, and most important, never discuss age, her own or Louise's. Louise was forever twenty-five and having a nine-year-old around prompted men to start counting. Third, no one wanted Rose. She should be grateful Louise was big-hearted enough to take in such a skinny, unattractive child. What Louise conveniently left out was the money Rose's mother had in her savings account at the time of her death. Rose had never known how much was there, and she'd certainly never seen a dime of it. It turned out to be the extra incentive Louise had needed to do what the social worker termed 'the decent thing.'

Soon Louise had nabbed herself a well-to-do new husband and Rose was shipped off to a private school in Eastern Washington — a turn of events that couldn't have made Rose happier.

Harper Academy was in Harper Falls. Rose had been informed by the oh-so-proper headmistress that it was a very exclusive school. She thought Rose should say thanks every day that she had a wealthy benefactor with connections to the Harper family, the founders, and trustees. Rose didn't know or care anything about who ran the school or the surrounding town. What mattered to her was the outstanding music program the school offered. When things with her mother had been at their worst, music would often be their only way of connecting. Being able to study, to learn new instruments, was a dream come true.

Rose had always known that her mother was an unhappy person. Maggie O'Brian was alone in the world; her heart given to a man who had gotten her pregnant and disappeared before Rose was born. Maggie assured Rose that her father would be with them if he could, that someday he would come back. Rose was too young to know what that meant; all she did know was that it made her mother sad. When Rose sang, sometimes her mother would smile. She taught herself to play the guitar. The old beat up instrument that she bought at a yard sale for one dollar had been her most prized possession. The simple songs she wrote weren't chart toppers by any stretch of the imagination. At the time, Rose's only goal had been to give her mother a few moments of happiness. What she couldn't understand at such a young age was that the depression that had a hold on Maggie O'Brian was stronger than a few well-meant songs. Maggie had crawled into a black hole and didn't want to come out. Not for her daughter, not for anything.

When Rose got her first look at the school's music room full of shiny new instruments, most of which Rose had never even heard of, it was all she could do to contain her excitement. She felt terrified that if it got back to her aunt that Rose was actually thrilled to be there, she would be taken out and sent somewhere else, somewhere without music. Inside, Rose jumped with joy. Harper Academy was where she was meant to be, and she wasn't going to do anything that might ruin her chances of staying.

Luck remained on Rose's side when it came to where she would live while attending Harper Academy, though at first she wouldn't have said it was *good* luck. There was housing for students, but when Rose arrived, it was the middle of June, and they didn't board students during the summer. A few townsfolk occasionally rented rooms to students when the dormitories were overbooked. The headmistress had suggested the Jones family because they had a daughter Rose's age.

Martin and Anita Jones and their three children lived within walking distance of the school though none of the children went to Harper Academy. When the headmistress explained to Rose where she would live, she had whispered this information, as though going to public school was some shameful secret. Rose didn't care — she was going to live with a real family. One that had children, and a mother and a father.

As the car from the school pulled up in front of the well-maintained two-story home, she could barely contain her excitement. She had spent the last six months hiding her natural curiosity and exuberance. Showing enthusiasm for anything was the quickest way to have it taken away. She hoped this family played and laughed and had a dog. Oh, please, let them have a dog.

Just then, as if someone had been reading her mind, a huge black and white dog came running around the house barking what Rose hoped was a greeting. She had pictured a much smaller dog, one that wasn't almost as tall as she was. The driver didn't seem overly worried. He skillfully maneuvered the animal away from the car door and helped her out.

"Don't worry, miss," he assured her. "That's just Barney. He's as gentle as a lamb."

As if to prove the driver's point, Barney chose that moment to swipe her hand with his large, wet tongue, and that was all it took — Rose was in love. She giggled and threw her arms around the dog's neck, feeling like she had made at least one new friend.

"Get your hands off my dog, rich girl."

Rose jumped back in surprise. She supposed the tall, slender girl with a mass of tangled black hair was yelling at her; she *was* the only one near Barney. But *Rich Girl?* Hardly.

"Tyler, what did your mother tell you?"

"I don't remember, Uncle Stan." The girl dug the toe of her scuffed sneakers into the dirt; her eyes not quite meeting the big man who had driven Rose from the school.

"We agreed to be nice, Tyler," a soft but firm voice admonished.

Another girl had joined them, smaller than the mean one and much friendlier. *She looks like a fairy princess,* Rose thought the first time she saw Jordanna Wilde. Her hair was an endless mass of pale-colored curls, and her eyes were the color of emeralds. Rose couldn't help wondering what it was like to be so beautiful.

"Hi." The girl's smile was warm and welcoming. "I'm Dani; I live next door. And this is Tyler. She's really nice when you get to know her." Seeing Rose's skeptical look, she added, "I promise. Before the summer is over, we'll all be best friends."

And they had been. It became a rare occurrence when one was seen without the other two. After school, holidays, and every summer, except one. For the next nine years, nothing could keep them apart. Now they were all back where it started. Nothing made Rose happier than knowing the two people she loved most in the world only lived a few blocks away.

"Finally," Tyler called out as Rose entered the coffee shop. "You leave us messages about some big news and then you're late. I ordered you your usual Earl Grey. Sit and spill. The beans, not your tea."

"Tyler was up all night working, so she's kind of wired. I made her order decaf." Dani always tried to curtail Tyler's caffeine intake. She wasn't very successful.

Rose looked at her friends and was amazed at how much they still looked like the girls she had met for the first time all those years ago. Dani still looked like a princess, with curling light gold hair and deep green eyes. But this woman was no damsel in distress. She was a kick-ass photographer who had fulfilled her dream of traveling the world. Afghanistan to Nice, war zones, or film festivals, Dani had done it all. Now she was based in Harper Falls, still flying out when the right story came along, but ready to put down roots and stop living out of a suitcase. She had just been hired to do a photographic history of the town in honor of the upcoming centennial celebration. A job that would keep her a homebody for the foreseeable future.

"We could have gotten together later in the day," Rose looked at Tyler with concern. "You need to get some sleep."

Tyler's eyes did look tired, but she had such an inherent vitality that it was hard to tell unless you looked closely. Much like the nine-year-old Tyler, the grown up one thumbed her nose at constantly worrying about her appearance. Her hair was piled into a messy bun on top of her head, and her jeans and baggy man's shirt had various colors of paint splattered all over them. Her high cheekbones and full mouth spoke to a mixed heritage that couldn't be easily pinned down. A bit of Native American, some Irish, perhaps a smattering of Nordic blood from way back. It was a spectacular combination of coal-black hair and pale gray eyes. She had a tall, slender, athletic body. What curves she had were subtle and sleek. She had the face and figure that could have graced fashion magazines. Tyler found the idea hilarious. She was an artist, period. She had nothing to do with the way she looked. Put *that* down to genetics and some randy Vikings. Some girls had once called her a mutt. Whether it had been out of spite or jealousy, it was a term Tyler happily embraced. Bluebloods, she'd spit with contempt, you could keep them. And the one blueblood whose name wasn't to be mentioned was the worst of the lot.

Early on in their friendship, it was Rose who felt like the mutt, and it would have been so easy to fall into the plain friend role. But Dani and Tyler didn't spend their time looking in mirrors. They were normal little girls who scraped their knees, climbed trees, and went shoeless from June to September. Before long, Rose stopped worrying about being an ugly duckling among swans. As a result, she didn't even notice when her body began to change. Her beauty had been a gradual thing. There were no sudden growth spurts, no overnight development of curves. By the time she was eighteen, she was almost as tall as Tyler, and her hair had taken on a rich auburn sheen. When the three of them went out together, people might notice Tyler and Dani first but they never overlooked Rose.

"What I need," Tyler said with obvious impatience, "is for the two of you to stop playing mommy and let me choose how much caffeine I consume or how many hours I sleep. Now, let's drop that boring subject and switch to a different one. How was your date with Dr. Dull? Did he live down to your expectations?"

"Well," Rose sighed, "there are a lot of ways to describe last night, but *dull* isn't one of them."

Tyler and Dani exchanged looks. The conversation wasn't starting the way they'd expected. They always shared postdate reviews. Tyler rarely dated any man more than a month but while they lasted, her men were hot and wild. Dani liked what she called the sexy professor type, intellectually challenging and easy on the eye. Rose usually began with how nice her date had been, nice restaurant, nice conversation, followed by a nice kiss goodnight. In other words, nice and dull. This new twist had them sitting up in their seats.

"We met at that place down on Maple Street, the one with the cotton candy-colored door."

"Not *Pink Tank*?" Dani cringed. "I thought I read that that place had been shut down weeks ago for health violations.

"You didn't eat anything iffy, did you?" Tyler asked.

"No." Rose sighed. "But my date did."

The evening had started out fine. She and Calvin had agreed to meet at the restaurant instead of him picking her up. Rose had thought the place seemed a bit dingy but otherwise it looked clean. They had a bit of pre-dinner chitchat. Well, he did most of the chatting. He spent most of the time telling her about his exciting work as an actuary.

"An actuary?" Tyler exclaimed. "Where do you find these guys?"

"Not every guy is a race car driver or extreme sports enthusiast," Dani reminded her friend.

"Before you two start the same argument we've all heard a thousand times, can I finish my story?"

Tyler and Dani both nodded and gave the tick-a-lock sign on their mouths.

"Everything was fine until the food arrived." Rose grimaced before telling them what happened next. "Calvin would take a bite and then make an odd face. He sniffed at the next bite and then held it out and asked me if I thought it smelled off. When I told him I wasn't sure, he just continued to eat his food, smelling everything before he put it in his mouth."

"How was your food?" Dani asked. Rose could tell they tried their best not to laugh.

"By that point, I had lost my appetite, so I didn't eat much," Rose admitted. "I kept telling him to send the food back but nothing would stop him."

"And?"

"And before he even finished, he started complaining that he didn't feel well. I took advantage of the situation and as soon as the bill was paid, I hustled us out of there. We hadn't gotten more than a few steps out the door when Calvin turned towards me and threw up all over my Prada pumps."

"Not the pale pinks ones," Dani gasped. "Off with his head."

"The hell with his head," Tyler interjected. "We're talking Prada. Pale pink suede Prada. Off with his balls."

The three friends finally gave in and burst out laughing. When Tyler suggested grabbing the nearest knife and tracking down Calvin's testicles, it set them off on another round of giggles.

"I wish I could have laughed last night," Rose said after they had calmed back down. "There I stood, unsuccessfully trying to shake the vomit off my shoes as Calvin stumbled off towards his car, without a single word of apology. If it hadn't been for the owner of the flower shop next door to the restaurant, I don't know what I would have done. She saw the whole thing and ran out with a garden hose. She got all the goo off me *and* the sidewalk and then gave me a pair of flip-flops to wear home."

"What a nice thing to do."

"She saved the day. Which reminds me," Rose reached into her purse and pulled out a couple of business cards. "From now on, if you need flowers get them at *Peony*. The owner's name is Lila, and she just opened up a few weeks ago. I want to send as much business her way as I can."

"Rose, I know we laughed, but I'm sorry your date turned out to be such a disaster." Tyler leaned over, giving her hand a squeeze. "At least you know *that* isn't likely to ever happen again."

"You're right," Rose agreed and plunged in with her big announcement. "So I wanted you both to know that as of last night, I am pulling out of the dating world. No more boring dates or bad dates or dates involving projectile vomiting. For the foreseeable future, I am officially a man-free zone."

"Come on, don't you think you're overreacting?" Tyler asked. "You could just avoid any dates that involve food."

"Or give it a week before you decide anything," Dani reasoned. "You might feel differently in a few days."

"Louise called."

"When?" Tyler and Dani exchanged concerned looks.

"Last night. She'd left a message on the machine." The old school landline and answering machine served the purpose of giving Louise access but making sure Rose never had to talk to her. No one else had the number, and Louise only used it for two purposes, to announce she was getting married, or divorced.

"So she found another sucker," Tyler's words dripped with disgust.

"It's one of her few talents." That and being a crazy, psycho bitch.

"Well, now I get your sudden moratorium on men. Louise, plus Calvin, equals celibacy."

"It's not like I slept with any of the guys I'd been out with lately," Rose reminded them. "I can take care of my needs just fine, so I might as well cut out the middleman."

"So Louise is getting married, again." It was hard for Dani not to shudder. "It was inevitable that she would call with the *good* news. I wish you would just rip that phone out and cut her off for good."

"And have her show up on my doorstep?" It had been almost twelve short years since Rose had seen Louise. The last thing she wanted was the woman to be anywhere near herself, or Harper Falls.

"Please, not another word about that whack job." Tyler paused for dramatic effect. "I have an idea."

Rose groaned. She loved Tyler, but her ideas tended to induce headaches. Or the police. Sometimes both.

"No."

"Just hear me out," Tyler smiled. "What you need to do is grab a gorgeous, hunky man and let him screw your brains out. One night, no strings attached."

"And this will help me how?"

"How could it hurt?" Tyler wanted to know. "Gorgeous man, great sex. On top of that, it will shake things up; get you out of your rut. You don't need to give men up; you just need to change them up."

"Since when are men better in bed just because they look good?" That hadn't been Rose's experience.

"They aren't, necessarily," Tyler conceded. "You would have to choose a guy with a reputation for pleasing women."

"Tyler, this isn't a great idea," Dani warned.

"And how would I find this sex machine?" Rose asked, ignoring Dani's objection. In spite of herself, she was beginning to see the appeal of this idea.

"We'll do a little research," Tyler assured her. "Ideally, you want to be familiar with the guy; he shouldn't be a complete stranger, not for a one-night stand. So, someone you know on sight but not someone you would run into every day."

"Guys." Dani tried to interject another warning, but her friends weren't listening.

"You're thinking someone from out of town?" Rose asked thoughtfully. Either Louise's call had scrambled her brains more than usual or she was actually considering this. There certainly was no harm in hashing out some details.

"We'll figure it all out as we go." Tyler tented her fingers as if thinking deep thoughts. "Right now, we need to start by asking around, subtly, of course. Men brag about their conquests, and so do women, right?"

"You certainly do," Dani teased affectionately.

Ignoring her, Tyler pushed on. "We know a lot of women. Some of them must know guys who treat the ladies well and aren't looking for long-term relationships. I'd give you one of mine, but we don't need to start sharing men."

All three women shuddered at the thought. They'd made it this far in their friendship without ever wanting the same man. There had been no crossover dates or lovers. Now was not the time to change that.

"I still have to think about it, Tyler." Rose wasn't going to commit herself to one of her friend's crazy schemes right away. She was interested, but if she gave Tyler the go-ahead, she was afraid of finding a guy in her bed that night. "Crap, is that the time? I have to go. Frank and I have a song to finish, and he should be calling in about fifteen minutes." Grabbing her purse, Rose exchanged quick hugs and was out the door.

Dani waited until Rose was out of the building before turning on Tyler.

"Are you out of your mind?"

"Often, but not at the moment," Tyler grinned. "And I know what you're going to say, so before you jump down my throat let me set your mind at ease. Rose is *not* going to have a one-night stand."

"Well, you were all for it a minute ago," Dani reminded her.

"I never thought it was a great idea." Tyler took a sip of her strong, dark-roasted coffee. She knew the owners, and they never served her decaf, not that Dani needed to know that.

"We both saw how Rose wasn't herself. That always happens after Crazy Louise calls. This time she'd just gotten back from the lousy date to end all lousy dates. She wasn't thinking clearly, and while she might have gotten over the no date thing in a few days, she would still choose the same kind of guy. She needs to rethink her dating strategy."

"With a one-night stand?" Dani demanded. "Rose is not the type. None of us is. And don't try to tell me you are because I know better. You talk a good game, Tyler Jones, but it isn't you."

"Would it make me a slut?" Tyler knew the answer. They wouldn't call their worst enemy a slut. It just wasn't a word they used.

"Of course not," Dani sighed. "Women who enjoy their sexuality the same as men are not sluts, whores, or whatever. Not all women can sleep with a man if they don't know him for a while. Rose can't, I can't, and you..."

"Never put out until at least the third date." It was as close as Tyler was going to get to admitting that she wasn't quite as *popular* as she sometimes made out. "Look, we both know Rose. She'll need at least a week to process, reprocess, and then think about it again. During that time, we'll work on her — remind her how much she really likes men. *The little dears.*"

"Can't live with them—" Dani laughed. "So what you're saying is bide our time. Try to rewire her brain a bit. And why does it feel like this whole thing has disaster written all over it?"

"Because you don't have my vision."

"I don't want your vision." Dani sometimes wondered why Tyler's *vision* didn't give her nightmares. "But I will concede your idea has potential."

"It's potentially brilliant, my dear." She drank the last of her coffee and jumped to her feet. "And now that I'm sufficiently re-caffeinated, I need to get back to my sketching. The ideas for the sculpture celebrating the town's centennial have to be submitted by the end of the month. And I plan on mine being so amazing that not even Queen Regina Harper will be able to reject it."

"Re-caffeinated?" Dani cried. Tyler gave her a hug before she dashed out of the coffee shop. "Oh, why do I even bother?"

Chapter Four

ROSE FELT LIKE she had a neon sign flashing over her head — *looking for a one-night stand, only sex gods need apply.*

The annual spring Lilac Ball had seemed like the perfect place to find a man — the right man. Now that she was here, she just felt awkward and conspicuous. It didn't matter that no one could know what she was thinking. She still felt oddly guilty. As though looking at every man she passed as a potential sex partner was a crime.

It had only been three days since Tyler's one-night stand suggestion, but Rose thought of little else. Of course, she knew what her friend was up to. Tyler didn't *really* want Rose to have sex with some random guy. At first, the idea had seemed too outrageous for words. The more she weighed the pros and cons, the more pros popped up. It wasn't about sex or finding a man. She had never been a boy-crazy teen or one of those women from a bad romantic comedy who lamented her rapidly waning youth. Rose did need *something* different. And if she got an orgasm or two out of it, all the better.

The Lilac Ball was a yearly event that raised money for the local hospital. Invitations went out months in advance. It was one of Regina Harper's pet projects, so she made sure everyone there had deep pockets. Not that you had to be a multimillionaire to attend. Regina just stacked the deck with wealthy donors — it wouldn't do for any of her functions to be anything but a rousing success. Tickets sold out within days, in part because it was a good cause. It was also one of the few times the doors of Harper House opened to any but a select few. Three hundred and sixty-four days a year, the residents of Harper Falls lived in the shadow of the towering mansion. But on one night in May, for the price of a ticket you could see how the other one percent lived.

Rose, Dani, and Tyler had attended last year and had gotten their tickets early for this one. There was an open bar and a constant stream of servers offering every kind of finger food imaginable. Rose was partial to the mini quiches.

The lilac theme filled the grand ballroom. Clear fairy lights covered the ceiling like millions of twinkling stars. The scent of lilac filled the air but didn't overpower. Vases of flowers occupied every corner. Both light purple and dark purple overflowed in controlled abandon. Rose thought they must have stripped every bush within a two-hundred-mile radius.

Rose had arrived earlier than Tyler and Dani — normally they would have come together. She wanted to look around and decide if she was going to do this. And she wanted to do it without any unwanted influence. They would be a bit horrified if they knew that she considered picking up a man tonight. Tyler had put the idea into her head, so she had no one to blame but herself.

Rose had to admit there were some very attractive men here tonight. The old adage that every man looked good in a tuxedo was spot on. The ball was formal, and all were decked out in their finest. The problem was finding out which ones were as good at sex as they were at having their suits impeccably fitted. She couldn't just go up and ask. Or could she? No, probably not a good idea. Beyond the embarrassment factor, who would tell the truth? What man would admit to being a lousy lover?

Then there was the real possibility of being turned down. Rose knew she looked good. The white gown she had bought the last time she was in New York clung to her every curve like it had been made for her, and it had. The designer herself had done the final fitting, and the style, while simple, suited her perfectly. It was sexy but not obvious. The modest neckline showed very little skin and the slightly flared skirt allowed her plenty of movement, so there was no need for a leg-baring slit. The effect was flattering — subtle. The back, though, was another matter altogether. The deep plunge showed off her toned, sleek muscles, ending *just* at the base of her spine. Business in the front, party in the back. The dress gave her confidence. And she was going to need all she could get.

She had been at the ball for almost an hour and still didn't see any sign of Tyler or Dani, which was good. Deciding to check on her makeup, Rose slipped from the ballroom. Just to the right was a discreet sign indicating the way to the restrooms. Giving herself a critical once-over in the ornate mirror, she decided all she needed was a fresh coat of lipstick. She had just removed the tube from her bag when two women entered the lounge area.

Rose immediately recognized one of them from her days at Harper Academy. To say that she and Jilly Underwood had never been friendly was putting it mildly. Jilly's family had money; Rose didn't have money *or* a family. As far as Jilly was concerned, that made Rose so far below her notice she might as well have been invisible. Even after Rose had transferred to Harper High, for some reason she had remained at the top of Jilly's enemy list — along with Tyler and Dani. Look up mean girl in the dictionary, you'd find a picture of Jilly Underwood. Sure, it was an old joke, but that didn't make it any less true.

The two women went to the mirror opposite Rose without acknowledging her. It seemed that nine years had done nothing to change Jilly's opinion.

"Jack Winston is here," Jilly's friend said in an excited whisper. "He is the sexiest man I have ever seen. Well, I guess Drew Harper is just as sexy. I wonder if *he's* here."

"I doubt it. Word is he won't even be in the same room with his mother, not that I blame him. That woman is colder than an iceberg. But I could care less about Drew," Jilly practically purred. "I've had my eye on

Jack since he arrived in town, and tonight I'm going to have him."

"I hear he is an animal in bed. Martha Underwood claims he kept her busy for three days straight with no breaks."

Not even to pee? Rose wondered.

"Martha is a liar. Not that I doubt that Jack is capable." Rose recognized Jilly's predatory smile. When she wanted something, the woman was never subtle. Between her bleached blond good looks and her father's money, she wanted for nothing. But when she *was* denied? That girl was an A-number-1 tantrum thrower. Rose had been witness to a few of them, and it was a sight to see — as long as you stayed out of spittle range.

"Why tonight? I mean he's turned you down every time you've come on to him," Jilly's friend put on a concerned face but Rose got the feeling the woman found Jilly's failures highly entertaining.

Jilly chose to ignore the jab, though her lips had that *I just sucked a lemon* look that was starting to become permanent, if the wrinkles around her mouth were any indication.

"I have it from a reliable source that Jack has spent the last week in the company of nothing but other men. Since I'm sure he's one hundred percent heterosexual, tonight he should be ripe for the picking. I'll get him on the dance floor, and before the song finishes, he'll be dragging me out of here. We might not even make it back to my place."

Jack Winston. Now there was a possibility. They'd met briefly a few months ago. Tall, buff, and good looks to spare. *And* killer blue eyes. Paul Newman eyes. It shouldn't surprise her that he had a reputation as a great lover. He wasn't just good-looking; he was — well — *yummy.* Just the man Rose was searching for. And if she could induce a Jilly-fit? That was a win-win for Rose.

But she had to get to him first. She casually returned her lipstick to her bag and made her way out of the ladies' room. Good Lord, her heart was beating like a hummingbird's wings. The adrenaline was good, she decided. It kept back the nerves. Mostly. Now she had to find Jack, proposition him, and get him out of there before Jilly could get her lethal claws into him.

Jack, blissfully unaware that he was about to be pursued by two very determined women, sipped a club soda and lime. If he *had* known that he was the object of their desire, he would have hightailed it for the nearest exit. The only reason he was there at all was because he'd promised Drew that he would represent the company tonight. Drew hadn't set foot in Harper House for over ten years, and nothing was going to change that. Being a charity they both wanted to support, Jack agreed to put in a brief appearance.

When a waiter offered him a glass of champagne, Jack politely turned him down. Inside he cringed at even the thought of anything alcoholic. He had never been a heavy drinker. Two beers was usually his limit. He could count on two fingers the number of times he'd gotten stinking drunk. Once had been during his first year of college after his team had handily won their homecoming game. He was eighteen and on a testosterone high. Surrounded by teammates and lots of free beer? You didn't have to be a rocket scientist to figure out how that would end.

Then there was last night. After a week of intense training with their security crew, he and Drew had let loose for the first time in a long, long time. Because the crew stayed at the compound, no one had to worry about driving. Like everyone else, Jack got caught up in the celebratory atmosphere. Tequila shots and plenty of them. Drew had nursed a hangover most of the morning. Jack was lucky to have been blessed with a metabolism that let him drink everyone under the table, and not suffer for it the next day.

Unfortunately, when he drank too much, he tended to become susceptible to suggestions. The more outrageous, the better. Oh, never anything terribly dangerous or illegal. Jack never lost his sense of self-preservation. If it was relatively harmless, then he was all in. In college, it had garnered him a tattoo — a rather large one on his right shoulder. It wasn't anything embarrassing, but it served as a reminder. Don't get fall down, stinking drunk — ever again. Last night, the drinks had snuck up on him. His body was overly tired, and it took less alcohol than usual to knock him on his butt. And on top of everything else, he was blessed with *TDR*, total drinking recall. No blanks in *his* memory. No, he remembered every idiotic moment of the mess he'd gotten himself into.

First, there was his hair, what little of it that was left. Sometime during the night, he'd mentioned his need for a haircut. Naturally, someone had the bright idea to get a pair of sheep shears that the previous owners had left in the barn. Sounded like a great idea to him. It would save him a trip to the barber. *Of course,* the rusty old things had still worked. Drew ran his hand over the dark stubble on his head. His hair hadn't been this short since he cut it himself and his dad ended up evening it out. At least that time they had been actual clippers meant for humans. He was lucky the drunken idiots hadn't taken his ear off. It was just hair; it would grow back. It was the second thing that he had agreed to that was the problem. Because of tequila and a stupid bet, he now had to be celibate for the next month.

Three weeks to be technical. The guys had been generous enough to count the prior week as part of the bet. Jack had no doubt he could make it; he wasn't a sex addict. It was just that knowing he couldn't have any was making him think about it more than at any time since he'd lost his virginity when he was seventeen. He hadn't gone longer than a week since then, and he had been looking forward to tonight. Every woman here looked particularly beautiful and he couldn't do anything about it.

He could have gotten out of the bet. This morning none of the guys remembered what had gone on the night before. Some of them remembered the bet but couldn't remember the details. However, Jack did — vividly. And his stupid sense of fair play made him fill them in — with every embarrassing detail.

The rules were simple but specific. He couldn't tell anyone about the bet. If he went out on a date, he could provide the woman with an orgasm as long as his dick didn't penetrate any part of her body. He wasn't allowed to let her pleasure him but if he came in his pants without manual help from her, that was acceptable. Masturbation? Hell, yes — thank God.

Jack sighed again. Good Lord, what were they, a bunch of twelve-year-olds? The bet had been Drew's evil idea — every single detail of it. If his dear, old friend hadn't spent the morning holding his head and looking like death warmed over, Jack would have kicked his ass. Then the jerk had the gall to laugh like a banshee when reminded of it. Jack's satisfaction in seeing Drew's head almost explode with pain was short-lived. Three weeks. Something told him he was going to be spending a lot of time in the gym, and with his hand on his dick.

Rose scanned the crowd. It shouldn't be hard to find Jack. He was a man that left an impression, which meant he was the exact opposite of the men Rose dated. For once, she was going to give in and go off her bland diet. For one night, she was going hot and spicy — she planned on gorging herself on beautiful man.

Her gaze stopped on a tall man with dark hair. He stood alone across the room, holding a glass and looking none too pleased to be there. Not terribly approachable. She almost moved on, but something about him made her look again. It was Jack. Well, no wonder she hadn't recognized him. Rose had been looking for someone with dark hair, but she thought it was much longer. She remembered when they met she'd had the fleeting desire to run her fingers through the thick, wavy locks — to find out if they could be as soft as they looked. But all that beautiful hair was gone. Though it didn't seem possible, he was even more attractive than before.

Maybe the hair had been a distraction. Because now when she looked at him, all she saw was his impossibly beautiful face — all sculpted cheekbones, firm but inviting lips and a jaw line that she found herself wanting to bite. She couldn't remember ever being turned on by a man's jaw, but there it was. Jack Winston was the total package. If his reputation held up, Rose planned on giving his jaw, and the rest of him, plenty of attention.

Looking at him, Rose had a moment of doubt. Maybe she should start a little slower and work up to a man like Jack. What the hell! Tonight she was splurging. After denying herself for so long, she deserved a treat.

"Champagne?"

Rose accepted the fluted crystal glass and swallowed down the contents in one gulp. Before the waiter could move on, she exchanged her empty for a full one. She might have been arming herself with false courage, but in the short run, it couldn't hurt. Right now, she needed all the help she could get.

Five more minutes, Jack promised himself. He was only supposed to put in an appearance; an hour should fulfill all of his promise to Drew. If he started inching his way towards the door, by the time he'd exchanged a few greetings and had shaken some hands, he'd be nicely situated to make a quick escape.

"Dance with me, Jack?"

Damn it, he'd been so close. He turned towards the voice, intending to politely turn her down. Dancing was not on his agenda for the evening. The refusal died a quick death the moment he saw who it was.

Rose O'Brian.

Her eyes were the color of rich amber. A man didn't quickly forget eyes like that. Sparks of red and gold shot through her shoulder-length hair. Growing up with older sisters, he knew that women had a knack for fixing their hair for occasions like this one. He'd coughed his way through enough toxic clouds of hairspray to remember that. However, Rose's hair looked silky soft, not lacquered to within an inch of its life.

Jack had felt a spark from the moment he'd met Rose. However, it had been obvious she didn't feel the same. He might have tried to persuade her. Wouldn't that have been fun? Two things had stopped him. *His* best friend and *her* best friend. Drew Harper and Tyler Jones had a history, one that had ended badly. Drew still wanted her, and Tyler crossed the street rather than take a chance of coming within ten feet of him. No, as tempting as Rose was, it just hadn't seemed worth the trouble their association might stir up.

Walk away, his inner voice screamed. *You're one week into that asinine bet, and this woman could turn out to be too much temptation to resist.* Man, was she lovely. It wasn't so much that her dress hugged her body, but it accentuated all the right places. The stark white material covered almost all of her creamy skin, leaving just the dip at the base of her neck bare.

It was a spot just made for a man's kiss. His kiss. She had the height of a model but way better curves. No jutting hip bones on Rose. He could easily imagine his hands cupping those full breasts. He'd be playing with fire if he held her in his arms for even a moment. And for the length of a song? Torture. The hopeful look in her eyes made it impossible for him to turn away. Okay, torture it might be, but since he couldn't bring himself to say no, he might as well enjoy it.

Without a word, Jack took her hand and swept her into his arms. One dance wasn't going to kill him.

"Someone's had lessons," Rose laughed with relief. She had thought for a moment that he was going to turn her down.

"My mother insisted that all her children learn to ballroom dance," Jack smiled as he remembered the battle of wills between himself and his mother. Holding Rose close, he expertly twirled them around the room. He never could win a battle of wills against his mom, but he hadn't made it easy for her. Every week, she'd had to drag her twelve-year-old son to the lessons, promising that someday he would get good use out of them. Someday he would thank her. Mom always won, and Mom was always right.

"How many children are we talking about?" she asked. Rose had heard the affection in Jack's voice when he'd mentioned his mother. Happy families always fascinated Rose. She'd lived next door to Dani's, but that was from the outside looking in. Tyler's parents were often barely hanging on by a very thin thread. Though she'd lived with them, she'd never felt very close to any of the Joneses except for Tyler. She'd always wondered what it would be like to be an integral part of a big, boisterous family.

"Six older sisters."

"You're kidding?" Rose laughed. "Were you tormented or spoiled rotten?"

"Both. It depended on whether or not they were mad at me or wanted to use me as their own personal dress-up doll."

"You didn't consider that torment?" Rose asked. Jack must have been a very interesting child.

"You'd think so," Jack shrugged. "But while they were putting mascara and eyeshadow on me, they forgot I was their annoying little brother and would talk about all things girls. You wouldn't believe what I learned, though I'll admit I could have done without their discussion about periods and feminine hygiene products."

Rose couldn't think of anything to say. How could she steer the conversation into a sexy direction with that image in her head?

"Sorry," Jack said as if reading her thoughts. "Not casual conversation appropriate. Did you grow up with any siblings?"

"No, it was just me and my mom." She wasn't going there. Too personal and even more of a mood killer than tampons.

Jack could feel the slight stiffening of Rose's body. Obviously not a happy subject.

"Why don't we just enjoy the dance," he suggested. "I'm going to head us out onto the balcony, no talking required."

Rose hadn't realized how warm the ballroom had become until the evening air enveloped them. It felt wonderfully invigorating, and she could feel the tension slip away. Spring was in full bloom. Lush greenery surrounded them and though a few other couples were already taking advantage of the mild May night, it wasn't difficult for Rose to imagine that they were completely alone — in their own little world. It felt as if the music played just for them. Dancing in the arms of a dangerously handsome man, a man she barely knew? It was a heady experience. She could feel the attraction, one she was sure was mutual.

It wasn't a romance. She didn't want that. This was about sex. She wouldn't let herself get carried away just because they were surrounded by all the fairytale trappings. This fantasy was of the carnal variety. No prince. No happily ever after.

Jack had hoped the night air would cool his libido. It hadn't. Rose smelled amazing, all warm vanilla and bright citrus. Then there was the bare skin of her back — smooth, tempting. He couldn't resist exploring her back until his hand hovered oh so close to that dip in her spine that would lead him to her amazing ass. *But you didn't grope your dance partner,* it was just wrong. That didn't stop his imagination from going where his hand couldn't. Firm and smooth with just the right amount of feminine padding. Made perfectly for a man to grip while she rode them both to satisfaction.

"Jack," Rose frowned as she called his name for the third time. "Jack, are you all right? You look a bit flushed."

He tried not to groan out loud. *Stop fantasizing, Jack. Not here. Not until you're back at your place — alone.* And, it had better be soon.

"I'm fine. It's been a long week, and I guess it's starting to catch up with me." Which was partly true. Hopefully, it was enough of an excuse to cover his fantasy lapse.

"Should we sit out the rest of the dance?"

"No, I'm fine. Really." He pulled her closer. The song would end soon, and he wanted to remember every detail of how she felt in his arms. "I'm glad you asked me to dance."

"Jack," she pulled back a bit so she could see his face. Damn, did her voice just squeak? She tried again, deliberately lowering the timbre. "Jack." Much better.

"Rose."

"Yes?"

"Nothing, I just thought we were saying each other's names." He put his lips next to her ear and whispered, "I like the way you say my name. Do it again."

"Jack."

"Nice," he breathed. "Husky and so damn sexy."

"Jack." *Stop saying his name and finish what you've started.* "Let's go to my place and screw our brains out." Hardly subtle, but she needed to get to the point.

Yes, Jack wanted to shout. Instead, he took her hand and led her to a bench situated at the side of the balcony that provided them some privacy.

"That was unexpected," he began after seating them both.

"Should I apologize?" Rose asked.

"No," Jack assured her. "It just surprised me. And as much as it pains me, I'll have to decline your invitation."

"Do you have a girlfriend?

"No."

"Boyfriend?"

Unoffended, Jack laughed. "No."

She leaned in a bit and whispered, "STD?"

"Nope; clean as a whistle."

"Erectile dysfunction?"

"Not at the moment."

Rose looked down, her eyes growing wide. Ok, impressive.

"Premature ejacula—" Jack put his hand over her mouth before she could finish.

"No premature anything." God, this woman was a hoot.

"I didn't really think so," Rose admitted. "So you just aren't interested. Fair enough. Thanks for the dance."

Jack put out a hand to stop her from leaving. "Can I call you?" *In three weeks?* He added silently.

"You don't have to feel guilty, Jack. I get it; I'm not your type." She gave him a friendly pat on the hand and stood to go. "The night is still young. Maybe you'll hook up with someone else." *Just please, not Jilly Underwood.*

"Are you going home?"

"No," she said as she turned and went back into the ballroom. "Like I said, Jack. The night is young."

Wait. Jack quickly reran their conversation through his head. *The night is young.* Did that mean she was going to find another guy to invite home? Like hell she was. He might not be having sex with Rose, but neither was anyone else. Not tonight, and not anytime in the near future. And after that? Well, there wasn't any point in jumping too far ahead. For now, whether she knew it or not, Rose O'Brian was his.

"Rose, over here."

She turned at the sound of her name, smiling and waving when she saw Tyler and Dani. They both looked amazing, Dani was in a black number that set off her pale hair to perfection and left her creamy shoulders bare. Tyler, who loved bold, jewel-toned colors, had chosen a deep amethyst sheath that added a touch of violet to her changeable gray eyes.

"How long have you two been here?" she asked, giving them both a hug.

"Just long enough to get a drink and scope out the room," Dani answered. "I thought last year was ridiculously ritzy. What will she ever do to top this?"

"Throw an outrageous amount of money at a bunch of party planners and pick the one that she thinks is up to her unrealistic standards," Tyler answered in a monotone voice. She drained what was left of her champagne. "I need something stronger."

Rose knew that Tyler hated coming to Harper House. It represented a painful chapter in her friend's life, pain that lingered to this day. To her, coming was a necessary symbolic gesture. Sort of a *screw you* to the lady of the house.

"I'm for that." Rose linked arms with her friends and headed towards the bar. "I just got rejected during my first attempt at a one-night stand seduction. I could use a little liquid solace."

"You did what?" Tyler demanded.

"Three brandies," Dani requested of the bartender. "Now, start at the beginning. Who did you try to pick up?"

"Jack Winston," Rose answered. "I know that he and Drew are best friends, Tyler. But he fit all the criteria, and I figured it would only be for one night. What could it hurt?"

"I could care less who he's friends with." Tyler frowned into her brandy then took a healthy swig. "I'm worried about you picking up some pervert and getting hurt."

"It was your idea."

"But I never thought you'd go through with it. And never this quickly."

"I know." Rose laughed at the expressions on her friends' faces. "Surprised? I knew what you were up to, Tyler. At first, I did not intend to do it. I thought about it some more and decided I'd look around tonight; make a mental list of possibilities. Then I overheard Jilly

Underwood going on about Jack's reputation in bed and that she was going to pounce on the poor guy. Well, it was practically my civic duty to save him from the bitch of the west."

"You should have been a Girl Scout, Rose," Tyler sighed. "Though I doubt there's a badge for saving an adult male from a man-eater."

Rose shrugged. "It's a moot point. He turned me down, and I've decided I'm no good at picking up guys."

"Good." Dani gave Rose's shoulder a quick squeeze. "What if he had agreed? For all you know, Jack Winston could have turned out to be a sexual deviant."

"I assure you I'm not."

Tyler and Dani spun around in surprise, but Rose just closed her eyes and wished the ground would open and swallow her up. *Jack*. How much had he heard? It didn't matter; every part of the conversation was potentially embarrassing. It was clear he'd caught the last part — the worst part.

"Jack," she began.

"I've changed my mind."

"Well, so has she," Tyler answered for her.

He ignored Tyler. "Would you like to leave now? We can stay and dance some more if you'd like. Whichever you prefer."

"No, let's go."

"Rose," Dani stopped her. "Are you sure about this?"

"You don't have to go," Tyler added.

She could see the worry on her friends' faces. They acted as if she were a virgin being sent to a fate worse than death.

"I'll call you both in the morning."

"Call us as soon as he leaves," Tyler insisted then sent a warning glare Jack's way as he escorted Rose from the room.

"Scared?" Rose asked as they exited Harper House.

"Your friend has perfected her *I'll kill you if you hurt her look*." Jack gave their tickets to the parking attendant. "How long has she been practicing?"

"Tyler was born with it." She thanked him as he helped her into her car. "But she would never kill anyone. Tyler likes to leave a lasting impression though. She goes straight for the balls." Rose couldn't help grinning at Jack's automatic grimace.

"Relax, there's only been one actual castration."

"And what was his offense?"

"Kicking a dog." She paused. "Maybe littering. As you've probably guessed, Tyler has her own idea of right and wrong. Just try not to get on her bad side, and you and your boys will be just fine."

"I promise to be on my best behavior. Ah, here's my SUV." He made sure her dress was tucked into the car before shutting her door.

"I'll wait for you just down the road and then you can follow me home. Oh, and Jack? This is a one night only invitation. If you're not okay with that, keep on driving."

It was a quick trip to town. The bridge across the Columbia River and into Harper Falls served only one purpose — to get people to Harper House and back. So, of course, the way was impeccably maintained. During the day, a beautiful panoramic view drew photographers and artists from all over the world. On a moonless night like tonight, it was like driving over a bottomless cavern; a bit creepy if you stopped to think about it.

Rose's thoughts were completely taken up with Jack Winston. Was the jumpy feeling in her stomach excitement or nerves? Probably both. Jack was a big departure for her, which was the whole point. That didn't stop the little voice in her head from asking if this was a good idea. The dance they'd shared had been brief, but there had been a definite attraction. She knew having sex with him would be no hardship but there weren't supposed to be any feelings involved. Less than five minutes in his arms and she could say without hesitation that she liked him. She could see them being friends.

Because of her work, Rose had met hundreds of people. Those with whom she'd spent any real amount of time? She couldn't say. However, very few she would call *friend*. To her, friendship constituted a lot more than social media sites or recognizing someone enough to give them a casual hello as they passed on the street. Friendship equaled intimacy, letting someone in. Rose could count her friends on the fingers of one hand. If she added one more to the small list, she still wouldn't need a second hand.

She pulled her car to a stop in front her garage, waiting until Jack's SUV pulled up beside her. She had to stop overthinking this. No friend zone for Jack. This was about here and now, and if things went as planned, she was about to get hot and sweaty with the sexiest man she had ever met.

Rose rolled down her window when she saw that Jack had jumped out and walked towards her.

"There's plenty of room if you want to park in the garage."

He leaned down, grinning. "Afraid your neighbors will talk if they see my SUV parked out here all night?"

"My reputation could use a little tarnish." Just last week, Mrs. Teasdale from across the street had given her a ten-minute lecture about using it or losing it. The woman was seventy if she was a day and her love life was hotter than Rose's was. "We don't get a lot of vandalism or theft around here but you never know."

"I'll take my chances and leave it out here. Do you want me to come in through the garage or would you rather let me in the front door?"

"Come on in the garage. Just watch your head while the door is closing."

Rose turned off the ignition but before she could even reach for the handle, Jack held the door open for her and took her hand.

"You're a throwback, Jack Winston."

Jack shrugged. "That's how I was brought up. Dad opened doors for every lady he met. He always said the only way to get respect is to show respect, and it's especially important to respect women."

"Hard philosophy to argue with."

Rose turned on the light. Was it customary to offer your one-night stand something to drink? She was about to ask jokingly when Jack spun her around and had her pressed up against the wall. Who could think about etiquette when you were engaged in the hottest kiss of your life?

Chapter Five

JACK WAS GOOD at thinking on his feet. Whether it was avoiding a three-hundred-pound linebacker intent on inflicting as much pain as possible or fixing a glitch in a software program just hours before they released it to the public. When he came face-to-face with a crisis, Jack never panicked. When Rose had announced that tonight was going to be a one-time thing — period — he came as close to freaking out as he could ever remember.

The original plan had been to get her away from the party. He didn't know if she had been serious about hitting on another guy but better safe than sorry. Then he was going to drop her off at her house giving her one quick and very chaste kiss. He'd ask her out for the next night, maybe dinner and a movie. For tonight, he would claim exhaustion. Besides, he would tell her the sex would be so much better if they got to know each other first. At one time or another, he was sure he'd heard his sisters say that. Of course, the truth was that *hello* was all the relationship development most guys needed. Sometimes not even that was necessary. Women appreciated a man who was willing to take it slow — also a bit of wisdom from his sisters. Thanks to that stupid bet, Jack had become a freaking snail.

Unfortunately, Rose wanted fast, tonight, and only tonight. How was a guy supposed to plan for that? One dance and he'd known Rose was different from any woman he'd ever met. The attraction had already been there, but this was more. *What* it was he didn't know. To find out, he had to convince a woman determined to kick him out after one night that there was going to be a whole lot more.

The kiss was pure improvisation. Bad idea, his brain screamed, but he had to have a kiss, just a brief one. The moment she made that little moaning sound and opened her mouth to his questing tongue, he knew he was a goner. Kissing Rose could never be brief; he planned on devoting hours to this one task. Eventually, he'd be able to write a thesis on her taste alone. It turned out kissing Rose was the best *bad* idea he'd ever had.

Rose drowned in pleasure like she'd never known, just from a kiss. Jack wasn't touching her any place but on the lips and yet she could feel it on every inch of her body. Long, sure strokes of his tongue made her ache for him to explore the rest of her with equal thoroughness. She needed to touch him. Why wasn't she touching him? She reached out, not caring where she started, just determined *to* start. Jack had other ideas. Before she could do more than skim her hands up his chest, he stopped her. She was at his mercy and loving every moment.

"I want you, Rose."

Even his voice was an erotic jolt to her already overheated system. She had gone from nervous to ready to explode in mere seconds. Jack's warm breath bathed her ear with every whispered word. Had her ear always been so sensitive? She couldn't remember. At the moment, she couldn't think of anything past the small patch of skin on the side of her neck that he slowly caressed with the side of his finger.

"Can you feel that, Rose?"

"Yes," she sighed. "More. Give me more."

"Close your eyes. Think of nothing but my touch. Is that enough?"

Rose moaned. Enough? God, no. She needed his touch; she needed everything.

"One finger giving you so much pleasure." He slowly moved the tormenting caress down her neck and to the top of her spine. All her senses zeroed in on that feather light touch as it made its way down the exposed skin of her back.

"Imagine, Rose, just imagine. If just one finger can set your heart racing, what could the other nine do?"

If he hadn't been holding her hands above her head, Rose knew her legs would have given out. She felt so much all at once and yet she wanted so much more. She wanted Jack — naked — now.

"I'm going to leave you, Rose."

She heard the words, but it took a moment for the meaning to register. Leaving? Was he leaving?

Rose's eyes popped open. He still stood in front of her, but he no longer touched her, no longer whispered seductive promises.

"What did you say?" One of them was crazy, and it must be her. She certainly felt like she was losing her mind. She could only imagine how she looked, her eyes wild, her breath coming in ragged gasps. Jack, on the other hand, looked calm, collected and utterly unaffected by what had just passed between them. She *was* crazy, but her sanity returned fast.

"Why did you start something you had no intention of finishing?" Rose demanded. "It's obvious that you're as aroused as I am. Why stop?"

Aroused was putting it mildly — and he was going to suffer for it the rest of the night.

"I don't do one-night stands, Rose." *Which was true.* "I have. In college, hook-ups were regular. But I'm not a kid anymore; I want more." He looked deep into her eyes. "I want more with you."

Well, crap. Crap, crap, crap, crap, exclamation point *crap*!

"And I don't. Want more, that is." She took a deep breath. All systems were almost back to normal, and her legs were able to carry her to the front door. "Thanks for seeing me home and high praise for one hell of a good night kiss. This is where we say goodbye, Jack. I'm sure we'll see each other around town, but that's it." She opened the door and stood aside so he could exit.

"I'll pick you up tomorrow night at six-thirty. Nothing fancy." He gave her a quick peck on the cheek and headed towards the driveway.

Open-mouthed Rose just stared at his retreating figure. Okay, so *he* was the crazy one.

"I'm not going out with you, Jack," she called out.

Jack gave her a backward wave and jumped into his SUV.

"Six-thirty."

Rose watched in disbelief as he pulled out and onto the street. The glow of the truck's taillights faded before she shook herself and went back into the house. What had just happened? How had she lost control? Had she ever really had it?

Rose removed her shoes and slowly made her way upstairs. She carefully took off her dress and hung it up. The original house had had almost no storage space, so Rose tasked the contractor to knock out the wall between bedrooms and design a huge master suite. New bathroom, walk-in closet; all the bells and whistles. For the first time in her life, she had a bathroom all to herself. No sharing counter space, no picking up someone else's wet, dirty towel. If there was hair in the sink, she knew it was hers, not her roommate's slovenly boyfriend. Everything had been lovingly handpicked and paid for *by* her. She didn't have to consult with anyone if she wanted bright yellow walls or bordello red bath towels. It didn't matter that she'd gone with neither. The point was she could have. That's where the real satisfaction lay.

She did her nightly bathroom routine of face washing and teeth brushing before slipping on her favorite nightshirt and crawling between the ultra-soft sheets that she had put on the bed fresh that morning. She plumped the pillows and settled back with a sigh. There was supposed to be a big, sexy man beside her right now. Well, *inside* of her if she wanted to get technical. Damn Jack Winston.

She reached over and picked up her phone. She decided to call Dani since she was less likely to push for details. Tomorrow she would badger as hard as Tyler would, but for one night, she'd let Rose keep her thoughts to herself.

"Are you all right?" Dani's greeting made Rose smile. They must have been more worried than she realized.

"I'm fine. Tucked up in bed safe and sound. And alone." Rose could hear voices and music in the background. She looked at her clock. Eleven-forty-six. It felt later. "You're still at the ball?"

"Tyler wanted to stick around for the witching hour, or as she puts it, when the witch shows up, sans broom."

Regina Harper never mingled at her Lilac Ball. She made one appearance, at midnight, to give a short speech thanking everyone for attending and the generous donations. People always grumbled. Why couldn't she do it at an earlier hour? Most of the guests stayed out of respect or fear. As a result, they donated more money than they might have if they'd been able to leave sooner. Raffle tickets were sold all evening and that alone was a major cash cow.

Tyler stayed because she was one of the few people who could put a crack in Regina Harper's icy façade. If you looked closely, she swore you could see little puffs of steam coming out of the grand lady's ears whenever she was aware of Tyler's presence. Well worth the price of admission.

"And you're stuck there being a good friend." Rose would have stayed too if it hadn't been for a certain asshole.

"Someone has to hold her back." Rose heard someone asking Dani to dance and her friend's quick refusal. "One of these days she's going to make good on her threat to douse Regina with a bucket of water."

"And get arrested for her trouble. Though if she started melting, it would be worth the risk." The bitter animosity Tyler felt for the Harper family had been stewing for so long, it was bound to spill over eventually. Rose and Dani secretly hoped it would take the form of Tyler and Drew ripping each other's clothes off. But for that to happen, they would have to be in the same room.

"So you're alone. Quick off the mark?"

"I have no idea." Rose punched the pillow beside her where Jack's face should have been. "He kissed me once and left."

"That was it?" Dani asked, surprise obvious in her voice.

"He said he didn't do one-night stands. Told me — not asked, mind you — told me we were going out for dinner tomorrow night. Then he got into his SUV and drove away."

"Are you going?"

"No," Rose answered emphatically. "Probably not. Oh, I don't know." She couldn't see Dani's smile, but she could imagine it.

"How was the kiss?"

"I'm still recovering my brain cells."

"That good?" Dani laughed.

"Too good," Rose admitted. "Is that another guy asking you to dance? Go, enjoy. We'll talk tomorrow."

"You sure you're okay?"

"Go."

Rose hung up and burrowed under the covers. Talking to Dani had helped; she and Tyler settled her. She was lucky to have them. Sleep felt within reach now. Any solution to her Jack problem could wait until tomorrow. As her eyes drifted shut, she had one final thought — that *had* been one hell of a kiss.

JACK HAD GIVEN up trying to sleep around three that morning and decided he might as well use the time to fiddle with a little problem he'd been having with a new program. His home office had everything he needed to do the job, but he'd driven the few miles to the office instead. He didn't need his bed as a mocking reminder of the sleep he wasn't getting or the sex he wasn't *going* to get for another three weeks. At least he had a clear objective in sight. Not just sex with some no-name woman but sex with Rose. Beautiful, funny, hard-headed Rose.

He didn't know why she was intent on the old 'love 'em and leave 'em' routine. Maybe some idiot had hurt her with promises of a future that never materialized? He didn't know Rose — something he planned to change very soon. She certainly didn't seem like someone who would judge all men on the behavior of just one. However, it didn't matter. She'd soon find out that *this* man meant what he said — starting with making good on the promise to take her out tonight.

"You look like hell." Drew, on the other hand looked refreshed, all signs of yesterday's hangover long gone. His hair was still damp from his morning shower, and he carried a large cup of coffee in one hand and a bag of donuts in the other.

"Kiss my ass and give me that coffee."

Seeing a man in obvious need of a caffeine fix, Drew handed over the cup without argument.

"I was going to ask how things went last night but by the look of you, I guess I don't need to." Sitting in the chair on the other side of Jack's desk, he put his feet up and took a big bite out of a maple bar. "Want one?"

Jack just glared at Drew's big feet over the rim of his cup, annoying but not worth the effort. Then there was his friend's choice of breakfast. Jack could never face anything sweet in the morning whereas Drew had deep fried fat with a heavy glaze to start most days. The thought made Jack shudder.

"Better now?" Drew grinned as he watched Jack drain the last drop of liquid.

"I might live. God, is it seven-thirty?" He'd lost track. "I think I've finally gotten a handle on the glitch in our new security program. A few more hours of fine tuning and it'll be ready for the last test run."

"That's great, Jack, but the matter wasn't pressing. There wasn't any reason to come in and work yourself into the ground. You may be able to go longer without sleep than anyone I know, but even you need to get some shut-eye now and then."

"Call it a case of hard cock syndrome," Jack said ruefully. "Oh, and don't take this the wrong way, but I hate you."

"Sounds pretty straightforward to me." Drew crumpled the empty bag and tossed it in the nearby trashcan. "So, who is she?"

Jack scrubbed a hand over his face and sighed. "You don't want to know."

"Sure I do. I might even send her thank you flowers if she's gotten *you* tied up in knots." Drew threw his head back and laughed. "You meet a woman you want to screw and for once in your life, you have to keep you dick in your pants. I'm loving that bet more and more."

"Screw you."

"Not if you want to win the bet," Drew laughed again. "Now tell me about this woman that kept you from your bed."

"I think I'll pass."

"I know you don't like to kiss and tell but—" Drew heard Jack's soft curse. "So there *was* a kiss. Must have been pretty memorable."

He'd only thought about it a couple hundred times.

"It was all right."

"Sure." Drew leaned back, his fingers steeped in thought. "Let's see. Who is a sexy woman that you're reluctant to talk about?" Drew's feet hit the floor with a thud. "You son of a bitch."

"What?" Jack jumped in surprise when Drew suddenly shot out of his chair.

"It's Tyler."

"Are you out of your mind?" For a moment he thought that Drew might actually throw a punch at him. Since Jack was fall-on-his-face exhausted, he wouldn't have been able to put up much resistance. He braced himself for the blow when Drew collapsed back into his chair; all the fight drained out of him.

"I'm sorry, Jack." The anguish on Drew's face was palpable. "I know you'd never do that. You want to hit me?"

"Yes, but right now it would be with all the force of a wet noodle. Get back to me after I've had something to eat and a couple hours of sleep." Jack pushed himself out of his chair. "And that's what I'm going to do. But, let me leave you with a piece of advice you don't want to hear. Make your move and soon. You've had ten years to figure out how to get her back, and you're damn lucky she's not married with a couple of kids."

He didn't wait for a response because there was nothing to say. They both knew Jack was right; it was up to Drew to do something about it.

"Hey," Drew called as Jack left the building. "You never told me the name of your lady."

Jack smiled to himself and kept on walking. *His lady*. He liked the sound of it.

ROSE'S HAND REMAINED on the old guitar; her eyes still closed as the emotion of the song drifted through, the last notes fading away

Dani had dropped by about an hour earlier, damp from the rainstorm that had blown in that afternoon. She liked to walk whenever possible, but she never remembered an umbrella. Fortunately, some borrowed clothing and a hot cup of tea had warmed her up in no time. They had settled in for a rehash of the night before and segued into Rose playing a rough draft of *Wishing*. It was a sample song for the movie of the same name. She had finally given into Sam Laughton's badgering, but she still wasn't sure she was the right person for the job. It was such a lushly romantic story, and her music had always been raw, sexual. Almost angry. Writing these songs would be a huge departure for her, and it had Rose questioning the judgment of *the* Sam Laughton. But even more, it had her questioning herself. On top of that, because the original songwriter had dropped out at the last minute, Rose had less than two months to finish five songs.

She waited for Dani's response, but none came. Was it that bad? As she opened her eyes, she heard her friend's sniffle. Tears streamed down her face as she searched through her purse.

"I don't have any tissues," Dani cried.

Rose grabbed the box from the nearby table.

"It's good?"

"It's us."

Rose nodded. In the movie, the song was about a young woman who struggled with loss. The loss of her mother, the loss of the man she loved. Going through her mother's things, she found a piece of paper with a list of wishes. Her mother had made them for her on the day she was born. When writing the song, Rose had pictured Dani and Tyler, and herself combined to make the one woman. Therefore, the wishes were for them. Rose felt a lump form in her throat. It meant so much that Dani had understood what she was saying with her words, the love she expressed for the two most important people in her life.

"You have to play this for Tyler." Dani dialed and blew her nose at the same time. "I'm so glad you agreed to do this movie."

Five minutes later, Tyler agreed. She was the least sentimental of them all, but Rose could hear the slight catch in her friend's voice after she heard the song. "Rose, it would have been a crime to let anyone else write the score. I can't believe you even hesitated."

"It's a love story."

"And?" Tyler and Dani asked simultaneously.

They were going to make her say it.

"And I've never been in love. I understand that people write about things they don't know. But I loved this book; you guys loved this book. It needs just the right touch. Nothing too sappy or sentimental."

"Which makes you perfect," Tyler reasoned. "Give it to someone who's in love and they'll turn it into sugary mush. What if the writer had just gone through a messy breakup? Then they'd make it cynical or give it too hard an edge. That song you wrote proves you have just the right feeling for the material."

"I want this so much," Rose sighed. "That's the first time I've admitted it even to myself."

"Then it's settled. Great material — great song — great writer. Now that that's settled," Tyler said. "Let's talk you into going out tonight with Jack Winston."

"No need. I've already decided to go."

"That's great," Dani exclaimed. "What changed your mind?"

Rose shrugged. "I like him."

"You knew that last night," Tyler reminded her.

""Okay, it's going to sound stupid." She took a breath. "He tucked my dress into the car before shutting the door."

"Now, why would that sound stupid?" Tyler's sarcasm practically dripped through the phone.

Ignoring her, Rose continued. "Jack helped me into my car and the hem of my dress hung out. We all know plenty of guys who wouldn't have noticed, or just not cared, and closed the door, probably ripping or staining the material. Jack made sure there was nothing hanging out before he closed the door. Closed, not slammed."

"That's sweet," Tyler smiled. "Kind of romantic."

"But he wasn't *trying* to be," Rose explained. "There was nothing calculated or staged. I never got the feeling he was trying to make a good impression. I'd say his mother brought him up right, which from our brief conversation is true. But—"

"Nature or nurture," Tyler finished her thought. "Just because someone teaches you how to treat people right doesn't mean you will."

"Exactly." Rose thought of her own childhood. No, she didn't want to go there. "Jack Winston is innately thoughtful. He's careful with other people."

"Gorgeous, sexy, kisses that make your brain cells explode and a good guy? Why aren't you running in the opposite direction?"

Because I might have finally found a guy who is worth running to. That was too scary to say out loud so instead, she kept it light. "It's one date, Tyler. We can talk about it again if he doesn't turn into Mr. Hyde."

"Oh, we'll talk," Tyler assured her. "Dani and I are in a dating slump, so we need you to give us a few vicarious thrills."

They spent a few more minutes going back and forth about nothing in particular, and then Tyler hung up, anxious to get back to work on her latest commission.

"Looks like the rain has stopped." Dani put her phone away and headed for the laundry room where her clothes were drying. "These are ready. I'll change and be on my way so you can get ready for your date."

"How are things with you, Dani?"

"Me?" Dani asked as she pulled on her jeans. "What do you mean?"

"Well, if we aren't talking about my love life then we're dancing around Tyler's situation with idiot boy Drew. We never seem to talk about you."

"We talk about me all the time," Dani protested. "I spent most of dinner last week telling you guys about how the work is coming on my photo studio. If you're talking about my love life? It's as Tyler said; I'm in a slump. Things will pick up, they always do."

Rose wondered. Of the three of them, Dani, at least on the surface, seemed the most easygoing. No childhood drama, a great career, her pick of men to date. But there *had* been a bump, a big one.

"You know if you ever want to talk about Portugal, Tyler and I will listen."

Dani sighed. Now and then one of her friends would bring up that time just after they had all graduated from college. Completely on her own and bursting with youthful ambition, she had taken a job with an online travel magazine, Portugal being her first stop. She had fallen in love for the first time. He was handsome, funny, and brutally honest. From the first, she had known that they only had a limited time together and that he could be sent someplace new at any time. They never talked about what he did in the military. He couldn't say, and she didn't want to know. One morning she woke up alone, and that was that.

She'd cried for two days straight, including a couple of incoherent calls to Rose and Tyler, and then she'd moved on. Those brief two weeks had been perfect. A snapshot of her transition from girl to woman, and, even though her friends knew most of the particulars, some things she kept to herself, locked away in her heart. Things she didn't want to talk about. She preferred to keep the past where it was — in the past. It was an old wound, uncomfortably deep. But not crippling. She needed her friends to understand that.

"You make it sound like I experienced some great tragedy, Rose." Dani gave her a genuine smile. "I met a man, it was amazing, and then he was gone. End of story."

"But you loved him."

"I did." Part of her always would. "But that was five years ago and he hasn't made any attempt to get in touch with me." She shrugged. "All I want is for him to be safe and healthy and happy. If he ever thinks of me, I hope he remembers our time together with the same affection that I do. I can't ask for anything more."

"I want you to be happy," Rose pulled her in for a warm, loving hug. "I want us all to be happy."

"I am," Dani assured her and she meant it. Dani believed wholeheartedly in love, and she intended to fall in love again. However, she wasn't going to lose sleep over it. When the right time and the right man came along, she would welcome love with open arms.

Dani picked up her purse and deposited her phone. "Now, can we drop it? Please?"

"Absolutely." Rose walked Dani to the door, insisting she take an umbrella just in case. She only lived a few streets over, but the clouds still looked threatening. "I'll see you tomorrow."

"Have a good time tonight."

Rose planned to. She gave Dani a final wave before glancing at the hall clock. Five-thirty. Last night he'd seen what she looked like when she pulled out all the stops. Tonight it was going to be a comb through the hair and a swipe of lipstick. Clean and simple.

JACK PICKED HER up right on time. He had on faded jeans and a black leather jacket that had seen better days, but it still looked incredibly appealing on his trim, muscular body. He wore a t-shirt that was the same intense blue as his eyes.

He leaned in and gave her a kiss hello. It lingered nicely, leaving her with the promise of more to come.

"Hello." His smile was warm and friendly. "You look amazing."

"Were you this tall last night?" She desperately wanted to run her tongue over her lips, just to see if he tasted as good as she remembered. But that would be weird. Especially with him watching her so intently.

"Were you this short?" After making sure her front door was locked securely, Jack took her hand and led her to his parked SUV.

"It must have been the heels," Rose reasoned and he helped her up into the cab.

"I wasn't wearing heels."

She rolled her eyes but couldn't help laughing. He was quick; she'd give him that.

"Where are we going?" Not that it mattered. She had one thing on her mind tonight. Sex. Sex with Jack Winston.

"I thought you might like to see H&W headquarters. We've pretty much finished all the renovation and upgrades." He glanced over at her and shrugged. "You'll be the first to get the grand tour. I hope you don't mind, but I've been dying to show it off."

Rose was flattered. She knew of at least a dozen women who would have lined up at the chance to have Jack Winston give them a personal tour. Everyone in town had been brimming with curiosity ever since he and Drew bought the land on Crossfire Hill. Those who had worked on the construction said it was a large compound with several buildings. The details remained scarce. In the beginning, rumors of course ran rampant. Some said it was a secret government facility and that Jack and Drew were some kind of mad scientists. Her favorite bit of gossip had them opening a sex club. Rose doubted very many people in Harper Falls even knew quite what a sex club was. Maybe she was wrong. Some of those books that no one admitted to reading were pretty detailed.

They'd had the road up to the compound paved, so the trip was much smoother than Rose remembered. The one time she had been up here was in high school when her date had taken her to the local make-out place. Rose hadn't protested. She'd never been before and was curious what all the fuss was about. Other than a great view, she and her date had left disappointed. Will Hazelton's sweaty groping and slobbery kisses had put Rose off car dating for the rest of high school. From then on, if they couldn't walk, she didn't go. Luckily, in college she'd discovered boys with much better technique and much better cars.

Jack pulled to a stop. It was still light enough to see the layout of the compound. There were three main buildings. One was all office space on the first floor. Another acted as on-site housing for when any or all of the crew was there for training. And the last stored equipment and a full-service garage. These buildings formed a semi-circle around an obstacle course and parking lot. Most of the time it was more space than they really needed but when it was in full use, they were glad to have the room.

"This is amazing, Jack." Not at all what she had expected. These weren't shacks in the wilderness but modern, attractive and built to last buildings. "You and Drew have houses up here, right?"

"Farther up." He pointed to a road that ran up into the trees. "We wanted to be close to work but still apart. We're within shouting distance of each other and the compound — but private. I'll show you some other time."

So he wasn't taking her back to his place. Since she had spent a good part of the day picturing him in *her* bed, she was fine with that.

"Come on," he said, hopping out of the SUV. He came around and helped her down. Taking her hand, he led her towards the main building. "No one's around right now but depending on the day, the place can really hop with activity."

She waited while he punched in an elaborate sequence of numbers on a security panel then leaned in for a retinal scan. *Very Mission Impossible*, Rose thought.

"It's kind of gruesome to think of what I'd have to do if I wanted to break in here."

"Most people are a bit squeamish when faced with popping someone's eye out," Jack laughed as he disengaged the last lock.

"Have you had any dealings with people who aren't? Squeamish, that is." She knew they were a security firm, but it had never occurred to her that they ever faced any real danger. Even though they looked like superheroes, she'd assumed Jack and Drew were the brains, not the brawn.

"Nope. And we don't expect to. But industrial espionage is big business, and since we develop programs to stop cyber-theft, it would look pretty bad if someone robbed us."

"But you still do personal security, being bodyguards and such." Rose couldn't get past the idea of someone removing one of Jack's beautiful blue eyes. "That can be dangerous."

"Rarely. Come on," he pulled her along through a luxurious reception area that they had decorated in rich shades of brown and cream. "My office is just down this hall."

Again, with the endless code and retinal scan. It might have been scary, but it was also impressive.

Jack's office was a geek's paradise. Besides the multiple computers and printers, Rose had no idea what most of the stuff did. She just walked around and took it all in. One entire wall was nothing but glass that framed an amazing view of Harper Falls and just beyond the winding waters of the Columbia River. Harper House was practically straight across. That must have been a daily middle-digit salute to Drew's estranged mother.

"Pretty spectacular, isn't it?" Jack came up behind her, not quite touching. He was close enough, however, for his warm breath to brush against her cheek. "Drew knew what land he wanted before we even found out if it was for sale. Of course, his office faces in the other direction. I doubt that I have to go into great detail as to why that is."

She would have loved to know what Drew had told Jack about the whole sordid mess, but she doubted he'd be willing to break his friend's confidence. She would have lost a lot of respect for him if he had.

"Can I see the rest of the place?" Rose leaned back against Jack's body. He was wonderfully warm, adding to the heat that had been building in her since their kiss the night before. Maybe they could abandon the tour and take advantage of that large, soft-looking couch across the room.

"Are you afraid I might have a sex room hidden somewhere?"

"So you've heard the rumors." Rose laughed.

"I thought that might have been what Tyler was talking about last night." Rose frowned in confusion. "She warned you that I might be a sexual deviant."

"Whips, chains, and ball gags don't make you a sexual deviant, Jack," Rose clarified. "In Tyler's book and mine, anything goes between consenting adults. What makes you a deviant is forcing someone when she in *any way* indicated that she isn't a willing participant. In other words, no means no."

"Was she, were any of you ever…?" The question seemed to stick in his throat. The charming rascal had quickly been replaced by a protective warrior. If she'd given him a name, she had no doubt he'd have exacted his own kind of justice.

"No," Rose assured him. "But Tyler had a friend in college who was attacked and beaten. She fought, but she was no match for him. The next day Tyler made us sign up for self-defense classes. Dani went on and got her black belt in karate."

"Dani? Really?"

"I know she looks like a delicate piece of porcelain but never come up behind her without warning. Tyler might rip your balls off, but Dani goes for the jugular."

"And you?" Jack asked, turning her into his arms. "What do you go for?"

She slowly ran her hand up his chest. She stopped over his heart, feeling the increased rhythm. The muscles jumped when she gently massaged the firm, heated flesh. Then before he could blink, she was behind him, his arm twisted into the center of his back.

"I lull and then attack."

"Impressive," Jack conceded. He could have easily gotten out of the hold, but he liked that she had some moves. At the moment, he liked her rubbing up against his back. "Now that you have me, what are you going to do with me?"

If this had been someone she really wanted to get away from, she would have kicked him in the back of the knee and run like hell. Jack had had plenty of time to use his superior strength to gain the upper hand. That told Rose he was in the mood to play, which was fine; so was she.

"Take off your jacket," she ordered. "Slowly. I don't want to have to get rough with you."

Laughing to himself, Jack removed his jacket, slowly, and tossed it onto a nearby chair.

"I like a man who can follow orders. Now turn around." When he did, Rose grabbed a handful of his t-shirt, pulling him down until they were eye-to-eye. "Kiss me, Jack. Like you mean it."

It would have been so easy to give her what we both want, Jack thought. Just lean in and take what she so sweetly offered, forget everything he'd decided that afternoon while he tossed and turned, still unable to sleep.

It took a while, but he finally came up with two reasons to hold off sleeping with Rose.

Number one, the bet. It was stupid, juvenile, and completely impossible to justify to anyone but himself and the group of idiots who had been too drunk to understand just how ridiculous they were being. Maybe it was a guy thing, but he just didn't want to give in and admit he couldn't keep his dick to himself for such a relatively small amount of time. On top of that, it was a bet that hurt no one. Outside of his overactive libido, it was a victimless crime, so to speak.

Then there was Rose. Beautiful, funny, confident, and oh so sexy, Rose. Two weeks ago, he wouldn't have hesitated. He would have spent last night in her bed, and he had no doubt it would have been amazing. But then what? *She* claimed she wanted a one-night stand. *He'd* never been with the same woman for more than a few weeks. Suddenly he had the chance to get to know a woman as a person. Sex wouldn't be the end game every night. People still went to the movies, held hands, and ended their dates with just a kiss or two. Stupid as it was, the bet had given him the chance to find out if he and Rose were compatible outside of the bedroom. A novel concept but, with Rose, he found the idea more and more appealing.

Instead of the full-on kiss she expected, Jack gave her a soft peck on the cheek. Sweet and affectionate. That seemed to be the order of the day.

"I haven't finished showing you around," he said, taking her hand. "And then I have a surprise for you."

Rose was already surprised. As Jack led her out of his office and to a nearby stairwell, she couldn't help but wonder what had just happened? She had been so sure he was about to kiss her and not like you'd kiss your kid sister. Something had changed in the short moment between him taking off his jacket and his lips landing on her cheek. Had she read him wrong? She didn't have much experience with men like Jack. Wasn't he supposed to be a sure thing? How hard could *that* be to read?

She followed Jack down two flights of stairs, the smell of chlorine becoming stronger with each step.

"There's a swimming pool down here?"

"Drew likes to swim every morning," Jack explained as they entered what Rose could only describe as a subterranean oasis.

"Honestly, Jack?" Rose laughed. "This is like something out of a movie. Who takes care of all this?"

"We have a guy," Jack answered. Several, actually.

She did a slow circle, trying to take it all in. The pool was large, not Olympic size, but big enough to do laps easily. It was surrounded by lush, green plants that thrived despite the lack of sunlight. Grow lights, she assumed. The room was humid but not overwhelmingly so.

"I don't hear any fans," she commented, still taking in all the amazing details. "But it seems fresh air is being pumped in."

"State of the art system, almost soundless." Jack enjoyed the changing expressions flitting across Rose's face. Wonder, amazement, humor. Mostly humor.

"I'd say boys and their toys," she laughed, "but this goes way beyond video games and giant TVs."

One day he'd show her the huge projection screen that they had hidden in the ceiling. Maybe when he brought her back for a late-night skinny dip.

Taking her hand again, he showed her the weight room and showers, and then led her down the hall to what looked like a dead end. Jack pushed a button, and the wall opened up to a hidden elevator. Rose gave Jack a *'you've got to be kidding me'* look as they entered.

"Rooftop," Jack said and the elevator started moving. "I know," he laughed. "But it's fun, right? We spend most of our time here. There's no reason it has to be all business."

The ride was short, so Rose had no time to do more than shake her head and smile. When the elevator doors opened, there were no words. All she could do was gasp.

Jack didn't need to look at the sunset; he could see it in Rose's eyes. They glowed, not just with the brilliant lights of the day's last moments, but with the joy she found in seeing it. It was a memory he would carry with him the rest of his days. Maybe, if he were lucky, over time he and Rose would create a few million more.

"It's like I'm seeing it for the first time." She turned to him, and he realized it wasn't the sun shining in her eyes; it was just Rose.

Getting ahead of yourself, Jack. Slow down. You don't want to scare her. Hell, he didn't want to scare himself.

"We designed most of this with a sloping roof so the snow will slide off easier in the winter. But I wanted a small section that we could use for lunch breaks or meditation, or this." He stepped aside letting her see the table he had set up earlier in the day.

Everything was set up for romance, Rose thought. Pale yellow china on an antique lace tablecloth. Flameless candles, practical but no less sweet, flickered next to fluted crystal champagne glasses. And in the center, a small vase of white peonies.

"I got the flowers from that new place down on Walnut. Is it weird that I got peonies from a place called *Peony*? Lila suggested them."

"You know Lila?" Rose asked in surprise.

"She's the sister of an old friend," he explained. "I knew she wanted to open a place of her own so I suggested Harper Falls."

"Small world," Rose whispered.

"You don't like them?" Maybe he should have gone for the cliché and bought roses.

"They're beautiful, Jack," she assured him. Someday she would tell him about how she'd met Lila but tonight wasn't the time to mention ruined shoes or projectile vomiting.

Jack smiled in relief. Holding out her chair, he seated her and then opened the waiting bottle of wine. "I know we had champagne last night but it seemed appropriate."

He handed her a filled glass and raised his own in a toast. "To romance."

Rose didn't drink. "What are we doing, Jack?"

He didn't pretend not to know what she meant. "I'd like to slow down, Rose. What would be wrong with us getting to know each other before we have sex?"

"There's nothing wrong with it, Jack. But you need to know there can't be any future for us."

"Why?"

How could she explain without sounding pathetic? It was such a 'poor me' story. She'd lived it and moved on. Mostly. Jack didn't need to know all the gory details.

"Do you see yourself married someday, Jack?" she asked. "Do you want children?"

"Yes, but I wasn't asking you to marry me, Rose."

"But you might." Did that sound egotistical? Maybe, but she needed Jack to understand. "I don't believe in marriage. Not for me."

"Rose…"

"Okay," she interrupted. She took a deep breath. "Here's the *Reader's Digest* version. My father left my mother and me before I was born. For the next nine years, she used a procession of men to fill the void until he came back. He was never coming back. But you couldn't tell her that. After she died, I was sent to live with the only relative that they could locate. I didn't know I even had an aunt, but here's her story. Louise marries for money. When she gets bored, she screws the nearest man and then she gets divorced. She's about to marry husband number seven. Lucky for some."

"Wow."

"Succinct, but accurate." Telling him this didn't just sound pitiful, it made her feel unclean. She wasn't responsible for Louise's actions, but they rubbed off nonetheless.

"I believe in love, Jack," she assured him. "Marriage between the right people can be beautiful and lasting. But I'm afraid I wouldn't even know how to begin to hold onto either."

"Then let's just take it a day at a time." Jack wanted to reach across and pull her into his arms. He wanted to tell her that she wasn't her mother or her aunt, but Rose already knew that. Maybe she was damaged; maybe he couldn't help her heal. But he could try.

"I don't know if I'll fall in love with you, Rose," he began. "I know I like you. I know I want to spend time getting to know you. Maybe I'll find out I hate your taste in movies, maybe you won't be able to stand the way I eat corn on the cob. Maybe we'll decide to be friends and forget about sex altogether."

Their eyes met for a moment, and they both started laughing, breaking the heaviness that had settled over the evening.

"Okay, forget the no sex part. But you get what I'm saying. Please, Rose. Give it a chance."

She wanted to. If Jack was still willing, even after everything she'd told him, then so was she.

"I'll agree but first you have to tell me something."

"Name it."

"How *do* you eat corn on the cob?"

Chapter Six

KISS ME JACK, *like you mean it.*
Believe me, it'll be my pleasure.

There was no smooth seduction, no easing in. There was no more teasing. She'd told him to kiss her, and he took control. His hands lifted, molding the shape of her head, firm and wonderfully sensuous. When his lips found hers, the taste of him filled her senses as his tongue entered her mouth, rubbing against her own. Jack's arms came around her, pulling her up until their bodies were in perfect alignment. As her breasts rubbed maddeningly against his chest, she wanted him to rip away every piece of clothing that prevented them from touching flesh to flesh. Her breathing became heavy, and every nerve seemed to center between her legs, right where his thigh rubbed with expert precision.

"Sweet," he groaned, coming up for air. "Like spiced honey. I want to spend a week tasting you. Your mouth," Jack swiped his tongue over her lips. "This spot right here," he whispered as he left a slow trail of kisses across her jaw unerringly finding the sensitive skin just below her ear. She thought she might come from just the feel of his lips on that spot. It was officially her new favorite erogenous zone.

"Touch me, Jack." He sensed a desperation in her voice that he'd never heard before. She needed his hands on her body, anywhere, now.

"I know what you need. Close your eyes, Rose. All you have to do is feel. I

promise I'll give you exactly what you want."

His lips continued to torment the spot below her ear but now his hands added to her arousal. He took his time, a slow journey, with a much too brief stop to tease her breasts. Go back. She wanted to scream. She could only manage a moan — part frustration, part encouragement.

He knew what he was doing. Building her up to heights she'd never experienced, the anticipation becoming almost unbearable.

"This is what you want, isn't it?"

Jack's fingers deftly unbuttoned her jeans, sliding the zipper down in one long, agonizingly slow motion. He teased the skin just above the top of her panties, one finger breaching the top and causing her to scream in hypersensitized frustration.

"Hurry, Jack. I need you to touch me."

"I am touching you, sweetheart." He laughed deeper than she remembered, the sound making her body clench with need. "Here, this is where you need my touch, isn't it, Rose? Tell me how it feels; tell me how close you are."

"So close." Finally. Jack's hand slid between her legs, his fingers finding the slick proof of her arousal. Yes, he knew the spot she needed him to touch. No hesitation — no teasing. Hard and insistent and oh God, he knew exactly what he was doing.

"Now, Jack. I'm coming now. Yes, just a little more. I can feel it, Jack, I can…"

What the hell? Rose sat up with a start; her body still poised for what she assumed would have been the best orgasm of her life. A dream orgasm. Well, that would have been a first. Just a few seconds more and dream Jack would have finished her off.

Still hazy from sleep, it took her a moment to realize what had awoken her. The computer was beeping. Right — Frank.

"You are officially my least favorite person ever." It wasn't Frank's fault that the closest she'd come to sex with Jack was in a dream, but his timing was lousy.

"Good morning to you too, sunshine." Apparently, Frank wasn't offended by her unorthodox greeting. "What have I done to incur your wrath so early in the day?"

Only awoke her from the best sexy dream ever. She'd fallen asleep on the couch waiting for Frank's call, and her subconscious decided to give her what she wasn't getting in real life. Unfortunately, she seemed doomed to frustration in her dreams as well.

"Sorry, Frank." She scrubbed a hand over her face. If she'd been alone, she'd have brought out her battery-operated friend but instead, she headed to the kitchen for a cup of hot tea.

"You caught me dozing," she explained over her shoulder.

"It must have been some dream."

"Not going to share, Frank."

He laughed. "My imagination is inventive enough. Jack Winston is definitely dream-sex material."

"I didn't say anything about sex." She set her cup down on the table by the computer. Last week, a few days after her rooftop date with Jack, she had mentioned him to Frank. No details, just that they had started seeing each other. Frank had wanted details; Rose gave him none. "And how do you know if Jack is *anything* worthy? When I mentioned him the other day, you said you'd never heard of him.

"There's this little thing called the internet. It's what's allowing us to talk right now."

"You're a riot, Frank." Rose frowned. "So you googled him?"

"You haven't?" Frank asked in amazement. "Honey, you have way more self-control than I do."

"It never occurred to me," Rose said honestly. "Is there much about him?"

"Plenty. Though most of it is several years old." Frank leaned in closer to the screen. "The spike in the number of pictures and articles happened about five years ago, right after that Karen Poe incident."

"Karen Poe, the movie star? Jack was involved with her?" Rose always *had* liked the actress' work, but she might have to rethink that.

"Honestly, Rose, I sometimes think you live under a rock," Frank said in amazement. "It was all over the news at the time. But never mind; let Frankie-boy fill you in."

"I could just look it up myself," Rose reminded him.

"And deprive me of spilling a bit of dish about your hunky

boyfriend?" Frank was appalled at the thought. "Since you were so closed-mouthed, I'll have to assume you know he and Drew Harper worked as personal bodyguards when they first went to L.A.?"

"He told me that." Why did she sound so defensive? It was just annoying that Frank knew more about that time in Jack's life than she did.

"Did he also tell you that he was Karen Poe's bodyguard while she was shooting *Lost Child?*"

"It never came up." Jack was *not* a namedropper. "I imagine he worked for a lot of famous people."

"But this was what put him and his company on the map." Frank paused dramatically before continuing. "Karen Poe was still an up-and-comer. She hadn't reached A-list status yet. But she'd made a few movies that generated her some buzz and, unfortunately, a stalker."

"So she hired Jack."

"The studio would only pop for a budget-friendly bodyguard and your boyfriend qualified."

"Would you stop calling him that?" Where Jack was concerned, Rose didn't know what they were. Maybe friends without benefits?

"Do you want to hear the rest of this?"

"Go on." She sighed when Frank just looked at her. Honestly. "Go on, please."

"So," he continued with a satisfied smile. "Nothing happened until the night of the movie premiere. They were on the red carpet when out of nowhere Karen's stalker jumps out of the crowd, intent on doing who knows what. Our hero steps in front of Karen, shielding her with his powerful body. And suddenly with one mighty uppercut, fells said villain and saves the day."

"That's unbelievable."

"Pretty impressive, huh?"

"Jack, yes. Your narration? Not so much."

"Everyone's a critic," Frank grumbled. "Shall I tell you what happened next?"

"I'm on the edge of my seat." Glancing down, she realized she was, literally. For all her teasing, Frank told a mean story, *and* it was about Jack. All that was missing was the popcorn.

"By the time he woke up the next morning, Jack Winston was a social media phenomenon. The video of the attack went viral. Twitter practically broke. Suddenly you weren't anyone if your body wasn't guarded by someone from H&W Security. It didn't hurt that both Jack and Drew Harper look like superheroes."

While Frank had been talking, Rose pulled up the video of the attack. Saving the beautiful movie star *and* unbelievably photogenic. Jack Winston was something to see. She wasn't the only one who thought so. The video had over five million views.

"Though no one would confirm, rumor has it that both Jack and Drew have been offered starring roles in action movies. Since we haven't seen their names up in lights, I assume they said no."

"Safe assumption," she murmured. Watching it again, she realized just how vulnerable he'd been. *What if the guy had had a weapon?* The thought made Rose shudder. She was grateful that Jack stayed behind a desk these days.

"So tell me, does he look as good in person?"

"Better."

"Lucky bitch."

Rose laughed. She was. She *really* was.

JACK HAD BUILT his house with privacy in mind. The trees that surrounded his home gave the illusion that he didn't share the mountain with another living human. Drew's house was a mere half-mile away, but you'd never know it. Standing on the old-fashioned wrap-around porch, Jack could just see where the southern end of the Columbia wound away from Harper Falls. He could look out, but no one could look in. Not unless they made a great effort, and then his security system let him know when visitors, welcome or otherwise, were coming.

Rose would be here at any minute. They'd been seeing each other for a week, and this was the first time she was coming to his home. Things were going well, amazingly so.

They had no fixed routine. One day they met for breakfast, the next she cooked dinner at her place. She claimed to have very little expertise in the kitchen but the simple meal of lasagna and tossed green salad had been terrific. She'd warned him about the state of her refrigerator before he put the wine into chill. However, it was hard to grasp what it was she meant until he actually saw it. Yogurt, bottled water, and orange juice. Healthy, he guessed, but limited. And it was an odd brand of yogurt, not that he was an expert. She told him that only one place in Spokane sold it, and she would stock up whenever she was in the city. And no, she interjected before he could comment; she wasn't going to order it online. She liked to pick out her own flavors, and she didn't know what she would be in the mood for until she was in the store buying it. Some people might find it odd that she was so defensive about yogurt but not Jack. He understood completely. He'd grown up in a household of eccentrics. Yogurt was nothing.

The sensor by the door went off telling him a car had entered his property. Jack glanced at the monitor and saw it was Rose. He had just started toward the porch steps when a bundle of brown and white fur came tearing around the corner, yapping like crazy. He went sailing past Jack until he realized the love of his life was now behind him. He tried, unsuccessfully, to stop his forward motion. The result was a heap of tangled puppy paws. Not to be deterred, he quickly righted himself and bounded up to Jack, pure adoration all over his face.

"My ferocious watchdog." Jack knelt down and gave the quivering mass a vigorous scratch behind his ears. It was a joke, of course. Jack had acquired Edgar the last time he'd visited his parents. Someone had dropped a box of puppies in their driveway. They were mutts, an indeterminable mix of breeds that had resulted in massively cute dogs that, if the size of the paws were any indication, were going to be quite large. His mother set about finding homes for all five but still had two left when Jack arrived. He needed a dog, she reasoned. He shouldn't be all alone in that big house. Jack said yes immediately. He had planned on getting a dog, and it never hurt to pile up the brownie points with Mom. He didn't have to pick between the two puppies. Edgar picked him by peeing on his boot five seconds after they'd met. It was love at first sight for both man and dog.

For all his size, Edgar was a bit of a fraidy-cat. He came running, in full out yap, whenever the surveillance system went off but lost his nerve when an actual car drove up to the house. His favorite hiding place was behind Jack, crouched down until he was sure the visitor was a friend and not a foe. For Edgar, within thirty seconds, everyone was a friend.

"Let's go say hi to Rose," Jack said just as her car came to a stop. "You'll like her; she smells amazing."

Rose turned off the ignition and sat for a moment taking in the details of Jack's house. It wasn't at all what she'd expected. She'd imagined something modern and sleek but instead he'd built a house that belonged to another era. Two stories and a full attic by the looks of it, painted white with dark green shutters. She knew he had a large family, but such a big house must be lonely when no one visited. Then she saw the huge puppy tumble his way down the stairs, a laughing Jack right behind him. Maybe not so lonely after all.

She barely had her door open when the dog was there. She wasn't sure if he was trying to push them both back in or drag her out, but either way he was irresistible.

"He's very friendly," Rose smiled as Jack pulled the puppy back enough for her to get out of the car.

"This is Edgar. I told him how good you smelled, and he was determined to find out for himself."

"He seems more interested in how I taste." The puppy's large, wet tongue gave her hand a thorough bath as she tried to pet his head.

"I don't blame him; I'm already addicted."

Sitting the wiggling Edgar down, Jack pulled Rose in for a long heated kiss.

"See," Jack said as he pulled back. "One taste and his affections have already turned."

Rose looked down to see Edgar staring up at her, his big paws resting on one of her feet.

"How big is he going to get?"

"The vet estimates he'll be well over a hundred pounds. I just hope by then he'll be better at controlling it. Come on, the casserole should almost be ready to take out. Would you like some wine while I finish the salad?"

"Sounds good."

Edgar ran ahead, disappearing around the house. Jack led her into the living room and made his way over to the kitchen. He'd chosen an open layout with hardwood floors and a huge gas fireplace that dominated the far wall. It was warm and inviting just like the man himself. She immediately felt at home, not that Jack would have let her feel any other way. It was a knack. One you couldn't learn no matter how hard you tried.

"Red or white?"

"Red. Is there anything I can help you do?"

"Food's under control. Take a seat and keep me company." He pointed to the row of bar stools. Rose pulled herself up onto the nearest one and set her wine down on the dark marble counter.

"I made one of my mother's recipes. I called her to ask what she put in it and was surprised to find out it was just something she threw together, never the same twice. She talked me through, and I think it turned out all right. Of course, I didn't tell her I was substituting beef for the tofu."

"You grew up a vegetarian?" Rose asked. Jack gave off a definite meat and potatoes man vibe.

"Mom tried." He finished buttering the bread and then wrapped it in foil and popped it the oven. "But given the chance, we all cheated. Even my dad sneaks out now and then for a burger. Mom pretends she doesn't know."

"Sounds like a system that works."

"It has for almost forty years." Jack opened the refrigerator and pulled out a bowl filled with lettuce. She could see some cucumber, carrots, and black olives sitting on top. He deftly poured on some dressing and tossed everything together then after plating two servings, finished it by shaving thin strips of parmesan cheese on top.

"By the time we eat our salads, everything else should be ready."

They didn't eat at the solid oak dining table. It looked like it would seat an army. Instead, Jack led her to the coffee table in front of the fire. It was still cool enough in the evenings that the blaze felt good.

"I hope you don't mind sitting on the floor. I like eating over here."

Rose settled in next to Jack, curling her legs underneath her. The plush area rug provided a comfortable cushion between them and the wood floor. They dug into the salad, an easy silence between them. Reaching for her wine, Rose took a sip. This was nice, relaxed. In a very short amount of time, she'd become very at ease with Jack. If it weren't for the *no sex* thing, she wouldn't have had a single complaint.

Get your mind off how sexy he looks in jeans and a pullover. Or how the pushed up sleeves showed off his strong forearms. Good Lord, had she ever been turned on by forearms before? Then again, lately it didn't take much more than Jack walking in a room for her libido to kick in. Or Jack sitting down. Or Jack licking his fork. It was getting hot in here; maybe sitting this close to the fire hadn't been such a good idea.

Had she worn that dress on purpose? Jack wondered. The raspberry-colored knit hugged her like a glove, cupping every luscious curve of her body. Curves he was becoming very used to dreaming about. Then he had to have the bright idea of sitting on the floor. The hem of the dress was now halfway up her thighs. She had fantastic thighs. Had the fire suddenly gotten hotter?

"A friend clued me into what a celebrity you are. Nice video, by the way."

"Ah," Jack shrugged. "You saw that."

"Are you blushing?" Rose teased.

"Flushed," Jack corrected her. "From the fire." God, he hated that video. It had followed him around for years. At least Rose seemed more amused than impressed. He'd lost count of how many women had come on to him just because of that one incident being posted online.

"You could have been hurt."

That surprised him. He couldn't remember a single person, outside of his family, who'd commented on the danger involved. There was none, not in that case. Rose was genuinely concerned.

"He turned out to be a flabby wacko. He could have hurt Karen, but not me or anyone else who had any experience and training."

"But," she turned to him. She wasn't that easily convinced. "Even out of shape wackos can carry weapons. What then?"

"In all the time I was in the business, I never got a scratch. Neither did Drew." Jack raised her hand to his lips. "But it's sweet that you care."

"Did you have sex with Karen Poe?"

"Well, when you change the direction of a conversation, you make it a big, fat, sharp turn."

"I'm sorry." Rose wanted to kick herself. Why had she asked such a stupid question? *Because sex is on your mind.* Why had he slept with Karen Poe but turned Rose down? *One has nothing to do with the other. Stop having a pointless conversation in your head.*

"I honestly don't care if you had sex with Karen Poe." She quickly tried to backtrack. "Not that I would blame you. She's gorgeous. You're gorgeous. Undoubtedly, you would have gorgeous sex."

"So we must have had sex." Jack liked that Rose was a bit flustered and maybe a little jealous. "We didn't. But we became good friends. In fact, I still act as her honorary bodyguard whenever she has a movie premiere. She thinks it's good luck."

"I don't want to know about the women in your past, Jack." She frowned. "Though if we are ever going to get intimate, we should discuss sexual health."

"I always use condoms and get tested every year when I have my physical."

"Me too." Then she clarified. "I make the guy wear condoms, that is. I give blood regularly, so I know I don't have any diseases."

"So we're good." Jack gave her hand another kiss before picking up their dishes and heading to the kitchen. "Looks like the casserole is hot and bubbling. I'll dish some up. Would you mind letting Edgar in? He should have worn himself out by now chasing uncatchable squirrels."

Rose opened the door prepared to call the puppy but instead found him waiting as if he knew she was coming. "Aren't you a good boy? Come on in."

She followed the bounding dog who paused to greet Jack before running back to the hall and out of sight.

"It's his dinner time too," Jack explained. Rose watched as he filled their plates with something that smelled amazing. He brought the dishes out and set them on the table. Their eyes met and held, and he must have read the questions she hadn't been brave enough to ask.

"We will have sex, Rose." He pulled her into a warm, gentle hug. Leaning back, he met her gaze again. "But I like what we're doing here. In just a week, I know so much more about you, and I *like* you, Rose. I hope you feel the same."

"I do." Rose snuggled deeper into his embrace. It felt good to have him hold her. "It's not like I've ever been that into sex. It's nice; sometimes it's very nice. But when the possibility of it isn't even on the table, you tend to think of it a lot more."

"First of all, when *we* have sex, it's going to be a lot better than nice."

"Bragging?" Rose grinned into his chest.

"Just stating the truth." Jack gave her a playful slap on the butt. "Second, the possibility is more than on the table. In fact, you see that?" He gestured with his head towards the huge dining room table. "We will have sex on that and on that sofa and on that rug. And in all likelihood, that kitchen counter."

"Now you *are* bragging."

"Again, just stating the truth."

Chapter Seven

ROSE LOOKED DOWN at the paper in her hand and then looked again. Still looking, she picked up her phone and hit speed dial.

"Had sex yet?"

"I'm regretting telling you about any of that." Tyler had been answering her calls with the same question for over a week. It was getting old.

"Sorry, that was the last time. I promise." Once Tyler made a promise, then it was written in stone. "So what's up?"

"Are there etiquette rules for when a guy sends you a doctor's report clearing him of any sexually transmitted diseases?"

"Say again?"

"I'd rather not." Rose looked at the paper one more time as if she expected the words to have magically rearranged themselves. It had arrived earlier that morning by messenger. Jack had told her last night that he was clean, and she believed him. Yet he'd still sent over documented proof.

"I hope we're talking about Jack because if random guys are sending you their medical records, well, there are some seriously weird dudes out there."

Rose laughed. Leave it to Tyler.

"But what do you think it means?

"It means you're going to be having sex with Jack Winston," Tyler said. "And sooner than later."

Rose did a little happy dance around her living room. Then a thought hit her. "Do I reciprocate?"

"I wish I was recording this so I could play it back to you at a later date." Tyler sighed. "I doubt there are any hard and fast rules for something like this. Wait, *is* there anything like this?"

"Tyler."

"But," Tyler continued. "I'd say yes, reciprocate. If he was thoughtful enough to let you know he's clean, then you should be equally as thoughtful. And the minute you hang up, I'm calling Dani and telling her every detail of this conversation."

"I wouldn't expect anything less. Besides, it will save me from having to do it."

"She'll call you as soon as I've finished," Tyler warned her.

"I know. But in the meantime, I'll have called my doctor and requested her to send the information to Jack." Rose was already scrolling through her numbers for her doctor's office.

"Then get at it. See you soon."

As Rose dialed, she thought about just how right Tyler was; this *was* weird. But it meant she and Jack were going to have sex — soon. For that, she could live with a little weird.

ONE WEEK LATER and still no sex.

Rose was curled up on her sofa binge-watching old *Seinfeld* episodes. Nothing new there. Tonight, however, she was curled up next to Jack. His arm was tucked snuggly around her shoulders, her favorite blanket covering them. His hand gently rubbed up and down her arm. It was nice, comfortable, and completely non-sexual.

They'd met for lunch the day of the medical records exchange. At first, Rose had felt slightly awkward but Jack had treated it as an everyday occurrence. It put her at ease, but it prompted her to ask if it was the norm for him.

"This is the first time," he assured her. "I want you to feel safe with me, in as well as out of the bedroom. I thought this might be one more way to do that."

She did feel safe with Jack. They saw each other every day, and they were developing a bond that was new for Rose. She had men who were friends and men she dated. She'd never known a man who combined the two. Jack's plan to get to know each other before sex was working. She still wanted him, desperately. And Jack was very affectionate. They had even had a few hot and heavy make-out sessions. But that was as far as it went. He always pulled back before it went too far. She'd never even seen him without his shirt on. He had traveled under her shirt one time, but the only bare skin touched was on her back. She was fine if it turned out that was all there was going to be. She just had to know one way or the other.

"I was wondering if you'd like to go out to *Tom Tom's Tavern* tomorrow night."

Rose lifted her head and frowned slightly. Had she missed something?

"I'm sorry," she said. "What, where?"

Jack laughed. Damn, Rose thought, he was so gorgeous. And funny and sexy. She liked Jack as a friend, but it was going to be torture never having him in her bed.

"Did I catch you dozing?"

"No." Rose sat up and ran a hand through her hair. "My mind was wandering a bit. What were you saying?"

"Saturday night, Drew and I are getting together with some of the guys on our security crew for drinks and pool. You've never hung out with Drew, and I thought this would be a good opportunity. You could invite Tyler and Dani if you want."

"Tyler and Drew in the same room for an entire evening?" It was a hard concept to wrap her head around. "It sounds like a recipe for disaster if they would even agree to it."

"He's an idiot," Jack said.

"Yes." You couldn't argue with the truth.

"And Tyler is—"

"The injured party," Rose interrupted. "I don't know what Drew has told you. I don't want to know. But what happened between them is all on him."

"There *are* two sides, Rose."

"And he's never tried to explain his. Not then and not in all the time that has followed." Drew Harper had hit her shit list ten years ago, and nothing had happened since to move him off. However, she would admit that he could be a dick head to Tyler and still be a good friend to Jack. If he wanted them to meet up, she was willing. Besides, how much socializing could you really do inside a crowded, noisy bar?

"I'll ask them but I can't guarantee that Tyler will show. Jack," she asked warily. "This isn't some ill-advised attempt at matchmaking is it?"

"I promise it's just what I said," Jack assured her. "Shall I pick you up?"

Rose shook her head. "I'll come with Dani and Tyler, if she agrees."

"Forming a united front?"

"Girl power never dies, even when you've become women. Can I get you something more to drink?"

"Only if you're getting something. Don't make a special trip for me."

Considerate. She had to add that to the growing list of Jack's stellar qualities. She grabbed one of the beers she'd recently started keeping in her fridge and poured herself a glass of water. Or maybe he was too considerate. It was time to find out.

Jack took the beer and smiled. "Thanks, sweetheart. Do you feel like more Seinfeld or are you in the mood for something else?"

Now there was an opening if ever she heard one.

"I've been thinking, Jack."

"I'm all for that. My sisters have informed me for years that the sexiest thing about a woman is her brain."

"Your sisters are so interesting. I'd love to…" Damn it, she would not let him sidetrack her. Jack was so good at that even when he didn't know he was doing it.

"I've been thinking," she began again, "that I like you. More and more."

"I like you too."

"And maybe we should stop the pretense and be happy with just that."

It had sounded better in her head. But she'd said it and the rest was up to Jack.

"Let me get this straight." He sat his beer down and turned towards her. "You want to keep on being friends, hanging out and so forth. But you never want to have sex. At least not with me."

"Hey, this isn't about what *I* want. I made my feelings clear on the very first night." Rose was annoyed that Jack was turning this back on her. "I agreed to wait — against my better judgment. And I know you keep telling me how much you want me but let's face it, Jack. We are firmly in the friend zone. And I've decided that I'm okay with that. So be honest with yourself and me. You're just not that attracted to me. You've tried. And I appreciate it. But let's forget about the sex so we can relax and just be friends."

Rose waited for a response, her stomach churning with nerves. She expected Jack to shrug it off. He was so easygoing, so quick to tease. Except that wasn't what was happening. And he didn't seem angry. However, *something* was in his eyes she'd never seen before. The warm blue had become icy steel. Rose wasn't afraid; she knew Jack would never hurt her. Nevertheless, she was less sure of where this was going.

"No."

That was it? No? No to what?

"This isn't over, Rose. It's just beginning."

"What does that mean?" she demanded. "I'm not talking about ending us altogether. I just thought—"

"Now's the time to stop thinking. Shut down that beautiful brain of yours and just feel."

She would have said more, she meant to, but Jack leaned in and kissed her and all she was capable of doing was what he said to do. All she could do was feel.

Just friends, hell no. It didn't take long for panic to take the place of the calm determination that made him so good at getting whatever it was he wanted. Whether it was a football scholarship or a multi-million-dollar company from the ground up, he had an unwavering belief in himself and his abilities. Rose was his; he believed it. If he hadn't been sure before, he was now. And it was time to show her.

Lord, the man could kiss. He didn't rush but savored the process. His tongue slowly traced the shape of her lower lip, bathing it with gentle swipes. He could take her blood to a low boil with just that one languid movement. His teeth upped the heat. Taking her lip and pulling just hard enough to sting, he then sucked it into his mouth to soothe any hurt he might have caused. But that didn't ease her growing need. Instead, she was suffused with flush that traveled the length of her body. His kiss was the source that fed her arousal, one that centered in that rapidly moistening place between her legs — a place that desperately longed for his touch.

"I'm going to taste you, Rose. After tonight, I'll no longer have to imagine how sweet you are. Your flavor will linger on my tongue like a fine wine. And I plan on savoring every sip."

Her clothes were suddenly an unnecessary burden. They were in the way. She needed them gone, now. Jack must have read her mind. He removed her top and bra with little effort and no resistance. The cool air felt like heaven against her overheated skin. No, that was wrong. Heaven was the feel of Jack's lips on her breast. His tongue lapped at her beaded nipple once, twice before his teeth bit down ever so gently. He moved to the other breast giving it equal attention. Rose's fingers gripped his head, afraid he might take away the amazing sensations coursing through her body. His short hair was surprisingly soft, but the bristled tips still made her palms tingle with increased sensitivity.

"Do you like that?" Jack asked biting her nipple a little harder than the first time.

"Yes, I like it all," she breathed. "More, I need more.

He chuckled knowingly, leaving her breast to make a slow path of moist kisses down her stomach to the open waistband of her jeans. When had he done that? It didn't matter. They were just one more thing that was in the way.

"Lift for me, sweetheart."

Rose raised her hips so Jack could remove her jeans. And the panties? No, he'd left them.

"I don't need those." Her voice was husky, unrecognizable.

"But I do."

"They aren't your size." She felt a little nervous again, which meant her brain started to be a bit of a smartass. This was where she always had problems. She needed to shut down her brain and just let her body feel.

Jack raised his eyes to hers. Deep, heated blue, not a trace of ice.

"Close your eyes, Rose. All the way. Can you feel what I'm doing?"

His finger was just inside the elastic band of her underwear. Rose swallowed.

"Yes."

"And that?"

His tongue. She gasped. One pass across that oh so sensitive bud. Then another but slower, this time drawing it into his mouth, material and all.

"You're killing me, Jack. I'm begging you…"

"I don't want you to beg, sweetheart." His voice vibrated through her center, causing her legs to jerk in response. "I want you to let go. Let go and just feel."

Rose could hear the passion in his tone, feel how his breath grew heavier, causing a coating of steam to envelop her overheated flesh. She gasped at the sound of material ripping and then his mouth was on her, his tongue opening the folds. There was no hiding; her legs were wide, welcoming his body, his touch. One finger, then two entered her easily, the slick, plentiful moisture easing his way. They matched their rhythm. His tongue, his fingers, her hips, moving together, taking her closer to fulfillment.

"Let go, Rose. Give in. Give me everything."

His words sent her over the top. A full body orgasm that started between her legs and fanned out to the top of her head and the tip of her toes. It seemed to be neverending. She would start to come down, and Jack would send her just a bit higher until there was no more. She was spent, a limp, thoroughly satisfied woman.

"Good?"

Rose would have laughed, but she didn't have the energy.

"There are no words. Thank you."

"I'd say the pleasure was all mine but let's just call it mutual."

Jack sat back up on the couch and pulled her into his arms. He brushed a soft kiss onto her temple and smoothed back her hair. "Cold?"

"No." She snuggled closer. "Give me a moment and I'll return the favor." She slid her hand down his chest towards the bulge in his jeans. "With pleasure."

Before she could reach her destination, Jack trapped her hand beneath his.

"This was for you, Rose."

She frowned in confusion. "But Jack…"

"Next time." Jack kissed her, sweet and tender. He tucked the blanket they'd been wrapped up in earlier back around her. "Shall I carry you to your bedroom or do you want to stay here?"

"Will you join me?"

"Not tonight," Jack said with genuine regret.

"Then I'll stay here." She snuggled deeper into the blanket. "Being in my bed all alone would be too depressing and I don't want anything to bring me down. I plan on basking for at least a couple of hours."

"I like the sound of that." He gave her a final kiss, sweet instead of hot. "I'll see you tomorrow night at *Tom Tom's*. Eight o'clock."

Rose watched him go and sighed. She could spend the rest of the evening trying to figure out Jack Winston, or she could do what she'd told him she was going to do. Her body felt loose, relaxed, still floating on a post-orgasmic high like nothing she'd ever known. The choice was easy, she basked.

Chapter Eight

TOM TOM'S TAVERN was located south of Harper Falls, outside the city limits and away from any restrictions that the town council put on places that served alcohol. You couldn't get a liquor license if you catered to an *unsavory element*. Tom Unger, owner and veteran of the first Gulf War, thought that was the only kind of element *worth* serving. The more unsavory, the better. As a result, it tended to be a rowdy crowd.

Jack ordered a round of beers for himself, Drew, and the five crewmembers joining them. It was purely informal and something they did from time to time to blow off steam. Whoever was free and wanted to come was welcome.

"Seems to be more strangers than usual." Jack didn't have to shout at the bartender, but it was a near thing.

Bobby Finn had worked at *Tom Tom's* since it opened. He was big and mean and kept the peace with intimidating looks and a Louisville Slugger that was always within reach behind the bar.

"Bikers," Bobby said with a shrug. "There's some yearly gathering down the road at the campground."

Great, bikers. Normally Jack wouldn't have had a problem with that.

However, he didn't know any of them personally and with Rose and her friends due to arrive at any time, he wondered if this had been a bad idea. The women's safety was too important, and there was no predicting who in the bar might have a short fuse when lit by alcohol and a surplus of testosterone.

Making his way through the crowd with seven long necks lifted over his head was a challenge, but he made it to their table without incident.

"If our business ever tanks, you could do that for a living."

Jack gave Drew the finger and passed around the beers.

"I was thinking, maybe I should call Rose and cancel. Too many strangers and they're getting rowdy early. It will probably be okay, but I don't want to take any chances with Rose and her friends."

"*Friend*," Drew muttered.

"What?"

"Tyler won't come."

Jack sighed. It had to be the hundredth time Drew had told him that Tyler would be a no-show. Usually while gritting his teeth. If Drew didn't do something about his feelings for Tyler, his dentist would soon be fitting him for a pair of dentures.

"Well, it's too late; there they are." Jack got up when he saw Rose come through the door. "We'll just have to be extra vigilant and hope these guys know how to keep their hands to themselves." On the way, he patted Drew's shoulder. "And it seems you don't know Tyler as well as you thought."

Drew's head shot around. Damn, he'd been hoping she wouldn't show almost as much as he was hoping she would. An entire evening of having her just within reach and knowing she wasn't his to touch. It had been ten years and her taste was still so vivid in his memory. He could feel the saliva pooling in his mouth just thinking about it. The problem was she hated him, and with good reason. He sometimes wondered if he could go back to those final days, would he do anything differently. The answer was always the same. His reasons had been solid, even necessary. He broke Tyler's heart and as painful as it would be, he would do it again. What he wouldn't do was stay away. He would find her and explain. He would make her understand. Now it felt like too much time had gone by, and he had no idea how to mend the cracks that had become chasms. Nevertheless, he'd figure it out, he vowed. He would find a way. Just then, Tyler looked up and caught him staring and for a moment, he thought he saw a hint of the love that used to shine so freely from those silvery depths. Unfortunately, it was replaced so quickly by the icy indifference he'd grown used to. He couldn't help but wonder if that flicker had just been wishful thinking. It felt like his whole life was becoming one huge wish, a wish to have Tyler in his arms again. Drew groaned. It was going to be a long night.

Jack made his way across the room as quickly as he could without physically removing the bodies in his path. The three newcomers already garnered attention, and he wanted to get them back to the table and out of harm's way as fast as possible. Sure, he knew he was overreacting. There were other women in the tavern, and he hadn't noticed anyone giving them a hard time. He'd always been protective of women, having six sisters will do that to a guy. This was different. Overprotective Caveman Jack was someone he'd never met before and doubted Rose would like. Well, too bad. She was his woman, and it was his right to take care of her.

"Great place," Rose said into his ear as he greeted her with a hug. "You've met Tyler and Dani. We were saying that we can't believe none of us have ever been here before." *Tom Tom's* was a place all kids aspired to sneak into. Very few succeeded and the few who made it past the door didn't make it far. Tom Unger kicked them out but not before he gave them a talking to that left their ears ringing for days. If they tried coming back again before they were twenty-one, they were banned for life. Rose and her friends had left Harper Falls well before they were old enough to get in. She'd wondered for years what was inside the rather nondescript dark brown building and now she would finally find out. It was loud, dimly lit and smelled a bit like stale beer and industrial cleaner. In other words, everything she'd hoped it would be.

"You all look beautiful." Jack took Rose's hand and ushered Tyler and Dani with the other. He was able to get them back to the table and seated without any problems. Yup, Jack decided; he was overreacting.

"What can I get the three of you? It's crazy in here, and you never know when a waitress might pass by."

"You went last time," Drew interrupted. "Stay here with Rose and let me go."

"Thanks," Jack said with a knowing shake of his head. Drew couldn't be around Tyler for two seconds without bolting at the first opportunity. Then again, he was only going for drinks. He had to come back.

"Whiskey, neat," Dani said.

"Same," Rose nodded.

Drew waited for Tyler's answer with a quizzically raised eyebrow. He would have waited all night.

"Tyler is driving so just bring her a club soda." Rose rolled her eyes at Jack but only because she knew Tyler couldn't see the gesture. It wasn't as though they were asking her to engage the guy in a lengthy conversation. Tyler had agreed to come. Telling Drew what she wanted to drink wouldn't have killed her.

After Drew had left to get the drinks, Jack made the introductions. The five security crewmembers — Terry, Linus, Carl, Mark, and Wade — were a bit younger than their bosses but just as physically imposing. None of them lived in Washington but were there for a couple days of training before their next assignments. Rose was still getting a grasp of the personal security side of H&W. She knew people in the music industry who had bodyguards, but they were with them day and night. Jack and Drew only booked temporary jobs. They lasted a few days, maybe a week at the most. From what Jack said, they were in high demand and if they had wanted, they could have expanded to a much larger operation. However, they liked it small and exclusive. Jack had laughingly told her it was classy, just like him and Drew.

They sat near one of the pool tables, and a couple of the guys just finished up a game.

"Want to play next?" Rose asked Jack.

"Just don't make a bet with her; she's a shark." Dani grinned.

Jack choked on his sip of beer. *Bet.* The word caught him off guard.

"Are you all right?" Rose patted him on the back. She exchanged puzzled looks with Tyler and Dani. What had they said?

"He's fine." Drew had just returned with the drinks, which included another round of beers for the guys. He set down the full tray and then gave Jack a hard slap on the back. Jack lurched forward, catching himself with his free hand.

"Thanks," he muttered to Drew. If looks could kill—

"Anytime, buddy. Now, did I hear someone mention a game of pool?"

Jack handed Rose a stick and then racked up the balls.

"Rose," Dani called to her. "Tyler and I are going to the bathroom. By the looks of the line, you should be up a couple games by the time we get back. Do us proud."

"Ladies first." Jack gestured towards the table.

"Are you sure?" Rose chalked her cue. She looked back at him before making her first shot. "Dani wasn't kidding about me being good. Her family had a table in their basement. Her dad taught me how to play, but it wasn't long before I could beat him most of the time."

"I think my ego will survive if you win." Jack wasn't worried. He knew that once he got a turn, he'd clear the table. Rose didn't give him a chance. Ball after ball fell into the pockets and all he could do was stand back and watch. Not that it was a hardship. Her hip action when she was setting up for a shot was mesmerizing. Her tight jeans hugged her like a second skin, highlighting a truly fine ass. By the looks on his friends' faces, he wasn't the only one who'd noticed.

"Hey, keep your eyes to yourselves," he grumbled.

"You can't blame them for looking," Drew pointed out. "And now that they've seen her, they're all wondering how you've maintained your virtue for the last two weeks."

"Do they doubt my word?" Jack demanded.

"Hell, no." Drew laughed. "They know you too well for that. You're starting to achieve legendary status in the control department. It's a good thing the terms of the bet lets you take care of your own business or you'd be going out of your mind." He gave Rose's swaying hips another look. "By the way, how's that going for you?"

"I never thought I'd say this, but if it was capable, my dick would yawn every time it saw my hand coming."

"Or every time it comes in your hand."

"Lately you have been a real laugh riot, my friend." Jack watched as Rose sank the last ball. "One more week," he groaned. God, she was even sexier getting balls out of pockets than she had been putting them in. He almost lost it when she racked them up for another game and crooked her finger, inviting him to join her.

Drew shook his head in amusement at how quickly Jack jumped when she called. His friend was a goner, no doubt about it. Was it love? That was for Jack to say. Either way, Drew couldn't have been happier for him. It wasn't easy finding a woman to love. Sometimes it was even harder holding on to her.

He'd been keeping one eye on the ladies room door just to make sure Tyler and Dani made it back to the table without being bothered. They'd been gone for some time and he was just about to go looking for them when Dani returned alone.

"Where's Tyler?" he demanded.

Dani gave him a look that was one-step up from how she'd look at something stuck to her bottom of her shoe. Okay, he got it. He wasn't her favorite person. He tried again, hoping he sounded a little less gruff.

"It's a rough crowd tonight, Dani. She shouldn't be wandering around alone."

Dani stared at him a moment before deciding he had a point. "She saw an old friend at the bar and stopped to say hello. See, there she is near the end."

Drew relaxed a bit when he saw Tyler was indeed at the far end of the long, mahogany bar. He tensed up again. She wedged herself tightly between two men, one of whom seemed more interested in getting *her* attention than the bartender's.

Drew knew that Tyler wouldn't appreciate his intervention, so he stayed where he was, but kept watching her just in case. Drew frowned.

The guy hitting on Tyler looked awfully familiar. Was that Craig Lowe? It couldn't be. Craig was in rehab and wasn't scheduled to get out for several more weeks. Drew shifted his angle to get a better look at the man's face. Shit, it was Craig, and it looked like he was drinking. Drew set his beer down with enough force to get the attention of a couple of the crew. He waved off their questions and headed across the room. Tyler might not want his help, but she was about to get it.

Tyler had lied to Dani. She hadn't seen an old friend. It was just an excuse so she wouldn't have to go back to the table, an excuse Tyler knew Dani had seen through but thankfully hadn't called her on. They both knew that the real reason she wanted to be on her own was Drew, no explanation needed. She hated that he could still make her feel anything. Anger, hurt, need, even longing. Ten years should have been enough time to purge her of those feelings. She wanted apathy. She wanted to be able to see him walking down the street and have no reaction beyond mild appreciation for an attractive man. Try as she might, she wasn't there yet.

She managed to find an empty spot at the bar and ordered a whiskey and soda. She didn't plan to drink it, but it didn't seem right to take up prime real estate and not spend some money. Just ten minutes, she promised herself. Then she'd go back and join her friends.

"Hey, baby." The man's breath had arrived before he did, sour with booze and garlic. Tyler groaned. *So much for alone time.* There always had to be one deluded drunk in the crowd and tonight she seemed to be the unlucky woman to draw his attention. At the best of times, her patience was thin; tonight it was like tissue paper.

"Not interested." Her words were sharp and to the point.

"Are you screwing Jack?" the man slurred. His eyes were swollen and extremely bloodshot. He kept squinting at her as if he couldn't quite make out her image. "Jack break the bet? Saint Jack sticks me in rehab and forgets all about me." He tipped her way, grabbing her arm to keep from falling. "Bets he can keep his dick in his pants and then screws you. Lies about it."

The guy was rambling, but Tyler got the gist of what he was saying.

There was some stupid bet involving Jack. Damn it, was he playing games with Rose? If he hurt her, Tyler would make sure *he* hurt a lot worse and for a lot longer.

"Wait," the drunk grabbed at her again to stop her from leaving. "Forget what I said. Jack's my friend." He was almost in tears. "Shouldn't tell secrets. Bros before Hos," he cried out, lunging for Tyler's breasts. Disgusted, she neatly avoided grasp, not even glancing back when she heard the distinct thud of his body crashing to the floor.

"Are you all right?" Drew pushed past a particularly large man dressed entirely in leather just in time to see Craig hit the floor.

"I believe you have some trash that needs taking out."

Drew sighed as he watched Tyler wind through the crowd. What the hell had Craig said? Drew caught Terry's eye and motioned him over.

"Can you get Craig back to his place?" Drew remembered that Terry and Craig used to hang together so he hoped he wouldn't mind being singled out to take care the guy.

"No problem, Drew. I visited him last week and he seemed to be doing fine." Drew helped him get Craig to his feet. "I wonder what set him off."

Drew made sure Craig was buckled into Terry's car before he reentered the bar. He hated to think what kind of crap the idiot had been spewing at Tyler. Technically, he wasn't responsible for Craig's actions but that didn't stop him from feeling a twinge of guilt. Even though he doubted she would accept, he wanted to apologize to Tyler. By the time he got back to the table, none of the women were anywhere in sight.

"What happened over there?" Jack asked with a frown. "Tyler practically dragged Rose and Dani back to the bathroom. Though she looked more like she wanted to punch someone than pee."

"Craig Lowe showed up and by the looks of him, he'd started his drinking long before he got here."

"Did he hurt Tyler?" Jack asked with concern.

"No, Tyler took care of Craig without any help." Drew smiled thinking about it. "I got Terry to take him home. Craig said something to Tyler that set her off. If it's possible, the look she gave me was even nastier than usual."

"I'm sorry, Drew." Jack felt for his friend. "But what could be so bad that she couldn't wait to tell them?"

"I don't know but I think we're about to find out."

Dani and Tyler returned, but Rose wasn't with them. Dani looked worried; Tyler pissed. Jack just wanted to know where Rose was.

"Rose wanted to get some fresh air," Dani told him before he could ask. She stopped him when he would have gone after Rose. "Give her a few minutes, Jack."

"A few minutes to do what? What is going on, Dani?" When she didn't answer, Jack gave up and headed for the door. Whatever the problem it wasn't safe for Rose to be outside alone. If she didn't want to tell him what was wrong, he could live with that for now. He wasn't going to stay inside and worry about her safety.

Drew watched with concern as Jack pushed his way through the crowd. He couldn't imagine what had happened and hoped Jack would be able to straighten out everything. As he raised his beer to his lips, he suddenly became aware of Tyler. Truth be told, he was always aware of Tyler, but now she was right next to him, her eyes fixed on the door through which Jack had just left. Drew shifted, for some reason feeling slightly uncomfortable. Tyler always avoided him like the plague so why was she suddenly standing mere inches away?

"Listen," she said, her voice flat and unemotional. "In all the years we've been friends, I've only seen Rose cry twice. Once, just after we'd met, when a stray cat she had adopted was run over by a car. The other time was when, after months of chemo and radiation, and prayers, we found out Dani's mom was cancer-free."

Drew started to speak, but Tyler cut him off.

"This is not a conversation; this is *you* listening to *me*." Seeing that he understood, she continued, "Rose has had plenty of other reasons to cry, reasons that are her own private business, but believe me there were times that if anyone deserved a good sob it was her. But she never did. She keeps it together as well as anyone I've ever known. I'm telling you this because tonight she came as close to tears as I've seen her in a long time. She was starting to trust Jack, not an easy thing for her. Your drunk friend let out enough details for me to figure out that you and your juvenile buddies made a bet and without telling her, Jack has pulled Rose right into the middle of it." Tyler paused to gauge Drew's reaction. His grimace and whispered *shit* told her she was right on target. It sounded just like something the Drew she used to know would have thought up. It seemed, at least in that regard, he hadn't changed.

"So I'm going to stand here," she said matter-of-factly. "And I'm going to wait for Rose to come back. If I see she's been crying, hell, even if she looks overly upset? I'm going to rip off your balls, put them under the heel of my boot, and grind them into dust."

Several of the crew who had been listening shifted uncomfortably in their seats. You could almost hear their silent groans. Talk about the ultimate ball buster. Tyler, whom they had all been secretly lusting after, had suddenly gone from sexy to crazy-ass scary in thirty seconds flat. They waited expectantly for Drew's response. There was no way he was going to take that from anyone, not even someone as gorgeous as Tyler.

Drew just nodded slowly and said, "Fair enough."

He saw the guys exchange astonished looks. He understood their reaction. He had his reasons for not having a harsher reaction and for him, it was a damn good one. What the crew didn't know was that for the first time in almost ten years, Tyler had said more than five words consecutively to him. On top of that, it was the first time since he was eighteen that he'd been this close to her for any length of time. It might have been all kinds of twisted, but he couldn't have cared less what she was saying as long as he could listen to the sound of her voice. And if she went for his balls? Well, he was almost positive he could stop her. But, he thought as he noted her well-toned arms, she would undoubtedly do some damage first.

Jack shoved his way through the door, his eyes searching for Rose. Luckily, she hadn't gone far. She stood a few feet away with her arms wrapped around her body; her head tipped back as she breathed deeply in and out. Jack took a step towards her then stopped. His first instinct was to pull her into his arms, to find out what was wrong and how he could fix it. However, he held himself back. Something had upset her and he didn't want to do anything to make it worse.

"Rose, sweetheart, what's wrong?"

She turned slowly and looked him straight in the eye. Her voice was flat and emotionless. "Tell me about the bet."

Well, shit, he hadn't been expecting that. Jack's brain did a swift assessment of the situation, analyzing how best to come at the problem. In the end, he did the only thing he could do; he told her the truth, every bit of it, from the very beginning. It only took a few minutes and during that time, Rose's expression remained blank. Jack had no idea what she was thinking.

"I know how it sounds." He said when he'd finished. In fact, it sounded even worse than when he ran the explanation around in his head. It had sounded awful in his head.

"So it had nothing to do with me?" Rose asked. Her voice was almost unrecognizable. She didn't sound anything like the happy, expressive woman he'd gotten to know over the past two weeks. It wasn't very encouraging — it scared the hell out of him.

"No, I promise you, the whole mess was just crazy bad timing." Jack lifted a hand. He wanted to touch her, to feel a connection. The look she gave him left no doubt that if he wanted all his fingers, he'd be smart to keep them to himself.

Jack finally understood what it meant when some said *the silence was deafening*. If she didn't say something, anything, soon he was going to jump out of his skin.

"Okay."

Well, something more than that.

"I believe you, Jack."

Jack felt the weight of the world lift off his shoulders.

"Thank you, sweetheart. I can't tell you how much it means to me that you trust me that much." Then realizing what all this meant, Jack grinned. "What do you say we get out of here, go back to my place, and spend the next week in bed?"

"Absolutely not."

"But, Rose…"

"After all this, do you think I'm going to let you lose that bet?" Rose asked in amazement.

Now Jack was confused. "There *is* no more bet. Once you found out, I lose. Besides, I deserve it for making the stupid thing in the first place."

"But you haven't lost," Rose told him. "The bet, as I understand it, was that you couldn't tell anyone. Well, *you* didn't. I found out from Tyler, who found out from your drunken friend. So—"

"So I didn't lose the bet," Jack finished. His Rose was very clever, indeed. "I regret making the bet, Rose. I'm sorry I dragged you into it. But," Jack took her hands in his, "it did give me the chance to get to know you and I wouldn't trade the last two weeks for anything, blue balls and all. I couldn't care less about losing the bet."

"Well, I care," she exclaimed. "I don't want Drew and those other assholes to win. One more week, Jack. And to make it easier for us both, I'm going to spend it in New York."

"That seems a bit drastic," Jack frowned. "I might not like it, but I can keep my hands off you for seven more days."

"I got a call this morning from a friend of mine who's recording one of my songs," Rose explained. "Things aren't going very well; she's clashing with the producer. I agreed to fly in and help. I'd only planned on being gone one or two days, but I think it would be best if I stayed the week."

"You *are* mad." Jack knew it had been too easy.

"I'm not," she assured him. "But I do need a little time to sort it all out in my head. It just feels a little strange, Jack. I can't tell you why because I don't know myself. I promise you this isn't some passive/aggressive move to punish you. I'm not trying to get the upper hand. Games like that are nothing but destructive. I would never do that to you."

Jack held open his arms and Rose sank in gratefully. He lifted her chin and gave her a long, hard look.

"One week," he said in a voice that brooked no argument. "This thing ends at eleven-thirty next Sunday morning."

"That's pretty precise." Rose grinned up at him.

"I have it engraved on my brain. Now," his voice was warm and affectionate. "Can I at least have a kiss?"

"Make it a week's worth." Rose pulled his mouth down to meet hers.

"Now that's hot. Want to share?"

Jack stiffened but didn't pull away from Rose. Instead, he slowly raised his head, getting a good look at what he was dealing with. Four burly bikers, arms heavily tattooed and muscled but a bit flabby around the middle. He could tell they'd had quite a bit to drink but were still steady on their feet. Carefully and with deliberation, Jack pushed Rose behind him, shielding her with his body. He breathed a sigh of relief that she didn't protest, didn't speak. He needed to get her back into the bar and out of harm's way. Pulling himself up to his full height, he shifted his stance, inching a bit closer to the tavern door.

"I don't share." He wanted to tell Rose to get ready to run. However, that was impossible so he would have to count on her knowing what to do when the time came.

One of the other bikers stepped closer. He was a little taller than the rest and a lot more ripped. "What makes you think we were talking to you?"

"I don't share, either," Rose called out. She tried to give them her best tough girl sneer, but Jack's body blocked her efforts.

"Why don't we go inside and I'll buy a round of drinks." Jack knew it was a lame attempt to avoid the inevitable, but he figured it was worth a try. He could handle the four of them, probably. He had Rose's safety to think about; that was his first priority.

"We can buy our own drinks, pretty boy. Right now, I have me a craving for some fresh ass, and I don't care which of you gives it to me."

Great, Rose thought, *equal opportunity rapists*. She knew what Jack had in mind, so she grabbed the waistband of his jeans and backed up toward the door. They weren't more than ten feet away and they were both fast. Just a few more feet and they could make a run for it. If they were lucky, somebody would come out and cause a distraction. Damn it, it was a busy place. Why hadn't anyone come out? It seemed they wouldn't be able to count on that, so they were on their own. Come on, just a little farther. Unfortunately, the bikers decided they'd had enough talk.

"Run," Jack shouted. He gave Rose a shove towards the bar then threw a hard punch, breaking the nose of the guy unlucky enough to be the closest.

Rose didn't hesitate. She heard the crunch when Jack's fist connected and gave a silent cheer as she threw herself into the noisy tavern. She needed to get Drew's attention and fast. Luck was on her side because it seemed the whole crew had been watching for them to return. Waving like a crazy woman, she gestured for them to come outside. Relief surged through her when she saw six powerfully built men carving a path through the crowd. She didn't wait for them to reach her. Jack was in trouble and needed her whether he knew it or not.

Bursting back the way she came, Rose saw Jack causing a lot of damage. This wasn't like the movies where the thugs came at the hero one at a time, and the others stood by passively until it was their turn. These assholes attacked all at once, getting in a few punches of their own. She could see that Jack was an amazing fighter, yet no matter how good he was, it was still five against one. Rose decided to do her best to improve the odds.

Jack caught sight of Rose out of the corner of his eye. *Damn it, why hadn't she stayed inside.* These guys were big, but they weren't trained fighters. They got in a few good licks that he would feel tomorrow, but he knew he would eventually take them out. He didn't need the distraction of worrying about Rose.

Suddenly one of the bikers howled in pain and hit the ground. Giving a quick glance, Jack saw Rose, fierce and beautiful, standing over the guy with a block of wood in her hands. She was poised to cold cock another one when the cavalry arrived. Once he had Drew and their security team on his side, the fight was over in less than a minute. Three of the bikers lay on the ground bleeding, but alive. The other two had stumbled off before the fight was even over, leaving their friends to fend for themselves.

A crowd had gathered around the combatants. *Where had they been when they could have been useful?* Rose wondered. She threw down the piece of wood and rushed to Jack's side.

"There's my warrior woman," Jack said pulling her to his side. "Are you okay? Did they hurt you?"

"Me?" Rose shook her head in amazement. He was the one with the split lip and scraped knuckles. "I'm fine, not even a broken nail. But we should get you to the hospital and let a doctor check you out."

"It's just a few bruises." Jack kissed her cheek, wincing slightly. "Nothing a hot shower and some antiseptic won't cure." He leaned close to her ear so only she could hear. "And by the end of the week, I'll be healed and waiting for you. If that's what you still want?"

She just smiled and whispered, "Eleven thirty-one, Sunday morning."

Jack grinned back, no grimace this time. One week. After everything they'd been through, it was going to be a piece of cake.

Chapter Nine

"THE FINAL TESTS show no glitches in the program. We should be able to have it on the market by September. This release is going to be huge, the biggest we've ever had."

Jack and Drew grinned at each other like little kids on Christmas morning. They had been developing their latest security software program for over three years, and finally it was done. Nothing was one hundred percent hack-proof; cyber thieves were getting smarter all the time. H&W Security was about to provide protection that was as close to impenetrable as possible, head and shoulders above anything else on the market. As a result, they would get a whole lot richer.

"Remember our goal back in college?" Drew leaned back in his chair with a satisfied sigh. "Millionaires by the time we were twenty-five, billionaires by thirty."

"Cocky little shits, weren't we?" Jack shook his head when he thought of the two of them, huddled together in a tiny workspace, bursting with ideas and ambition. They hadn't even considered the possibility of failure. Here they were ten years later, just months away from getting everything they'd always wanted. Whoever said be careful what you wish for was a fucking idiot. They'd wished, dreamed, and worked their asses off. And it was better than he could have imagined.

"To our first billion."

"A whole year ahead of schedule." Jack tapped his cup against Drew's.

"Thirty seemed like such a foreign concept back then. Now I can hardly remember what eighteen felt like."

Jack looked at his friend trying to picture him back then. It was harder when you'd spent almost every day with someone, worked and played beside them. They had pictures, however. The one that hung in the lobby showed the two of them, arms slung over each other's shoulders, fresh out of college and ready to take on the world. They couldn't have known just how quickly everything would change, that success would come first as bodyguards *then* as software moguls. Nevertheless, as they sat here, about to accomplish one of their biggest dreams, they were just as eager to push toward new ones. Jack knew that no matter what else changed, Drew would always have his back. If, God forbid, they lost it all tomorrow, the two of them could dig in and build it up again just as they always had, together.

"I got a visit from Terry this morning," Drew said, reaching over to refill his cup.

"Is there a problem?" Terry Moss was one of their best bodyguards, in high demand and reliable.

"He took Craig home Saturday night and stayed with him until he dried out. When he couldn't get him on the phone yesterday, he went to check on him and he'd gone."

Jack frowned. "I know he and Terry are friends but I can't work up a lot of concern for Craig. We tried to help and he paid us back by causing trouble. I hope he gets help, but it's no longer our responsibility."

"I agree." Drew stood, needing to stretch after sitting for so long. "Terry's main reason for stopping by was to make a confession. It seems while he was visiting Craig in rehab, he told him about the bet. Terry thought it would give Craig a laugh and help him feel like he wasn't out of the loop, that he was still a part of the crew. Terry was sick that he'd been the one to spill information that Craig used against you."

"Terry can't take responsibility for Craig's actions. I'll call him later and make sure he knows I'm not angry with him."

"Good." Drew lifted the cup to his mouth then thought better of it. He needed something solid in his stomach, not more caffeine.

"Any word from Rose?"

"Nope." Jack looked at the calendar on his desk. Still Wednesday. He found himself checking several times a day as if he could will the time to pass. Rose had promised to be at his house on Sunday morning, but she had also insisted they not talk while she was in New York. She said she needed to sort everything out in her mind. Jack had agreed; what else could he do? Craig had dropped a bombshell and Rose had left town before Jack could begin to clean up the mess. At least he knew she was coming back; this was her home. He just had to hope she came back to him.

"Damn, Craig," Drew said disgust.

"The timing could have been better," Jack conceded. "And it didn't help to have it come from someone else. To be honest, I hadn't figured out what I was going to say. I didn't know how I was going to explain why I hadn't told her from the start or why we'd made the stupid bet in the first place. It all came out — wrong place, wrong time — but Rose was amazing. She believed and forgave me. I'm just afraid she'll spend the week we're apart deciding I'm not worth any more of her time."

"Tyler said she almost cried." Drew relayed what Tyler had told him while they had been waiting for Jack and Rose to come back in the tavern. "She's invested, Jack. I don't think she'll give up on you for something that happened before you started seeing her."

Jack felt a constriction in his chest at the thought of bringing Rose to the verge of tears. He wanted to make her smile and laugh. He wanted to hear her moans as he brought her pleasure again and again. He never wanted to be responsible for making her cry.

"Jack?" The voice of their assistant, Pam Stoddard, called out from the intercom. "I know you said you didn't want to be disturbed but I have a bit of a situation out here."

Jack and Drew exchanged surprised looks. Pam was unflappable; in fact, neither of them could ever remember her losing her cool.

"What's the problem?" Bulletproof glass and locks that you could only disengage from the inside would have stopped anyone from gaining unwanted entrance, so they knew Pam wasn't in any physical danger. Jack checked the security camera feed on his computer screen just to be certain. The lobby was clear but outside there was a woman. She was tapping her high heel-covered foot, obviously impatient at being kept waiting. Jack couldn't get a good look at her face, but she was dressed in a figure-hugging black dress cut low in the front to show off an attention-grabbing amount of cleavage. Her dark hair fell in artfully styled waves down her back. Large sunglasses hid the color of her eyes, but her lips were a bright, fire engine red. Not a woman who was trying to hide in the shadows.

"Anyone you know?" Jack asked Drew.

"No, but she's a looker."

"She doesn't have an appointment, does she, Pam?"

"No," Jack could hear the dislike in Pam's voice. "But she seems to think you'll want to see her even though she is refusing to tell me who she is or what she wants."

"I'll handle it."

Jack hit the button that connected him to the outside intercom. "This is Jack Winston. Can I be of assistance?"

"Jack," she woman practically purred. "How are you?"

"I'm sorry, but have we met?"

"Well, not technically." She smoothed back her hair and adjusted her breasts. Jack couldn't decide if she was unaware of the camera or was giving him a show. "I'm Louise, Louise Hoover."

Jack looked at Drew, but it was clear he was just as lost.

"Now don't be coy," the woman continued, her voice running like warm syrup. "I know you're keeping company with Rose."

Rose? This woman knew Rose? Well, that wasn't going to get her in. She needed to stop being so cryptic and provide some actual information.

"Well, shit," Drew thought.

Jack pulled his hand back from the intercom button. "Do you recognize her?"

"I think that's *Aunt* Louise." He emphasized the word aunt; Tyler would say it that way.

"Rose's aunt?" Jack frowned. Rose had only mentioned the woman once, but he'd gotten the distinct impression they weren't close.

"Right." Drew gave the woman on-screen a closer look. "I don't know much about her but I do know she's trouble, Jack."

Jack considered for a moment then rang Pam. "Let her in, Pam. Take her to the small lounge and offer her something to drink. I'll be down in a few minutes."

"Tell me what you know," Jack said as he pulled on his jacket.

"Not much," Drew admitted. "When I started seeing Tyler, she and Rose and Dani had been friends for a long time and they kept each other's secrets pretty tight to the vest. I do remember Rose's aunt took her out of school one year a few months before the end of the term. I didn't see the aunt. She just showed up and the next day Rose was gone."

"When was this?"

"Let me think." Drew closed his eyes and ran his fingers roughly over his scalp. Jack recognized the gesture as one Drew used when he tried to figure out a software problem. "I was a sophomore, so that made Rose a freshman. She must have been about fifteen."

"But she finished school here in Harper Falls, right?" Jack developed a sick feeling in the pit of his stomach.

"She was back that fall. Not to Harper Academy, but Harper Falls High." Drew met Jack's concerned gaze and shook his head. "I don't know what happened, Jack. Since we weren't at the same school anymore, I didn't see her every day but she seemed different. Quieter, I guess. We didn't hang out with the same crowd, so I can't give you any details, but Rose was the kind of girl you noticed. I don't have to tell *you* that. For a while, it was as if she'd lost her spark. And that girl always had plenty of spark. By the next summer, when Tyler and I started dating, she was back to her old self."

"On the outside," Jack observed grimly. "Whatever *Aunt* Louise did to her is still influencing how Rose lives her life — at least her love life."

"And you think you're going to get answers by meeting with that woman?"

Jack shrugged. "I doubt she'll tell me anything with words but I want to get a feel for the woman. I want to get some idea, no matter how small, of what Rose went through."

"Hey, if you end up strangling her, you know you can count on me to help you get rid of the body."

Jack knew Drew was joking, mostly. The point was Drew had his back no matter what.

Jack paused outside the lounge and pulled in a few calming breaths. He had always had a long, slow burning fuse, but with just the little he knew about this woman, he could feel his blood simmering. It wouldn't take much to get it boiling.

Louise Hoover certainly knew how to set a scene, Jack thought as he entered the lounge. He searched his brain for the right word for how she had herself arranged on the sofa and decided *artfully* best described it.

Jack supposed she was trying to look casual and unconcerned as she leaned against the cushions, her arm resting on the back of the sofa. There was nothing relaxed about it. She had herself on display. She had crossed her legs in a way that had the hem of her skirt riding several inches up her thigh. Not *too* far but enough to show off how trim and shapely they were. When she saw him enter, she gave him a slow, welcoming smile and leaned forward so that the first thing he would notice was her breasts. However, just to be sure, she took a deep, cleavage-enhancing breath.

"Hello, Jack." *The woman was good,* Jack thought. With just those two words, she had made it seem like they already knew each other — really well.

"If you're in town to see Rose, I'm afraid you've missed her." Jack waited for the lie he knew was coming.

"Oh, dear. I had so hoped to spend some time with her. It's been much too long." She leaned even closer, cleavage first. "She's always so busy. I can't tell you how many times I've wanted to see her only to have her brush me off. Since I'm here, maybe we can get to know each other. I'm sure Rose would love for us to become *good* friends."

And there it was. It was such an obvious come on. He knew what she was doing, and she knew he knew. He wondered if she expected him to jump her right here at his place of business. Some men would, some probably had. Just the thought of having those slick, red lips anywhere on his body made Jack shudder.

Enough, Jack thought. Five minutes in and he'd gotten what he needed. The woman was a calculating bitch. She'd slithered into town and made a beeline for the man she knew her niece was seeing. She was in seduction mode before Jack had even entered the room. What was she after? A way to hurt Rose? Or was her main goal Jack's money? Both would be his guess. Well, *Aunt* Louise was going to leave town empty-handed on both counts.

"I find it odd that you've never mentioned that you're Rose's aunt."

"Oh, there's such a small difference in our ages, I never think of her in that way." The ever so brief tightening of Louise's mouth told Jack that she didn't like being reminded of the fact that she and Rose were related. "She never called me anything but Louise so I tend to forget. Now, why don't you take me someplace cozier and I'll show you just how little like an aunt I really am."

"That is a bad line, Louise." Jack slowly shook his head. "Even if I was the slightest bit interested, I would hesitate after you threw that one at me."

It was obvious that had thrown her, but she was a gamer. She wasn't going to give up *that* easily. Jack was sure she had quite a catalog of routines in her arsenal, ones she'd been perfecting for years. He didn't want to play anymore. It was time to send the woman on her way.

"This isn't going to happen, Louise. Not now, not tomorrow, not ever. Pack your bags and get out of town before Rose returns."

"She'd believe me if I told her you came on to me, that we had sex."

Five minutes with the woman and Jack was exhausted. He couldn't imagine what it had been like for Rose to spend months at her mercy. Louise was pure poison wrapped in a silky but ever hardening shell. In a few more years, she wouldn't be able to hide her brittle exterior with honeyed words and artfully applied cosmetics.

Jack didn't bother to reply, he just waited for Louise to gather her purse and escorted her to the door. Seeing them enter the lobby, Pam quickly disengaged the lock. Jack restrained himself from forcibly pushing her out of the building, but it was a close thing. He waited long enough to see her drive away before heading back to his office.

He needed a drink. They didn't keep anything harder than beer at work, so he grabbed his keys and headed home. Along with the drink, he wanted a long, hot shower. And Rose; he wanted Rose. There was no point in looking at the calendar. Three more days. He just hoped she missed him even half as much as he did her.

Chapter Ten

"WHAT ARE YOU doing?"

Rose looked over her shoulder as Frank entered the kitchen. He had on his *'Don't Mess with The Sex God'* t-shirt that she had given him for his last birthday. It didn't do any good to point out that it had been a gag gift. Frank took it as the complete truth.

"If you insist on me stating the obvious, I'm making popcorn." She waved the already popped bag at him. "I was also being a good guest and giving you and Len a few minutes alone to cuddle. But since you're here, you can grab the drinks."

Frank and Len had insisted that Rose stay with them instead of in a hotel. They had a spacious two-bedroom loft in Greenwich Village, so she readily agreed. It was great having the extra time to catch up, and since the men had long ago dropped their party-boy lifestyle, the three of them spent the evenings talking and watching movies. Popcorn and diet whatever were the nights' snacks of choice.

"I mean what are you doing in New York when you have a gorgeous, sexy man back home just waiting to ravage your body the moment you get back? And don't say you're here for work; you finished holding Felicity's hand two days ago."

It had turned out to be a bit more than handholding.

When Felicity Pike had called her on Saturday morning practically in tears, Rose had agreed to fly to New York and smooth over the differences the singer and her producer had. Felicity was an artist which when translated, meant temperamental diva. She was also talented enough to get away with the occasional outburst. Rose loved the way Felicity sang her songs. The producer was, well, a producer. Tommy B. was a control freak. It was his way or the highway. Rose was there to help them find a happy medium, something not usually in her job description. She knew them both and they all wanted to release the best possible product. Hit records meant prestige and money. That was something none of them could argue about.

What she thought would be one afternoon of calm negotiations and ego stroking had stretched into three days of long hours and upset stomachs. The result was two of the best sounding recordings of her material that Rose had ever heard. Felicity had been grateful. Tommy B. said he owed her one. Rose promised herself *never* again.

"Just a few weeks ago, you were saying how much you missed me. Are you tired of me already?" Can we please change the subject? As busy as she had been, Jack had never been far from her thoughts. The return airplane ticket that she had tucked away in her suitcase seemed to send out a beacon to remind her that she was due to fly home tomorrow.

"The bet ends on Sunday. I just wondered why you're waiting until the last minute to go home."

She had told Frank and Len the whole story. At first, they had been outraged that he would involve her in something so ridiculous. As the week progressed, their sympathies had made a definite shift. She wasn't sure how Jack had become their best pal when they'd never even met, but she started to feel like *she* had done something wrong.

"I was needed here in New York." She didn't have to look at Frank to know how lame he thought that excuse was.

"Ready to get back to the movie?" Not waiting for her answer, Frank picked up the tray of drinks and left the kitchen.

Fine, Rose huffed, following behind. Hadn't she said that she didn't want to talk about it?

Setting the bowl down on the glass coffee table, Rose grabbed her drink and dropped into her chair. She felt a little like pouting but Len, sweet, happy, Len, would have none of that.

"You have got to see this video a friend told me about this afternoon." He picked up the remote and hit play.

Rose watched as a group of men dressed in nothing but jockstraps gathered on some open field. "I'm all for gay porn, guys, but maybe you'd rather be alone to watch this."

"It isn't porn," Frank informed her. "Though it has made me rethink my opinion of that little town you live in."

Rose sat up in her chair. That was happening in Harper Falls? Peering closer, she realized that the field did look vaguely familiar.

"You guys ready to pay up?" a voice off-camera asked.

Jack. That had to be Jack holding the camera. And that was a practically naked Drew giving Jack the finger.

"Uh, Rose." Never taking his eyes from the screen, Frank reached for the bowl of popcorn. "You never did say what the stakes of that bet were."

"I never found out." She recognized some of the guys who had been at the tavern Saturday night. "Oh, my God. They're going to run the obstacle course. But why aren't they completely naked?"

"Honey, the last thing a guy wants is for his man bits to flop around." Len leaned in closer. "And some of those things they're jumping over and under, not to mention crawling through, look like they might scrape things up pretty bad." Both men grimaced slightly.

"Would you look at that red-haired giant?" Frank sighed. "I'd consider giving you the boot if he came calling."

"I'd consider giving you the boot if any of them came calling." Len gave Frank an affectionate kiss and then whispered, "Or maybe I'd keep you and invite them to join us."

"We'd have to get a bigger bed."

Rose had tuned out their banter. This was fantastic. By themselves, every one of those guys was spectacular. As a group, those muscular, well-toned bodies would cause a sensation. Women were going to be stampeding to Harper Falls by the thousands. And since Drew was the only one who actually lived there, he was going to be a busy boy indeed. She picked up her phone and sent a quick text. Tyler and Dani had to see this.

They'd ended up running it three times before finally turning off the TV. It had been better than any of the movies they'd planned to watch. Rose was still laughing when she suddenly realized that today was only Friday. Why had they paid off the bet two days early? She mulled the possibilities when her phone chimed signaling that she'd just received a text. Seeing that it was from Jack, she quickly opened it.

Schedules are going to be crazy for the next month, so the guys got together today to pay off the bet. You should get a kick out of this. After the message, he left a link to the video. Smiling, she saved the text knowing it was something she would want to look at again.

"So at the risk of you biting my head off, I'll ask again. What are you doing here when you have a man waiting for you? A man, I'll remind you, who has nothing to keep him from jumping the first available woman who walks by."

"I hope you aren't suggesting that Jack would wait three weeks to be with me and then give it up to another woman?" Rose looked at Frank as if he'd lost his mind. She had no doubt that Jack would remain celibate until she got there. Frank was right about one thing. What was she waiting for? Why didn't she get online and book the first available flight home?

"I'm going to clear up the dishes and then go to bed." Len gathered everything onto the tray and headed for the kitchen.

"It's not about the sex, is it, Rose?" Frank patted the cushion next to him. Rose didn't hesitate. She snuggled into Frank's embrace, her head resting on his shoulder. "If that's all it was, you would have been gone by now."

"Jack is different, Frank."

"You mean he's not boring?"

"Definitely not boring," Rose confirmed. "He makes me …"

"See the possibilities?" Frank finished for her.

Rose sighed. Possibilities she hadn't thought existed, at least not for her.

"No offense? But why aren't you one of those stereotypical gay friends that women have in the movies?"

Frank laughed. "You mean the ones that flit around wearing pink spandex and give the heroines fabulous makeovers?"

"Exactly."

"First of all," he pointed out, "you don't need a makeover. Second, I gave away my pink spandex about the same time I quit flitting."

"So I'm stuck with the smart friend who thinks he's always right and usually is."

"And that makes me stuck with the beautiful, talented friend who'd better get packed so she can get to the airport." He reached over and opened the side table drawer, pulling out a piece of paper. "This says your flight leaves in two hours. If we hurry you should just make it."

"I love you, Frank."

"Of course you do," Frank called after her as she raced out of the room. "What's not to love?"

Frank had been lucky enough to find the man he wanted to spend the rest of his life with. He wanted the same for Rose. To get it, she had to open herself up. She needed to let someone into her life. Maybe Jack was that person. Maybe it was finally Rose's turn.

Chapter Eleven

JACK WAS TIRED. Tired of looking at the clock, tired of worrying about when Rose would come home. And when she did, whether she would come to him. She hadn't answered his text. Should he be worried about that?

Going for a run had been a good idea. Work off some excess energy, clear his mind. His favorite music was blasting. No earphones necessary. He was on his property, with no one to complain about the noise. As he and Edgar started up a particularly steep hill, he felt himself relax. He couldn't will Rose to return any sooner so he might as well give into the joy of nature and a ridiculously happy dog.

Jack didn't like letting the puppy go out into the woods alone; there would be plenty of time for that later when he was full-grown and no longer afraid of his own shadow. Therefore, every morning when the two of them set out for their five-mile run, Edgar was in canine heaven. He slowed down as he approached his house, stopping to look at his panting companion.

"You go get yourself a drink and something to eat." Jack let them in and headed for the stairs. "I'm going to take a shower and then work for a few hours. You know where to find me if you need me."

"Has he started talking back or is his answer implied?"

Jack had imagined Rose right there, in his bed, so many times that he blinked a few times, afraid he was seeing things.

"You're naked." At least he hoped she was. Rose sat up in his bed, the sheet tucked underneath her bare arms.

"I hope that's okay." Rose enjoyed Jack's slightly stunned reaction to her unexpected appearance. It helped dispel the nerves she'd been battling ever since her plane had touched down. "Drew let me in and he told me to make myself at home so…"

Fascinated, Jack watched as Rose traced the edge of the sheet with her index finger. He suddenly became aware of everything. How the dark blue of the material made her skin look like fresh cream, all warm and smooth. He wanted to lap up every inch until they were both so crazy with need that they forgot about the world outside this bedroom.

"I've missed you." His voice sounded deeper, raspy. Almost desperate. Yes, desperate. He hadn't known if she would come back to him and now that she was here, so many emotions ran through him. He was a jumble of lust and relief. But there was also something new. Something he wasn't ready to name. It was too soon, too soon for both of them. Jack felt a shift inside of himself. This moment was important; a beginning that meant so much more than sex.

"I've missed you too."

Rose couldn't take her eyes off him. Big, strong, beautiful Jack. He was sweaty from his run and outrageously sexy. Was it weird to want him to skip the shower so he could cover her with his hot, glistening body? She knew how he would taste. Salty, masculine. Like Jack.

"Rose…"

"Are you nervous, Jack?"

Was it possible? Smooth, funny, oh so confident, Jack. Could he be feeling as jittery as she was?

"A little bit," he admitted.

They smiled at each other. It felt good to know that they were both a little unsure, that this meant something.

"I'm going to take a shower," Jack said, pulling his sweaty shirt over his head. "When I get back? Well, I hope you haven't anywhere to be for the next forty-eight hours. I have weeks of fantasies built up and we are going to do them all." He paused before going into the bathroom and looked over his shoulder. He met her gaze with his blue eyes full of promise. "On second thought, make that seventy-two hours. You never know what new fantasies might occur to me."

As the door shut, Rose fell back against the pillows. Now that was the Jack she remembered. Hearing the shower start, she settled down under the covers, her hand smoothing a wrinkle from the ultra-soft cotton sheets. She felt her body relax, maybe for the first time since she'd gotten on the plane for New York.

The flight home had been uneventful, giving her plenty of time to run scenario after scenario through her mind. Should she call Jack and let him know she was coming? Should she just show up at his door? What if he wasn't home? What if he was with another woman? Okay, forget the last one. She wasn't worried that Jack would give into his pent-up lust and sleep with someone else. He knew she was coming home, eventually.

That made her nervous. She hadn't responded to his text. She hadn't been in touch all week. Jack had told her he understood. She wondered if the situation had been reversed, would she have been okay with Jack going off and not talking to her? Maybe Jack was just a better person than she was. Maybe he was pissed and was one of those people who kept their anger inside until it built up to one huge explosion.

Rose groaned. She knew what she was doing. She was making problems where there weren't any. She'd promised Frank and herself that she would be open to the possibilities, and that's what she was going to do. For once, she was going to live in the moment and see what it would bring.

She heard the shower stop. Rose shivered with an anticipatory tingle. Jack didn't seem like the kind of guy who spent a lot of time on his post-shower activities so she knew there were just moments until he would come through the door. Other than that all too quick preview of him without his shirt, this would be the first time Rose would see him naked. Good, God. She salivated. And why not? Jack was amazingly drool-worthy with his clothes on. The thought of him clean and slightly damp from the shower caused her entire body to heat. She shifted again but suddenly couldn't find any comfort. She needed Jack. Knowing he was near and that soon he would be with her was almost too much for her to take. *Open the door*, her mind screamed. *Now, open it now.* She gasped when the door swung open as though she had willed it to happen. She grinned. Maybe she had.

Then Jack emerged, and she couldn't think at all.

She drank in the sight of him sure that anything so perfect had to be a dream. He seemed bigger with just a towel wrapped around his waist. It was amazing what wonders clothing could hide. Over six feet of long muscled male. Bronzed skin, lightly dusted with hair seemed to glow as he walked towards her. He moved like an athlete. Strong, confident strides that ate up the distance between them in no time.

Her hands wanted to touch him, anywhere, everywhere. His impossibly flat, firm stomach seemed to call out for her mouth to trace the ridges; her tongue eagerly memorized every smooth, muscled inch.

"Lose the towel." She wasn't asking, she was pleading.

Jack let the cloth fall to the floor. Eyes wide, Rose gasped. Mother Nature had been very kind to Jack Winston, and she was about to be a very grateful beneficiary.

"Rose, sweetheart," Jack stepped back when she would have touched him.

"Oh, come on, Jack," she groaned in frustration. "I've been a very good girl. Now it's time for my reward."

"It's just..." Jack grabbed her hand before it could touch his erection. "You know it's been a while. I need to warn you that this first time might be fast." He met her gaze with obvious embarrassment. "Really fast."

"You don't think I'm ready to go off like a roman candle on the Fourth of July?"

"It's just that I pride myself on my ability to last a lot longer than a minute. But the way I feel right now, I'm not sure I'll make it *that* long."

She was touched that even now, hard and needing release, he thought of her pleasure. Deliberately, Rose pulled her hand from his and ran it lightly up his arm. She shifted to her knees letting the sheet fall away, leaving her as bare as he was. She brought her hands to his face and cupped it. Feeling the smooth skin beneath her thumbs, Rose realized he had taken time to shave away his morning stubble. Hard and soft, strong and gentle, he was a delight of different textures. Leaning in, careful not to bring their bodies into contact, she traced the line of his firm jaw with her lips. She took his earlobe between her teeth and bit just hard enough to elicit a growl of pleasure from him. The bite hadn't been hard enough to cause any real pain. Just to be sure, she bathed his entire ear with her tongue, ending right where she'd begun, at the lobe. She pulled it into her mouth, sucking as if it was a different part of his body; one that she died to get her mouth on.

"Christ, Rose," Jack hissed. "I love what you're doing but I'm about to embarrass myself and come all over your stomach. You have to stop, now."

Rose made a protesting sound in the back of her throat but let Jack pull away. Who knew an ear could be so sweet?

"I love the way you taste," she breathed, running her hands across his chest. She knew he was in a state of high arousal and she tried to be good, really she did. She kept finding these wonderful places to play with. Ah, his nipples. It had felt so amazing when he had bitten hers. Would he like it if she did the same?

"Don't you dare!" Jack tugged on her hair until her head was tipped away from his chest and towards his face.

"Sorry," she said, not at all contrite. "I keep getting distracted." Rose finally gave into the one thing she'd wanted since he dropped his towel. Smiling innocently, she let her hand travel the short distance down his chest to grab hold of his straining erection. She felt a small twinge of guilt when she saw how hard Jack was gritting his teeth.

"Relax." She soothed the rigid line of his jaw with her other hand. "I wouldn't want you to ruin that beautiful smile by breaking some teeth."

"Then let go of my dick."

Sighing with obvious disappointment, Rose did as he asked. "Do you remember what you said to me the night you, you know…" now was not the time to blush, "went down on me?"

"Sweetheart, right now I'm having trouble remembering my name."

"Fair enough," Rose chuckled. "You told me it was all about me. At that moment, you were there to give me pleasure, not to receive it." She kissed his shoulder, then his cheek, and finally his lips. "Right now is about you; don't think about anything but what you need and how you want to get there."

"I have a choice?" Jack closed his eyes, enjoying how the sound of her voice washed over his skin like a cooling caress only to have her lips heat him up again. It was the sweetest form of torture.

"Always," she breathed against his mouth. "The choices are infinite but right now, I'm going to help you out and narrow it down to three. And remember, it's all about you. What you want."

She scooted back so he could see all of her. When she was sure that she had his slightly glassy-eyed attention, she began.

"Would you like my hand?" Rose held it up and made a slow motion to mimic what she would do to him. "My mouth?" Raising a finger, she slowly slipped it into her mouth, in and out, in and out.

"I'm about at my breaking point, Rose," Jack warned, his eyes transfixed on the glossy digit as she ran it over her lips. He felt dizzy. He moved his feet further apart, locking his knees. Knowing what was next he held his breath.

"Or," Rose slid her hand down her body with an excruciating deliberation. "My pussy." She moved that same finger that had moments before been in her mouth down through the slick, sensitive folds. She kept her hand to the side so he could watch as she penetrated herself for just a moment. Showing him the proof of her arousal, Rose left a wet trail up her body then circled one tight nipple until it glistened with her juices.

Jack couldn't stand it any longer. He swooped down, pulling her nipple into his mouth, savoring the taste of her. Oh, yes, he remembered that sweet, heady taste. And there it was — that little moan she made in the back of her throat. The sound that had been teasing his restless dreams ever since the first time he heard it.

For a moment, Rose let herself give into the pleasure of his mouth on her breast. Gathering her resolve, she pulled away, her skin cooling quickly and longing for the return of his touch.

"I told you; this is about you."

Jack ran his tongue over his lips, seeking every little drop.

"Believe me," he said, "it was my pleasure."

"And me helping you," she glanced down at his weeping penis, "will be mine. Now, what shall it be? Keeping in mind that just because you chose one doesn't mean the others will then be off the table. This is just to take the edge off."

Jack wasn't sure he was in any condition to make a conscious thought. All he knew was that his dick screamed for him just to do something. When his eyes roamed to that lush, warm mouth, his decision was made.

"Good choice." Rose took his hand and pulled him down so he was sitting on the edge of the bed. Giving him one last kiss on his shoulder, she slid to the ground and positioned herself between his legs.

Jack sucked in a deep breath. Now here was every heterosexual male's dream come true. A gorgeous, eager woman kneeling in front of him, her mouth poised to do wicked things to his cock. He raised his eyes to the calming picture that hung on the wall across the room. Concentrate, make this last. Green hills, contented cows, gently swaying trees — Rose's hands running along his legs. To hell with that stupid painting, his attention needed to be completely on the woman whose only goal was to give him pleasure. He would savor every moment of this no matter how long it lasted.

Truth be told, Rose was pretty much running on instinct. She'd done this exactly twice before, and though the guys seemed to enjoy it, she hadn't. Everything had seemed mechanical and slightly embarrassing. They had been by-the-numbers blowjobs, over and done as quickly as possible. It felt different with Jack. She had offered this because the thought of taking him into her mouth was appealing, exciting. His penis wasn't this alien object waiting to do its business and the hell with her needs. He was beautifully made. Long, thick and hard. However, she didn't find him the least bit intimidating.

Bracing her hands on his thighs, Rose raised her gaze to his. What she saw gave her all the courage she needed. Jack's blue eyes blazed with need and tenderness. He ran his hand through her hair, not with aggression, not to pull her closer, but to sooth and encourage.

Holding his eyes, she swiped the pooling moisture from the top of his erection. He tasted clean and masculine. She could see how he tried to control himself, how desperate he was not to give in too soon. That's not what she wanted. Rose wanted Jack wild with need, coming apart in her mouth. She wouldn't let him hold anything back from her. She gave him a final lick and then took his length into her mouth.

Jack almost lost it. Between the incredible suction of her mouth and the visual of Rose, his Rose, taking him with such enthusiasm was better than he could have anticipated. He was so close. She pulled away just long enough to lightly scrape her teeth across the head of his penis and then she pulled him back into her mouth. Jack knew he'd reached his limit. He tried to tell her, give her time to pull away but his orgasm hit with a force so strong all he could do was grip the bed and let out an exultant shout.

After taking all he had to give, Rose sat back. She wiped the side of her mouth, unable to hold back the laugh that bubbled up inside of her.

Jack had collapsed onto the bed, unable to stay upright a second longer. Hearing Rose's laugh, he cracked open one eyelid.

"That's a joyous sound." He held out his hand for her to join him. Jack sighed with contentment and wrapped his arms around her, pulling her close. "Are you all right? I was afraid I might have..."

"Drowned me?" she finished for him. She laughed again when Jack winced.

"I may have had a bit of a reserve stored up. I meant to warn you but there at the end, my mind melted down into a pool of pure bliss. I couldn't have spoken if my life depended on it.

Rose kissed his cheek then snuggled closer. "I'm not complaining," she assured him. "I liked it, all of it."

"So you weren't doing it just because you thought I wanted you to.

"I found out a long time ago that if you do things only to please other people, you're never going to be happy." Feeling her shiver, Jack pulled the comforter over them. "If I get on my knees for you, Jack, it's because I want to. I will say that was the first time that I've enjoyed it. And I've never finished and wondered right away when I would be able to do it again."

"I'm always at your disposal. And now that my heart has recovered, and the rest of me is well on the way, let me have the pleasure of taking care of you."

"Can we wait just a bit?" Rose asked. "It feels so good just to lie here in your arms."

"And it feels good to have you here. I got this gigantic bed because I'm tall and I like to spread out when I sleep, but lately it has seemed lonely."

"I'm sure Edgar would keep you company," she teased.

"Edgar does not sleep with me." Jack ran his hand down her back; the movement natural and affectionate. "He has insinuated his way into every other corner of this house, but my bed is off limits."

"Are you sure he knows that?"

Jack looked over to the foot of the bed to see Edgar watching them, head cocked to one side and tail wagging furiously.

"You don't think he saw us, do you?" Strangely, Rose found the thought more embarrassing than if a human had seen them.

"Don't worry, he won't tell anyone." Jack stood up and shooed the reluctant dog out of the room. "I'm playing with Rose right now but if you're a good boy, I might convince her to join us later for some outdoor fun." He gave Edgar a quick scratch behind the ear, then firmly shut the door.

"Jack," Rose said, thoroughly enjoying the view. She could get used to naked Jack.

"Yes, Rose." Jack rejoined her in bed, sliding down so that they were face-to-face.

"I know I'm not telling you anything you don't already know, but you have a rather rabid-looking bunny tattooed on your shoulder."

"It's a jack rabbit, not a bunny," he informed her quite firmly. It wasn't so much a case of out of sight, out of mind, but he'd had the tattoo so long he forgot until someone else noticed it. He could tell Rose was curious, so he settled them under the covers and told her the story of how he got it.

"Seriously, Jack," she laughed several minutes later. "You can never get drunk again. I shudder to think about what you might get talked into next time." Then after a minute, she suddenly made the connection. "Of course. Jack. Rabbit. Was Jack Rabbit your nickname in college?"

Jack considered changing the subject. She didn't need to know the truth. Since it was only mildly embarrassing, what harm could it do? Besides, he'd sworn to himself never to lie to Rose again, even by omission.

"No, not a nickname. It's my actual name."

"Your parents named you Jack Rabbit? It's on your birth certificate?"

"My full legal name is Jack Rabbit Run Winston. Go ahead and laugh; if you hold it much longer, you might blow a blood vessel."

"I'm sorry." Rose collapsed in a fit of giggles. "I think I could have suppressed it if you hadn't added the Run."

The word set her off again and Jack patiently waited for her to finish. It wasn't an unusual reaction. Exactly why very few people knew his full name.

"Done?"

She thought for a moment. "Yes," she said decisively. "I'm done. But do you mind if I ask how they came up with such an original name?"

"Mom thought that with six girls my dad needed a boy."

"*Needed?*" Rose asked. "What did your dad think?"

"I doubt Dad cared," Jack shrugged. "Not that he didn't love having a son; he was great at all those dad things like playing catch and teaching me to spit. He loves my sisters with all his heart. Another girl wouldn't have mattered to him, just more to love."

Rose felt a pang of envy, but just a small one. It would have been nice to grow up with siblings and a mother and father. In her experience, Jack's family wasn't the norm. Sometimes family, any family caused more pain than pleasure. No, she was glad that Jack had happy childhood memories, but Rose had found her family with Tyler and Dani. Sisters of the heart. She figured she was better off than most.

"So what does that have to do with your name?" Rose prodded.

"Patience, my dear. There's a process to telling a story, and you can't rush it."

"Fine." Rose gave him an affectionate shove. "But I need a visual aid to go with your story. Turn over and let me get a better look at your bunny."

"Why does it sound dirty when you say bunny that way?" Jack rolled over so his back was to her. "And it's a rabbit," he reminded her.

"Finish your story, Jack Rabbit Run." Rose traced her fingers over the snarling rabbit. It was beautifully done — a work of art. Considering the drunken state Jack had been in when he got it, he was lucky it hadn't turned out to be a cute little Easter Bunny.

"As I was saying, my mom decided even before I was conceived that I was going to be a boy. She read up on the subject, ate boy foods and did boy exercises."

"I had no idea there were such things." Rose replaced her fingers with her lips, outlining the tattoo with lingering kisses.

"Oh, you'd be surprised." Jack moaned when Rose ran her tongue along his shoulder blade. What was he saying? Oh, right, his name. What was his name?

"If you want to hear the rest of this, you'd better stop that."

"Don't you like it?" She gave the rabbit one final kiss before wrapping her arms around his waist so she could spoon him. "I want to hear the rest. I'll be good, I promise."

Having her naked body rubbing his back wasn't helping his concentration but it sure as hell felt good. Might as well enjoy. He pulled her arms tighter until she was molded to him completely, and then continued.

"But what made my mother certain all her efforts had worked was what happened the day my dad took her to the doctor to confirm her pregnancy. It seems that just as they were leaving the house, a brown and white rabbit jumped up onto the porch. Mom being Mom, she decided it was a sign. And then when the rabbit ran off into the field, well, she knew what she was going to name me."

"I like your mom," Rose said. "And I'm growing very fond of this jackrabbit."

"And me?" Jack turned to face her. "How do you feel about me?"

His words teased, but Rose felt an undertone of seriousness she wasn't comfortable with. She liked things light and playful and didn't want to go any deeper; not now, maybe not ever. Therefore, instead of answering his question, she shifted the subject to one she was more than happy to deal with. Sex and how amazing Jack made her body feel.

"So far I like you just fine and I can tell there's a certain part of your body that *really* likes me." She nudged his growing erection with her pelvis. "That is for me, isn't it?"

The moment had passed and he didn't want to push Rose where she didn't mean to go. It was early days. He knew his feelings were farther along than hers were and that he couldn't rush her. That didn't stop him from wishing she wouldn't shut down that part of herself whenever he got too close. He shifted, tangling his legs with hers. He had no complaints about getting to know each other physically; he was all for it. The rest would come; he just had to be patient.

"All yours. But this time *I'm* going to take charge." Making her gasp with how quickly he moved, Jack rolled her under him. He braced his arms so they bracketed her head then leaned down and whispered, "This time? Your pussy."

"Again, good choice." Her breezy quip was quickly cut off by Jack's blistering kiss. She suddenly had no desire to talk. Kissing was so much more fun.

"This is it, Rose." He gave her another hard kiss; one that told her playtime was over. "Remember when you wanted me to take you home and screw your brains out? Three weeks has felt like an eternity, but there's no turning back now." He moved his hand between her legs, testing her readiness. "Unless you want me to?"

Rose growled in frustration. She pulled his mouth back to hers and wrapped her legs around his hips. After three weeks of foreplay, she was more than ready. Their kiss was wild and out of control. Lips were bitten; tongues dueled; finesse had been replaced by raw need. Jack entered her with one firm stroke, filling her, and making her gasp. They stayed that way for several moments, unmoving — savoring the connection.

Jack raised his head. He wanted to watch the play of emotions on Rose's face. What they shared wasn't some random fuck, and he needed to know she felt the same. If she couldn't say it with words, let her tell it like this.

He pulled out slowly. Her eyes had turned a hazy amber. Just as he threatened to leave her warm depths, he paused, tormenting them both. One second passed, then two, wanting her to be just as desperate as he was.

Rose tightened her legs around his hips, trying to pull him back. Already she felt empty, and it was an emptiness only he could fill. No matter how hard she tried to bring him back, he wouldn't budge and she wasn't strong enough to make him. She rubbed her breasts against him hoping for some relief but it only added to her frustration. Everything felt so good, but she needed more. At the end of her rope, she reared up and bit him, hard, on the neck. Hard enough to leave her mark on him. She wanted to send a message. Move, now.

Finally, Jack thought with satisfaction. He entered her again, reveling in the way her body welcomed him. Her tight grip was like nothing he'd ever known. Home, he was home. Rose was the answer to every question. Their bodies knew it and so did he.

How could this be happening so fast? Rose wondered. Sex, even at its best, had always been a gentle journey towards a pleasant destination. This felt like she was about to burst out of her skin. Scorching heat blazed through her veins. Could she survive if her blood boiled? At that moment, she didn't care. Jack took her someplace she'd never been and the ride was wild and terrifying, and she loved every minute of it. His strokes were hard and sure. She was there, so close. Then she spiraled over, bliss suffusing every inch of her body. She knew the instant he joined her, his shout of release giving her another blast of pleasure.

Jack collapsed on top of Rose. He hoped he wasn't crushing her but at the moment, he was unable to move. He found just enough energy to lift his head and graze her cheek with an awkward kiss. He could feel her breath against his cheek and see the rise and fall of her breasts. Her eyes were closed, but there was a slight smile curving her lips.

"How are you doing?"

"Shh." Her smile deepened. "This moment needs to be savored."

That sounded good to Jack. He untangled their bodies and settled back against the pillows, pulling her into his arms.

"You go right ahead and savor." He smoothed her tangled hair back from her face — such a lovely face. "When you're finished, let me know. By then, I should be ready for the next round."

Rose had just enough energy for one good chuckle. "Don't start making promises you can't keep."

Jack pulled her in for another smoldering kiss. "Never."

DOGS WERE FORGIVING souls. Floodlights illuminated the yard making it easy for Rose to watch as Edgar chased his ball with never diminishing enthusiasm. There were no hard feelings for being kicked out of the bedroom. However, it wasn't as if they'd completely forgotten him. Jack had dutifully checked on him every few hours, filling food and water bowls, and letting him out to do his business.

It was well after dark when they finally took a prolonged break. With three incredible orgasms and plenty of pillow talk under her belt, Rose was ready for a shower, clean sheets, and food. Jack told her that it was a beautiful, roomy shower and insisted they should conserve water by sharing. Rose soon found out that Jack's definition of roomy meant spacious enough for twelve very friendly adults. As for saving water, by the time they had finished, she figured those twelve adults could have showered alone, twice.

Jack threw on a pair of jeans and a t-shirt before going down to start dinner. He had offered to help her make up the bed but as soon as he showed her where he kept the clean linen, she shooed him out of the room. She learned fast that Jack's superpower was outrageously fast recovery time. She didn't think the bed would ever get made if he were *helping* her. Not that Rose complained; she wasn't an idiot. She needed sustenance. She had plans for later and that required keeping her strength up.

An hour later, having refueled with bacon, eggs, and toast, they kept their promise to play with the dog. Edgar trotted over and dropped his slimy ball at her feet. He looked so proud that she was careful not to grimace when she picked it up. He'd welcomed her without reservation and had no problem sharing Jack. She didn't want him to think she found anything about him objectionable, not even his spit.

"Nice arm." Jack watched her throw sail into the trees. He had six sisters and a mother who would hit him upside the head if he ever accused anyone, man or woman, of throwing like a girl. There were degrees of competence and Rose obviously knew what she was doing.

"Which one of your friends is responsible for that?"

Rose laughed. Jack had figured out that where one friend went the others followed, not always enthusiastically, but never wavering in support. Baseball had been Dani's thing.

"Never tell Dani she can't do something." Rose shook her head as she remembered the third summer she'd spent in Harper Falls. "When she heard some of the boys saying girls couldn't play baseball, she got her father to coach us in secret. Dani had a wicked spitter. And yes," she held up a hand when Jack would have protested, "I know it's an illegal pitch. She struck out Billy Paul, the most obnoxious of the bunch, and then never played again. She proved girls could play, and I learned how to throw a rocket from third to first."

"I wish I'd known you then."

"I was five inches shorter and skinny as a rail." She knelt down to praise Edgar for all his hard work then grinned at Jack over the dog's head. "You wouldn't have given me the time of day."

Jack thought about his twelve-year-old self and had to agree. Not because of how Rose had looked, but because at that age, he had considered all girls to be weird, even his sisters. They giggled a lot and didn't like to get dirty. What could you do with a girl? Boys were much more fun. It would be a whole two years before he figured out that not only could girls be a lot of fun but they also smelled considerably better than boys did.

"You're right." Jack pulled her into his arms. "But only because all girls have cooties."

"*Boys* are the ones with cooties, fella."

"I'll show you my cooties if you show me yours."

Rose gave him a considering look then shook her head. "You can keep your cooties to yourself. Besides, I've already seen everything you've got."

"Is that right." Jack grabbed her, throwing her over his shoulder and heading for the house. Figuring this was a new game, Edgar trotted happily behind them. Locking the door behind them and setting the alarm, Jack told the disappointed dog to stay. "I think I still have a few things to show you."

"Jack," Rose yelped. "Put me down." She struggled, which earned her a hard swat on the butt.

Jack took the stairs two at a time. "Stay still or you'll make me drop you."

"That hurt." Rose was about to return the favor when suddenly she flew through the air landing on the bed with a bounce. Jack was on top of her before she could regain her breath.

"Show me," he grinned as he unbuttoned her jeans. "I'll kiss it and make it better."

Laughing, Rose let him strip off her pants. Jack knew how to have fun in bed, something new for her. The playful lover, the thoughtful lover, the intense lover, she'd found them all in him. As his lips soothed her, quickly igniting her passion once again, Rose wondered what other things she would find out about Jack. What unexpected things she would find out about herself.

Chapter Twelve

TWO DAYS OF sexual bliss, a man who could make her laugh, and a dog. Rose hated for it to end, but the real world called them back.

She closed her suitcase and sat it on the floor. Smoothing the comforter, she grinned when she thought about all the action the bed had gotten in the last forty-eight hours. Not that they'd confined their activities to the bedroom. Jack was very inventive, and if she were the type to blush easily, she'd be beet red in almost every room in the house.

"Let me get that." Jack came in and picked up her bag. "Are you sure you have to leave?"

"Are *you?*"

About an hour ago, Jack received a call from Drew reminding him of a conference call they'd had scheduled for weeks. Besides, she needed to get back to work. Sam Laughton expected a progress report and she wanted to tell him she would have the songs done by the end of June. He wanted her to deliver them in person to his Paris studio. A month ago, she would have been tempted. Sam was attractive and very interested. Not her usual type, but tempting. Now she had every reason to stay in Harper Falls because of a different man who was not her usual type. Rose refused to think of the implications or of the knot in her stomach that formed when she thought too far ahead. She enjoyed the now and a knot-free stomach.

"I should have turned off my phone." Jack took her hand as they descended the stairs. "Unfortunately, Drew lives just down the road. No getting away from work when your partner can be at your house in less than five minutes."

Edgar woke with a start as they came out of the house. He had been dozing in his favorite spot, but the moment he saw them he was wide-awake and wiggling, easily beating them to the SUV. Jack opened the back passenger door and let him jump in the car.

"He gets so excited about going with me and then sleeps for most of the trip." He laughed, giving the puppy a scratch before closing the door. He turned to find Rose staring.

"What?"

"Your hair is growing." Rose knew she stated the obvious, but it had just hit her how much longer it had gotten since the Lilac Ball. She sighed. She hadn't thought a man could be any more gorgeous than Jack had been that night. Yet there he was unshaven, hair at what should have been an awkward stubbly stage, and wearing jeans and a flannel shirt that had seen better days. If anything, he was sexier. Rumpled suited Jack Winston.

Jack ran a hand over his head, grimacing slightly. "It couldn't have gotten any shorter. Don't worry. My hair grows very fast. In a few more weeks, it will be back to a reasonable length."

"I liked it," she mumbled hoping her voice was too low for him to hear.

"Yah?" Jack helped her into the truck then jogged around and hopped in behind the wheel. "I didn't think the look worked for me."

She knew Jack wasn't searching for a compliment. Most guys would have expected her to elaborate on her comment, to stroke their egos. Jack didn't need any affirmations. She'd never met a man who was so comfortable in his own skin. He was who he was and he didn't need to be complimented every five minutes to feel good about himself.

They shared a companionable silence during the fifteen-minute drive to her house. Rose expected Jack to drop her off and head straight to work so she was surprised when he followed her inside. He set her suitcase by the stairs. Something bothered him. He had a habit of rubbing the back of his neck when he was troubled.

"Can we sit?" Jack waited for her to take a seat before he joined her on the sofa.

"What's wrong?" Rose couldn't imagine what could suddenly be bothering him. Before they'd left his place, he had seemed completely carefree.

"I would have told you this before but I didn't want anything to ruin our time together." He took a deep breath. There was nothing to do but just say it. "Rose, your aunt came to see me last Wednesday."

"What did she want?"

Jack couldn't have guessed what Rose's reaction would be, but he'd expected something more than a flat, monotone question.

"I'm not sure. She did this creepy come-on routine but it was so obvious and over the top, it's hard to believe she was serious."

"Oh, she was serious." Rose felt all the happiness that she'd experienced during the last two days draining out of her body. Just knowing that Louise had been nearby was enough to suddenly make her fifteen years old again, trapped in a horror show that was her aunt's life. Harper Falls had always been a safe haven from that. A place Louise avoided thinking it beneath her notice. Now she'd tried to sprinkle her unique brand of poison on Jack.

"You should go." Rose needed to be alone, to find her heaviest blanket, and burrow inside. She had to find a way to combat the cold seeping into her bones.

"Let me call Drew and tell him I can't make it." Jack had never seen Rose like this. It was almost as though she shrunk into herself. He took her hand, alarmed at how icy it had become.

"No," she pulled away. It took all the effort she could muster, but Rose forced herself to stand. With deliberate steps, she walked to the door. Grasping the knob, she pulled it open and leaned against it for support. "Go to work, Jack."

"I'm not leaving you alone. Jesus, Rose, you're trembling."

"I'm tired." She couldn't explain it to him. She didn't want him to see her like this. She was crawling into a hole that was dark and confining, one that took a lot of time and effort to climb out. Jack couldn't be a part of that.

"I'll go, but only if you promise to call Tyler or Dani. Hell, call them both." She started to protest, but Jack wasn't going to budge on this. "Call them, Rose. I'll be in my SUV, but I'm not driving away until I see one of them arrive."

"Fine." She wanted to be angry. But she couldn't generate enough heat to do more than pick up her phone and hit speed dial. Satisfied that she wasn't going to be alone, Jack finally left.

Rose watched the door close then shuffled back to the sofa, sinking into a boneless heap. With a sigh, she raised the phone to her ear.

"Dani?" It wasn't until she heard the catch in her voice that Rose realized Jack had been right; she needed her friends. "Can you come over? And bring Tyler."

IT TOOK SIX hours and endless pots of tea but Rose finally felt warm again.

Tyler and Dani had arrived within minutes of her call. There were no long explanations necessary. While Dani gathered thick socks and a downy comforter, Tyler heated the water for tea. She also called the local diner and ordered hot soup to be delivered. From then on, it was just a matter of them being there. Bracketing her on the sofa, lending their warmth unconditionally.

At some point, she must have dozed off, the exhaustion finally pulling her under. When she finally opened her eyes again, her head felt a little fuzzy, and she found herself stretched out on the couch alone. The clock on the far wall read four o'clock and since it was still light outside she figured that was p.m., not a.m. Slowly, she became aware of muffled voices coming from the kitchen. She wasn't surprised. Dani and Tyler wouldn't have left her by herself.

"Ready for more soup?"

"Bathroom." Any more liquid and she would float away.

When she came back, Rose felt like she just might be on her way to being counted among the living. It was amazing what brushing her teeth and splashing some cold water on her face could do for her outlook on life.

She found her friends waiting for her in the living room. Though they didn't say, it was obvious they were still concerned. This had hit quicker and harder than ever before, and neither of them had any prior experience to draw from.

"I was happy." Rose didn't know how else to begin. "I had no defenses to fight it because I'd let them all down. Jack must have thought I was crazy. He didn't even say her name — just *your aunt* — and I was practically catatonic."

"He didn't leave until we got here," Dani pointed out.

"If he's smart, he'll never come back."

"That's crazy and you know it." Tyler would only let her wallow so long. Now that Rose had her feet back under her, it was time for some tough love. "When you were fifteen, you had no choice. She was your legal guardian; you had to go with her. But she can't hurt you now unless you let her."

"Two years of therapy and I'm still a mess. A mess with a train wreck attached." Rose finally felt a stirring of anger. "I can't force the bitch to stay away. Now that she has the scent, she's bound to make another run at Jack — especially since I'm involved with him."

"You don't think Jack would..." The thought was too disturbing for Dani to finish.

"God, no." The last thing Rose worried about was Jack being seduced by Louise. "But if I keep seeing him, I'm going to have to tell him everything."

"What exactly are you worried about, Rose?"

"What *aren't* I worried about?" Rose paused to gather her thoughts.

Most of her worries were irrational but knowing that didn't magically erase them. "The last time I talked about any of this was to my therapist and that was almost ten years ago. I'm happy to say I rarely think about it anymore."

"That's good." Dani squeezed her hand.

"But what if I tell him and he thinks I've blown it all out of proportion?"

"Rose—" Tyler began.

"No, hear me out. I wasn't physically harmed, not really. There are people who go through much worse, for much longer periods of time."

"She drugged you," Tyler exclaimed. Unfortunately, it was all too easy to conjure up the image of Rose, too thin and hooked up to an IV, lying in a hospital bed. "She took a laughing, happy girl and, in the course of a few months, turned her into a withdrawn bundle of nerves. Jack won't try to diminish that."

"No," she agreed. Jack would be compassionate, which brought her to her biggest fear. "I don't want him to see me as a victim. If he knows everything, I suddenly become *that girl with the troubled past*. Jack grew up in an Ozzie and Harriet world. Why would he want to take me on?"

"*Ozzie and Harriet?*" Tyler scoffed. "*Jack?*"

For the first time in hours, Rose smiled. "With a few minor differences. The Nelsons were in black and white — Jack lived in vivid Technicolor." With an even bigger smile, she added, "And Jack would never get a G-rating."

"More like...?" Tyler urged.

"Most days, PG-13. In private? XXX."

"Oh, we will need details," Dani declared. "But for now, I'll give you some advice and I hope you take it. There was nothing wrong with your life before you started seeing Jack so if you break up with him, it won't be the end of the world. But he makes you happy, Rose. And there's something to be said for a man with XXX sensibilities. I say take a chance. Go for the happy."

"And the great sex," Tyler chimed in.

"There is that." Rose would have to think on it. For now, she wanted to clear her mind of her problems and binge out on someone else's.

"I have *Outlander* on my DVR. Anybody for ice cream and some time travel?"

JACK WAS PISSED. It didn't often happen, and it never lasted long. Oh, he could hold a grudge with the best of them. He'd never let it consume him. He'd put it away and deal with it if and when the problem reared its head. But, for the most part, Jack Winston did not stew.

Drew had given Jack plenty of room for the past few days. Whatever had happened with Rose ate at Jack, and while he didn't know the details, he understood that his best friend was in a bad place. It was his duty to either leave him be, get him drunk, or find something for him to hit. He'd done the first, and he knew that after what happened the last time, he couldn't get him drunk again. That only left one option.

"Get off your ass. We're going to the gym."

"Fuck off." Jack didn't bother to look up; he just growled and went back to work.

"Downstairs, now. If I have to come back up here to get you, there will be blood." Since he knew not all of it would be Jack's, Drew hoped like hell Jack followed him.

Jack didn't hurry. In fact, part of him hoped Drew *would* come back. A little spilled blood sounded good about now. After thinking about it for a few minutes, he finally gave in. Shutting down his computer, he headed to the gym. It was a short trip but by the time he got there, he was ready to rip Drew a new one.

The last few days had been hell. He hadn't slept more than a few restless hours each night; Rose wasn't answering her phone and his pride wouldn't let him beat down her door. The last thing he wanted was Drew trying to help him work out his frustrations. He slammed into the gym expecting a one-on-one confrontation. What he found was Drew and five hulking strangers in workout clothes.

"You want to explain?"

"You need to hit something; these gentlemen have volunteered."

Jack gave Drew a *'you have got to be shitting me'* look. "I repeat. You want to explain?"

"We have a few openings with the security crew and these guys have applied. Let's call this their preliminary interview. If they can get through you, they move on to stage two."

Jack could have argued. There was no such thing as a preliminary interview. However, he was in the mood to hit something. Earlier that morning, he'd gone several rounds with a punching bag but since it didn't hit back, he hadn't procured much satisfaction.

"Give me a minute to change." He took a moment to look at his would-be opponents. They were big and looked strong, but they were young. "You guys take the time while I'm gone to think this over. And you," he called to Drew. "Fill them in on what to expect. I don't plan on taking it easy. If any of them wants to back out, don't let the others give them a hard time. In fact, the ones that leave might just be the smartest guys in the room."

Chapter Thirteen

ROSE PULLED HER car to a stop. The parking lot outside H&W Security was fuller than she'd expected. She hoped to find Jack alone so they could talk without any interruptions. Maybe now wasn't a good time. Then when would be? She was here, and she needed to get this over with. She'd been ignoring Jack's calls and pretty much hiding out for three days. He deserved an explanation. After that, the rest was up to him.

Before she could even hit the intercom button, the doors clicked open. Surprised, Rose looked over at the reception desk to see Pam waving her in.

"Thank goodness. I'm afraid they're going to kill him."

That didn't sound good. Should she panic? In spite of her rather inflammatory greeting, Pam seemed relatively calm. Rose decided to save her panicking until she had a few more details.

"Who's going to kill whom?"

"Five brutes, in the gym, with Jack."

Jack and brutes were all Rose needed to hear.

"The stairs are to the right," Pam called out after her.

She remembered. It only took her a minute to get down the two flights but then she had to stop and get her bearings. Pool, then weight room, then gym.

It seemed awfully quiet, Rose thought as she hurried towards the door at the far end of the pool. If someone was trying to kill Jack, shouldn't there be yelling? That night outside the tavern she distinctly remembered a lot of yelling.

Afraid of what she was going to find, Rose hit the door at a run. There was no yelling, but the three guys on the floor groaned up a storm. She was relieved to see that none of them was Jack. She didn't see him anywhere, but she did see Drew. He didn't seem overly concerned about the bruised and bleeding men and at the moment, she wasn't either.

"Is Jack all right?"

Drew grinned and nodded. "*He* hit *them*," he indicated the men who were helping each other stagger to their feet. "And then he hit the shower. You'll find him in there."

Jack leaned his forearm against the tile and let the multiple jets of water beat over his body. It hadn't been much of a contest. Big kids, little training equaled three big booms and a couple of bloody noses. They'd be fine. More hurt pride than anything else. Jack, on the other hand, was no longer angry, which meant the adrenaline that had been keeping him on his feet had worn off. All he wanted was to finish his shower and head home. Well, he also wanted Rose, but there wasn't anything he could do about that right now.

"Need your back washed?"

His eyes popped open, but he didn't straighten. Instead, he watched under his raised arm as Rose removed the last of her clothes and walked towards him through the steam and water. She pushed the lever on the soap dispenser, letting the liquid pool in her hand. Moving behind him, she rubbed the soap into his back until a lather formed and ran down his spine. The scent of lemon filled the shower, sharp and clean. Jack put both hands on the wall in front of him. He arched his back, savoring the feel of her soap-slicked hands as they moved up his tense muscles, stopping so she could firmly massage the space between his neck and shoulders.

"Relax; let me take care of you."

Rose could feel the knots under her hands slowly loosen. Moving closer, she rubbed against him, her nipples hardening. She followed the disappearing soap with a trail of soft kisses. He smelled so good, like nothing else, masculine, clean — like Jack. She slipped her hand around his body wanting to feel his arousal. She wanted to give him pleasure. Before she could reach her goal, Jack took her and pulled her in front of him. He lifted her hands above her head and pinned them to the wet tile with one of his. His mouth opened over hers, greedy and demanding as the water cascaded over them in warm waves.

They didn't speak but Rose saw everything that she needed to know in his clear, blue eyes. He needed her, wanted her. Lifting one of her legs, he hooked it around his thigh. Bending just slightly he began to enter her, slowly, inch by agonizing inch. Her eyes never left his; their breathing synced in perfect unison. There was no hurry; the build was gentle but intense. Minutes passed or was it hours? Time didn't matter. As they reached their peak, they came together, the rush so powerful she felt her legs begin to buckle. Jack had her, his strong arms keeping her safe as they floated slowly down to earth again.

Jack gave her one last kiss before reaching over and turning off the water. Guiding her from the shower, he took a large towel and dried her hair.

It felt good to let him take care of her. She closed her eyes and just relaxed as he wiped the moisture from her body and then quickly did the same to himself. He found her clothes and handed them to her before he dressed himself.

"Is your car outside?"

Rose nodded. They silently made their way through the building. She wondered where everyone had gone. Drew must have cleared them all out for which she was grateful. She'd been so intent on finding Jack that it hadn't occurred to her that someone might walk in on them while they were in the shower. Not that either of them would have noticed. But still, it would have been embarrassing to find out later that someone had observed them.

After setting the alarm, Jack led her to his SUV. He assured her that her car would be fine, but that was the least of her worries. She'd run what she would say to him repeatedly in her mind and on the short trip to his house, she thought it through one more time. Now that the moment was almost here, she realized no amount of preparation could help. She would say her piece and that would be that. The unknown was frightening. What would Jack's reaction be? Before she said anything else, she needed to do something. After he had let them both into the house, Rose began to apologize.

"I'm sorry, Rose."

That threw her for a moment. Jack had nothing to be sorry for.

"Jack—"

"Sit, please." She did, expecting him to join her. Instead, he paced.

"I shouldn't have dropped the news about your aunt's visit so abruptly," he began after a few moments.

"Jack, you couldn't have anticipated my reaction." Rose was horrified to think he'd been feeling guilty for the last few days. "It was extreme, to say the least."

"I got a little glimpse of what your aunt is like." He finally joined her on the sofa. "Will you tell me about her? About what she did to you?"

"I wish I had some great revelation I could share with you, Jack. I spent a lot of time in therapy looking for one." It hadn't been a complete waste of time, but there hadn't been any magic answers either. She was still screwed up, just to a lesser degree.

"I told you that I was sent to live with my aunt after my mother died. What I didn't tell you was that she didn't just die; she committed suicide."

Jack was shocked. "Rose, I'm so sorry. I had no idea."

"Very few people know." Rose closed her eyes; it was such an ugly subject. "I felt guilty." She'd never admitted that to anyone besides her therapist. Not even Dani and Tyler knew. For some reason, she needed to tell Jack.

"Why?"

"I loved my mother and I think, in her way, she loved me. I tried so hard to cheer her up. The first song I ever wrote was silly and so bad, but it made her smile." Rose cringed when she thought of it. Ninety percent plagiarized and one hundred percent crap. It was all it took to get her hooked; music became her passion — her escape.

"After she died, I cried. Maybe that was when I cried myself out. Tears don't come easily to me anymore. I missed her. But I also felt free. I was nine years old and I'd never felt like a kid."

Jack took her hands, hoping to give her a bit of comfort. God, they were like ice. "Let me get you something hot to drink."

"I'm fine, really." It felt so good when he cupped her hands in his, sharing his warmth, making it easier for her to continue.

"It took about a month for the authorities to track down a relative. They asked me about my father, but I couldn't tell them anything. My mother never told me his name." Rose remembered fearing that no one would want her. "When she thought I couldn't hear, my social worker told another woman that she doubted my mother even knew his name, but that wasn't true; she just didn't like talking about him. Then, when they finally found my aunt, I was so excited. I started creating all these fantasies about how beautiful she would be and how she would love me and take care of me." Rose scoffed. "Well, she *was* beautiful."

"They just turned you over to her?"

Rose understood Jack's outrage, and was touched by it.

"All I know is that a few days after they located her, Louise swept in, with her makeup perfect and every hair in place. She charmed everyone, including me. We left; I was with her for a few months and then she found a new man who paid for me to come here to Harper Academy."

"You're leaving something out, Rose."

"It wasn't that bad the first time I was with her," Rose assured him. "Louise had just started dating the man who would become husband number three." Chester Freemont was a widower with a lot of money and a little girl about Rose's age. When he found out his new girlfriend could provide his little angel with a ready-made playmate, Louise used Rose as a way to upgrade her status to wife. Though she made it clear in no uncertain terms, Rose was never to call her *Aunt* Louise. She only slipped once, and Rose found out that Louise knew how to slap and pinch — hard. The bruises were hidden by long sleeves and Rose never forgot again.

"So you lived with her, the new husband, and his little girl?"

"Shirley was her name." She was spoiled rotten. The last thing she wanted was another child around to take any attention away from her. Rose hadn't been there two weeks before she was shipped off to the most remote location they could find.

"Louise was happy to get rid of me and I was happy to go. Harper Academy was a dream come true. Dani and Tyler's families welcomed me in as if I was one of their own. For the next few years, I was happy, unbelievably so. There was no reason to think it would end. I'd almost forgotten that Louise even existed, so why would I think she would come back into my life and turn it upside down?"

"Drew said that one day you were in school and the next you were gone." Jack braced himself for the next part of her story. His gut was already in a knot. He couldn't begin to imagine how hard it was for her to tell him — to relive it for him. He wanted to know. He wanted to understand. However, he didn't want to cause her any more pain.

"I need to finish, Jack." Seeing the concern on his face, Rose gave his hand a squeeze. "It isn't bad as you think it's going to be, so don't worry. I just want you to hear the rest."

With a nod, Jack settled back to listen.

"It was about the same time of year as it is now. I was fifteen and looking forward to getting out of school for the summer. Dani, Tyler, and I had lined up jobs taking care of people's yards. Dani's dad let us use his lawn mower and other equipment, and we figured to make a good chunk of money. Then Louise showed up. No warning. She told me to pack a bag and get in the car."

At first, Rose had been more confused than scared. Tyler's father was away on business and her mother was easily intimidated. When Anita Jones tried to protest, Louise pointed out that she was still Rose's legal guardian. It was her right to take Rose and no one could do anything about it.

"Mrs. Jones was no match for Louise, but Tyler wasn't going to let me go without a fight. She dared Louise to call the police."

"You have to love Tyler." Jack cheered the teenage hellcat. Unfortunately, he knew how the confrontation ended.

"She was my hero," Rose agreed.

She'd often wondered what would have happened if she'd stayed and fought. Would things have turned out differently? Who knows? In the end, Rose left with Louise without any fuss. Tyler's parents had been so good to her she couldn't stand to think of them getting in trouble because of her.

She had packed one bag, got in the rusty Ford Escort, and left the only real home she had ever known. She made Tyler promise to say goodbye to Dani for her. They hugged and promised to keep in touch. Rose had her phone and they planned on talking as often as possible.

As soon as Rose fell asleep in the car, her phone "disappeared" out the window.

"What the hell was her game?" Jack's meeting with Louise had been brief, but she hadn't come across as the kind of woman who would wake up one morning with the burning desire to play mother.

"Louise was riding pretty low, maybe as low as she'd ever been. Why she hated me, I don't know. But for some reason, she got it in her head that if she was going down, she was taking me with her."

Rose found out quickly that Louise loved the sound of her own voice. Most of what she had to say concerned how horribly life had treated her. Seven hours of almost non-stop complaining, most of which made little sense to Rose. Names she'd never heard; people she'd never met. Rose finally realized that Louise wasn't talking to her; she was just talking. Rose would have listened to music, but she'd already lost her phone, she didn't want to take a chance on losing her iPod too. Instead, she composed music in her head. By the time they reached Boise, she had three songs written.

"Boise? Why Boise?" Jack realized his entire body clenched. He took a deep breath and tried to relax. He wasn't very successful.

"That was where she had arranged to meet up with her current boyfriend, Gus Plank. He wasn't up to Louise's usual standards, but she was at that *'beggars can't be choosers'* stage."

Along with writing songs, Rose had been forming a plan. She knew she'd been an idiot to let Louise take her out of Harper Falls and away from anyone who could help her. So now, she was on her own and this time she had to be a lot smarter. If she could get to a public library, she could use one of their computers to email Dani and Tyler and let them know where she was. She doubted Louise would go to the police but just in case, Rose didn't want to involve her friends' parents. They could send her the money to buy a bus ticket home and they'd figure the rest out once she got there. She never made it to a library and it wasn't long before she was incapable of contacting anyone.

"We only stopped in Boise long enough to pick up Gus Plank. He was huge, Jack. For the first time, I was afraid. I didn't need to fear Gus; it was Louise. She was relentless. She wouldn't let me sleep longer than an hour at a time. She would sit next to my bed and whisper what she was going to let Gus and his friends do to me when we arrived at their cabin. I knew I had to get away from them, but I was never alone. I think she started putting something in my food because I had no energy."

They moved around from small town to small town; their routine never varying. Rose was terrified of getting to "the cabin," the place where Gus and his friends would do terrible things to her. Between the lack of sleep, Louise's nightly threats, and the drugs, just one month after the nightmare had begun Rose had become a jittery mess of skin and bones. She didn't have any appetite, but Louise made sure she ate a few bites. Rose wanted to refuse, but she didn't have the strength to keep the food from being forced down her throat. She had no idea how much longer she would have lasted if Gus hadn't come to her rescue.

"He seemed like such a doormat. Louise dictated every move. Gus almost never spoke but when he did, it was to agree with Louise." Rose gratefully took the cup of tea that Jack had finally insisted on making for her. She let the heat seep into her hands; it felt wonderful.

"It took the son of a bitch a month to finally help you?" Jack was so disgusted he could barely grind out the words. "He was as crazy as Louise."

"You're probably right. But something finally made him help me."

"What happened?"

"I have no idea."

Every day became just like the last, so Rose had no idea what had made that one different. She knew they had stopped, and she thought she could remember Louise complaining about needing to go to the bathroom. Suddenly Gus lifted her out of the car. The next time she was aware of anything she was in a hospital in Harper Falls, hooked up to an IV.

"I didn't know how I got there. Later, Dani told me that her father had received a phone call in the middle of the night telling him where he could find me. He didn't hesitate, Jack. He drove for hours to some no name town in Montana on the off chance the guy on the phone told the truth. Knowing that someone cared that much helped me get back on my feet, that and two friends who practically lived at my bedside. Tyler and Dani willed me to get better. I don't know what I would have done without them."

"The police?"

Rose shrugged. "They questioned me but the only thing I could tell them was who I was with and that at one point, we were in Boise. To be honest, Jack, I'm not sure they believed any of it. I think they saw a runaway who had gotten in over her head and finally called home when things got too bad. Louise and Gus had disappeared. A few years later, I read that he was in prison for armed robbery. I heard from Louise about a week after I sold my first song."

"She wanted money?" Jack held it together, but not by much.

"No, at the time she just offered me her *sincere congratulations*. She wanted to let me know that she had married again and that he was a *very* wealthy man. I was in shock. I couldn't move. Hearing her voice brought it all back again. My mind shut down just like the other day."

"Was there anyone there to help you?" Jack hated the thought of Rose going through that alone.

Rose shook her head. "I was living in New York and my roommate had gone away for the weekend. Thank goodness. Tanya was never very good in a crisis. I crawled into bed and didn't budge for two days. After that, I was more prepared. It wasn't often that she called. When she did, it was either to complain about how awful her soon-to-be ex-husband treated her or how she had nabbed the perfect man, perfect meaning rich. I would change my number, but she always managed to get the new one. When I moved back to Harper Falls, I made sure she had the number of a landline I had installed just for her. For whatever reason, she was satisfied with that. She would leave the occasional message, and I would erase it."

Rose rolled her neck. Almost done. "She's never tried to see me. I don't know what changed. Her coming to see you makes me wonder what other nasty surprises she has up her sleeve."

Unable to stand it another moment, Jack pulled her into his arms, burying his face in her hair. "Jesus, Rose," he breathed, taking in her scent. "Jesus."

Rose just held on. Feeling the slight tremor vibrate through him, she tightened her arms and let him process everything she had told him. It was a lot to take in, especially all at once.

"The other day was a fluke, Jack." Rose hated that she'd let Louise get to her. She was stronger than that; she'd made herself stronger. "She can't hurt me; she holds no power unless I give it to her."

"I wish I had taken Drew up on his offer."

Had she missed something? "What offer?"

"The other day when Louise showed up at our office, he said, if necessary, he'd help me bury the body. If I'd known then what I know now, I would have happily strangled the psychotic bitch."

"I'm glad you didn't know. She's not worth it."

Jack leaned back just enough to smooth her hair from her face. He gently kissed her, and then pulled her firmly into his arms. He couldn't let her go, not yet. He couldn't get the picture she'd painted of her frail body in a hospital bed out of his head. How close had she been to not making it? How much longer could she have lasted being dragged from town to town? Being drugged and tormented.

"How can you be so calm? So together?"

"Time, therapy, and amazing friends." Sometimes she wondered how much good the therapy had done. She still had issues, big ones. Talking about her mother and Louise had made things easier to cope with.

"I know it was a long-winded explanation, but I hope you understand a little better what happened the other day. Though it was a bit extreme."

"After what you just told me? I'd say you handled it pretty damn well." Slipping his arms under her legs, Jack stood and carried her up the stairs. "We're going to take a hot bath, jets set on high. And then have something to eat."

Jack was relieved when Rose didn't argue. He felt shaky, and he needed her to let him take care of her tonight. He dimmed the bathroom lights and filled the tub. As the steam began to fill the room and swirl around them, he gently removed her clothes before lifting her and settling her into the hot water. He quickly shed his clothing and joined her, positioning her between his outstretched legs. He pulled her back against his chest and wrapped strong, protective arms around her waist.

Before long, Jack felt himself begin to relax. Rose was safe, no harm could touch her; he wouldn't let it. Hearing her deep, steady breathing, he realized that she had fallen asleep. Dinner could wait. Right now Rose needed rest more than she needed food. He needed... well... all he needed was Rose.

Chapter Fourteen

"I'M TELLING YOU, it won't work, Jack."

They'd been having the same argument all morning. Or Rose had been arguing. Jack smiled indulgently or patted her hand as if he was placating a ten-year-old. Or he kissed her. As frustrating as it was, that was her favorite.

Rose had awoken after ten solid hours of sleep, wrapped in Jack's arms. It had been an emotional evening and they had both crashed like the dead. Snuggling closer, Rose looked at Jack's sleeping face, relaxed and rested, and realized she felt the same. She felt lighter, almost buoyant. If she never told that story again she would be happy, but telling Jack had been liberating.

Now she had to free Jack. Unfortunately, he wasn't cooperating.

"Nothing that happened to you was your fault and it certainly shouldn't stop you from living your life to the fullest."

How to explain? "I know it seems that this is about what happened to me that summer, but it isn't." The look Jack gave her told her he wasn't buying it. "Really." The man was impossible. "You know there's a big difference between charming and bullheaded."

"I can't be both?"

"Oh, boy," Rose thought, could he ever. But that didn't make him any less frustrating.

"One more time," she sighed. "Are you listening?"

"Always," Jack smiled. There was the charm.

"This is about me. I know myself, Jack. I don't do relationships."

The fact was she'd had sex with Jack more times than with any other man. Probably because the others hadn't been worth a repeat performance. What she did know was if she could have seen a future with anyone, it would have been with Jack. She wasn't going to tell him that. He didn't need any more encouragement.

"I don't recall asking you for a relationship. In fact, I haven't asked you for anything but a chance to get to know you better." Jack shook his head as if baffled by the conversation.

"I'm descended from all kinds of crazy, Jack. There's my mother and Louise. And don't forget a father who had no problem leaving me to be brought up by the poster child for antidepressants. My family tree should be ripped out by the roots and the ground salted." Why wasn't he running for the hills?

"I know what's bothering you." Jack smiled as if he had a secret.

Okay, she'd play along. "What's that?"

"You think that eventually I'm going to ask you to marry me."

That was her problem? She thought about it for a moment. Maybe he was right, and it was a problem. A big one.

"I'll never marry you, Jack."

"You would." Jack watched Rose with amusement. He could tell she struggled not to knock him upside the head.

"No. *Never.*" Now, *there* was the stubborn.

"You *would,*" he qualified, "if you loved me."

"I'm not going to fall in love with you, Jack."

"I'm not saying you will." Jack's clear, blue eyes stared at her, unwavering. "What I said was *if* you loved me, you would marry me."

Rose didn't know why, but this seemed like a trap. She ran his words over in her mind, but finally gave up.

"Fine. But since the first isn't going to happen, neither is the second."

"As long as we're in agreement."

Had they agreed? Technically, she supposed they had but to be honest, Rose still tried to figure out what exactly it was that they'd agreed. Jack had driven her to pick up her car then followed her into town. They never had gotten around to dinner the night before and they were both starving. *Pansy's Diner* was packed with the usual morning crowd, so they had to wait a few minutes for an empty table.

"Well, I'll be. I wonder what Harry Eisner is doing in Harper Falls." Jack waved at a man seated at the counter. "Do you mind if I leave you for a minute, Rose? I want to say hello to an old friend."

"Go ahead. I'll grab a table if one opens up and you can join me there."

Jack gave her a quick kiss before heading across the room.

"Well, isn't that cozy."

Rose sighed. She would recognize the dulcet tones of Jilly Underwood anywhere. Apparently, Jack's kiss had not gone unnoticed. If Rose was correct, Jilly was a bit annoyed. *Now, wasn't that too bad?*

"Hello, Jilly. Beautiful morning, isn't it?"

Jilly glared at her, glanced over at Jack, and then glared again.

"I *hate* you."

Rose watched as the woman slammed out of the diner, almost taking out another woman who had been entering.

"Are you okay?" Rose asked. "Lila." She smiled when she recognized the owner of *Peony*. She had called in several orders but hadn't been back to the shop since the night Lila had come to her rescue.

"I'm fine." Her dark auburn hair was piled up in a messy bun. The style was like Lila, casual and sexy. She wore a loose, long-sleeved blouse that matched the soft green of her eyes. "Who was the sour puss?"

"An old nemesis who thinks Jack Winston could do a lot better — with her."

"Do you know Jack?" Lila let out a delighted laugh. "He's the reason I chose to open my shop in Harper Falls."

Rose remembered Jack mentioning that in passing.

"Jack told me that he knew you but not any details. I think he's friends with your brother, is that right?"

"I kind of knew him when we were kids back in Oregon. He and my brother would hang out and I was the annoying little sister." Lila grinned at someone over Rose's shoulder. "Hey, Jack. I'm glad to see you picked the right woman."

"Lila," Jack greeted her with genuine affection. "Did I pick you?" he asked Rose. "I thought you picked me."

"That doesn't sound right." Rose gave him a wide-eyed look. "But you should know if it hadn't been for me, you could at this very moment be having breakfast with most annoyingly vapid woman on the planet. You can thank me later."

"And you can explain later." He slipped his arm around her waist. Lila thought it looked completely natural — nice. Like he'd been doing it for years. If she ever heard from her wandering brother, she'd have to let him know that it looked like Jack Winston had finally met his match.

"I see there's a table opening up. Will you join us?"

"No thanks, Jack. I just stopped in to grab some coffee and a muffin. Thanks to Rose, I have more orders to fill than I can handle, which is why I'm happy to say, I hired some full-time help." She gave Jack and Rose each a quick hug. "I left Tammy alone, so I need to grab my order and get back. See you soon."

"I like her." Rose took her seat in the booth expecting Jack to sit opposite her. Instead, he sat on the same side, making her slide over. Rose gave him a disgruntled look, which he chose to ignore.

"I'm glad Lila is making some friends. How did the two of you meet?"

Rose imagined that most people who met Jack thought he was easygoing and accommodating, but she knew better. For all his charm and smiles, Jack seemed always to get in his own way. It was like being sneaky quick. He thought he had the upper hand, but before he knew it, he had smoothly acquired what he wanted. With an exasperated shake of her head, Rose filled Jack in on the night she met Lila.

ROSE SPENT THE rest of the day in her studio.

She had finished several songs for *Wishes*. The big climactic love song was giving her trouble. She knew why. Love songs, like love, weren't her thing. She wrote about sex, heartache, and betrayal. But love? She could write about what she didn't know, but more often than not, it didn't ring true.

A series of notes had been swirling around her brain for days. Picking up her guitar, Rose strummed the strings, hoping to chase down the elusively faint melody. After the better part of an hour, and no results that didn't sound like a commercial for a feminine hygiene product, she growled in frustration and put away the instrument. She couldn't break through a wall, and right now, she didn't have any idea how to do it. In a few days, she would try again. Find a way to come at it from a different angle.

There were plenty of other things to keep her busy. Like the dreaded paperwork. It was something that eventually had to get done. What better time than when her creative juices seemed to have dried up. Sam Laughton might not like her putting *Wishes* on the back burner, but her accountant would be ecstatic.

An hour later, receipts and expenses duly recorded, Rose felt she'd earned a break. Her stomach agreed. Peanut butter and jelly sounded good. But did she have any jelly? Or bread? Or peanut butter? Her practically empty cupboards screamed the answer. No! Not even a stale cracker. Since for once she didn't feel like having yogurt, it was grocery shopping or the diner. She looked around for her phone. Maybe she could get Dani or Tyler to meet her at Cable's Market. It was always more fun to shop when she had her friends with her.

Wait a minute. *The phone.* Rose suddenly had one of those slap yourself in the forehead moments. Why hadn't she thought of it before?

Forgetting about her stomach, Rose marched across the house to the little room where she stored things that she might need someday but, for now, she wanted to keep out of sight. Sort of the equivalent of a junk drawer. Before she could enter the room, the doorbell rang.

"Hey," Tyler greeted Rose as she opened the door. "I needed to get out of my studio and have some human contact. Want to get some lunch?"

"You're timing couldn't have been better." Rose grabbed Tyler and practically dragged her into the house. "I'm about to cleanse my house of old demons."

"Shouldn't we get some sage to burn?" Tyler asked. Then she saw what room Rose was taking her into. "Or maybe we're going to burn something else? Please?"

"Not burn." Rose looked at the phone and answering machine that she kept shoved back in the corner. Out of sight, but never quite out of mind. She'd always thought of it as her last line of defense. An unspoken agreement that kept Louise out of Harper Falls. Well, that agreement had been broken. And then some. It was finally time to cut her last link to *Aunt* Louise.

Rose ripped the phone from the wall jack and headed towards the garage. "I'm going to run over it with my car."

"And imagine that it's a certain someone's head?" Tyler smiled at the graphic image.

Rose grinned back, hitting the automatic door opener. "Great minds think alike." Putting the phone under her back tire, Rose climbed in the car. "Want to get in? After I've ground this to dust, we can head to the diner. Killing a bitch, even symbolically, works up an appetite."

Chapter Fifteen

"**I** CAN'T BELIEVE the two of you smashed that phone without me."

Rose passed Dani the guacamole. She and her friends were having lunch at a new restaurant that had opened the week before. Boasting the only Mexican cuisine in town, it was doing a brisk business, and if the bright, fresh flavors of the homemade salsa were any indication, they shouldn't have any problem keeping their clientele.

"My garbage hasn't been picked up yet this week, so if you need to say your goodbyes, the bag of pieces will be available for viewing for the next two days."

"Believe me. I won't be doing any grieving." Dani sipped her icy margarita, licking the salt from her lips. "Just one question, then we'll bury the subject along with the phone. Do you think she'll turn up when she finds out the phone is out of commission?"

"She already fouled the air that I breathe."

"Great title for a song," Tyler quipped to lighten the mood.

"It's been done." Rose smiled reassuringly at her friends. "I'm not going to worry about it. I got my panic attack, or whatever it was, out of the way. I would have preferred not to do it in front of Jack. Whatever power she still has over me is less than it was last week — less than it was yesterday. I'm turning that evil phone room into a half-bath. Win-win."

"Seems fitting that people will be do their business in the place that used to house the shithead box."

"Okay, enough about that." As far as Rose was concerned, the subject was permanently closed. "There's an extremely handsome man in a chef's coat coming this way. You know how to pick them, Tyler. Good-looking and he cooks? Very nice."

"Maybe he has a brother who hang glides," Dani said. "What? I want to learn. Why shouldn't my instructor be gorgeous? Way to bust a slump, by the way."

"Right now it's all about the sex," Tyler grinned. "If we ever get to the talking stage, I'll be sure and ask if he has any hang-gliding brothers."

Tyler had met Max Rivera, the owner/chef of *Bienvenido*, two weeks ago when she was loading a sculpture into her van for delivery. Max jogged by, saw Tyler and after they had exchanged pleasantries for several minutes, he had asked her out. Max was busy opening his restaurant; Tyler had a backlog of commissions to get done. Neither had the time or inclination, to start a romance. The sex was great and she liked him. Friends with benefits and food.

Max turned out to be charming and he was obviously fond of Tyler. Rose and Dani gave their silent approval. After all, that was what this outing had really been about. As her friends, it was their job to make sure the man in her life, no matter how temporary, was worthy of her. Max passed with flying colors. So much so, that Rose couldn't help wishing he could be more to Tyler than just a way to scratch an itch. In her way, Tyler was as screwed up about love and relationships as Rose. Different reasons, same results. Then there was Dani and her lost love. If she weren't so sick of therapy, Rose would suggest they find a psychologist who gave group discounts.

After lunch, Rose headed over to the high school. She had been asked to be a judge at the annual talent show. Back in the day, Rose had participated, coming in third. She wasn't a performer. Early on in her career, producers had taken one look at her and decided she could be a star. A woman with her face and killer songs that she wrote herself? She must want to be on stage, right? Wrong. Rose knew where she belonged, and it wasn't performing in front of screaming fans.

Harper Academy had given her a solid start with her music. She'd learned so much and, even more importantly, the teachers there had encouraged her dreams. Looking back, Rose was glad she hadn't been able to go back for her sophomore year. There had no longer been any money from Louise's husband, correction, ex-husband, so Rose had spent the next three years with Tyler and Dani at Harper High.

Harper Falls' public high school had been remodeled and modernized about five years ago, but Rose soon found that not much had changed. Kids still milled around the halls, waiting until the last minute before scurrying to class. Principal Harriman still ruled with an iron fist, and a heart of mush. She greeted Rose with a hug.

Rose remembered how lost she had been those first few months, still recovering both physically and mentally. Mona Harriman had taken Rose under her wing, making sure she adjusted to her new school. The woman had been a rock, and Rose had never forgotten.

"I should have warned you. We're having an assembly to introduce this year's judges."

"What, now?" Rose looked down at her faded jeans, yellow button-down shirt, and black loafers.

"You look great," Principal Harriman assured her.

"At least let me do a quick stop at the bathroom to check my hair."

"Of course." They detoured into the designated door. "Girls, the bell has rung. Get to the gym. And Clare, spit out that gum. The next time it ends up in another girl's hair, you're going to have to explain to your parents why I had to suspend you."

The girls scrambled out of the bathroom, suitably chastised.

"You haven't lost your touch." Rose applied some lip-gloss, her eyes crinkled with humor.

"I love my students. Now and then, they need a verbal kick in the butt. Which reminds me, how's Tyler these days?"

The two women exchanged grins. Tyler had been an instigator. To her credit, she rarely caused any real damage, if you didn't count a smoke-filled chemistry lab. She was the champion of those who couldn't look out for themselves. Rose and Dani did their share, but Tyler was the fiercest. There wasn't very much bullying when she was around. And though Principal Harriman didn't condone a vigilante approach, she could have used a few more students with Tyler Jones' sense of justice for the underdog.

After Rose had made sure she was as presentable as possible given the short notice, they headed for the gymnasium where the students had assembled.

"Is this a new thing? Introducing the judges?" She clarified. "It wasn't done when I was in school."

"Word of your participation has caused a bit of a stir." She held the door open for Rose. "Rather than have them all rubbernecking at the talent show, it was suggested that if you are introduced to them now, it might temper the excitement on the actual night."

"I'm surprised any of them even know who I am." People wanted to meet the singer of the songs, not the writer.

"I believe a picture of you with Beyoncé has been making the rounds."

Now the light bulb went on. "Ah, yes, celebrity by association. They're going to be awfully disappointed when they find out that she and Jay-Z rarely drop by for a chat."

Rose exchanged brief hellos with the other four judges. She didn't know any of them, but she imagined they were a bit surprised by all the hoopla that went along with a high school talent show. In fact, most of them looked like they wanted to be anyplace but here. Only Carl Fuller appeared to be enjoying the spotlight. Owner of Fuller's Feed and Seed, Carl considered himself a big man in town and he took an instant liking to Rose. Overcompensating for the noisy student body, he leaned over and shouted in her ear, "If you ever need any flower seeds, you let me know. I'll give you a big discount, if you know what I mean?"

Honestly? The kid in the last row of the bleachers knew what he meant. Grimacing, Rose stepped away. She moved so that the other judges were between her and *seedy* Carl. Did that line ever actually work? And at a high school assembly? Carl needed to learn some manners. Where was Tyler when she needed her?

Principal Harriman quieted the students with her patented silent stare. Thirty seconds, Rose counted. Impressive.

"We are very fortunate to have five distinguished members of our community with us today. They have graciously agreed to donate their valuable time to judge this Saturday's annual talent show."

Each of the judges received a polite smattering of applause. When the principal introduced Rose, she was relieved that her reception was only marginally more enthusiastic. Not bad, nothing embarrassing. Then it happened. One of the little smartasses had to call out, "Who was your boyfriend when you wrote *Grind?*"

Ugh. Five more minutes and she'd have been out of the building. Now she had to deal with hormonally charged teenagers and fellow judges who were giving her looks ranging from disgust, to increased interest by Carl, the seed man.

Principal Harriman quickly brought things back under control. Rose didn't offer to answer any questions. No matter what she said, it was a no win situation. Parents didn't want their children having a Q&A with the writer of sexually explicit songs. Who could blame them?

"I'm sorry about that." The students were back in their classes and the other judges had left. Principal Harriman insisted on walking Rose to her car.

"You have nothing to apologize for. They're just kids."

"My school, my responsibility. I don't like any guest to be embarrassed."

"That was nothing. In fact, it was pretty mild." Rose gave the principal a considering look. "Were you embarrassed, Principal Harriman? By the song, not the question."

"First of all, call me Mona." She held up a hand when Rose would have protested. "You'll get used to it. Secondly, I have heard it before,

Rose. In fact, my husband and I have been known to play it when the mood strikes."

"Mona." Rose ran the name through her brain a few times. It wasn't *too* strange. "I'm a bit disturbed to hear that from my former principal but I'm thrilled to hear it from my friend."

"I don't suppose you'd like to confide in me… you know?"

Rose laughed at Mona's sheepish question. She unlocked her car door and tossed her purse onto the passenger seat. "I could tell you, but…"

"Right, I understand. Besides, who would keep all those *little darlings* in order if I were dead?"

Rose was still laughing as she started to pull into her driveway. At the last moment, she changed her mind and drove until she was in front of Tyler's studio. Her exchange with Principal Harriman was too good to keep to herself. Her friends were the only ones who would appreciate it *and* keep it to themselves. While she waited for Tyler to answer the door, she called Dani to come over. Rose suddenly realized she hadn't stopped grinning since she left the school. Who could blame her? *Mona Harriman liked to get down and dirty to 'Grind.'*

IT WAS LATE afternoon when Rose decided to surprise Jack at his office. As she approached the gates, she wondered if she should have called first. She pulled to a stop as a guard approached. This was new. She hoped nothing was wrong.

"Are you expected?" The guard had a clipboard with a list of names.

"No. What's going on? Is everyone all right?" Had something happened to Jack?

"I'm sorry, miss, but without an appointment, you're going to have to turn around and leave."

"Look, I don't want to cause any trouble." Rose knew the guard wouldn't be out here if Jack and Drew didn't think it was necessary, so she was trying to be pleasant. If he didn't tell her if Jack was all right, she was going to storm the gates.

"Then turn your pretty little ass around and get out of here."

Pretty little ass? Really? Rose grabbed her phone. This guy's *ugly big ass* was about to get her foot up it.

"Hey, sweetheart. I was just thinking about you." Rose relaxed. Jack answered after the first ring. If something had happened to him, it would have taken at least two.

Before she could tell Jack her situation, the guard leaned down to her level. "Look, I can't let you in, but why don't you give me your address and I'll come by in a few hours after I get off." He looked her up and down. "Then I can help *you* get off."

"Martin, let Miss O'Brian through the gate and then get your things and clear out. You're fired."

Rose wiggled her phone at the stunned man. She almost felt sorry for him. Almost. Help get her off? That was the second time today someone had clumsily propositioned her. Was she wearing a sign that read *Open for Business*?

Jack waited for her, opening the door almost before her car came to a stop.

"Are you all right?" He pulled her into his arms. "Did that asshole touch you?"

"I'm fine. But what's going on? Are you expecting some kind of an attack?"

"Come inside and I'll tell you all about it."

Rose waved at Pam as they passed. Everything looked normal in here. Whatever was going on, no one seemed to be terribly concerned. Before she could get an explanation, Jack had her in his office and pushed up against the closed door. His kiss, hard and demanding, drove all questions from her mind. The world could be ending and she wouldn't care. All she needed was more of this, more of Jack. His tongue sought out hers, running slowly along the roof of her mouth before finding hers again, twining together in a sensuous game of tag. Jack's teeth gently bit her lower lip then sucked it into his mouth.

"I've missed you." He laid a trail of hot kisses along her jaw until he found that place, just under her ear, that drove her crazy. Her knees would have buckled, but Jack wouldn't let her fall. His strong arms lifted her, carrying her to his desk.

"Honestly, Jack?" Rose moaned the words. "The desk? The rich businessman? Isn't it a bit of a cliché?"

Pushing everything out of the way, Jack lowered her until her back was flat on the cool, smooth surface. "You know why it's a cliché, Rose?"

"Why?" Her breath caught when Jack ripped her shirt open, buttons scattering in every direction. Her bra was unfastened and removed as if by magic.

"It's a cliché because it works so damn well."

He pulled off her jeans and panties in one quick motion; her shoes flying across the room. "Beautiful," he breathed. His hand drifted across the slope of her stomach, settling between her legs. "So soft, so wet."

"Jack," she moaned. His fingers drove her higher, finding the perfect balance of pressure, knowing just when to advance and when to pull back. "Inside me, I need you now."

Rose gripped the edge of the desk with desperate fingers. She watched, panting, as Jack pulled his shirt over his head, tossing it in no particular direction. He made quick work of the rest of his clothes until he was as naked as she was, standing between her open thighs. Erect. Ready.

"Tell me again, Rose." His voice was a low growl. "Tell me what you want."

She reached out, grasping his erection. "You, I need you."

"Then take me."

His entrance was a long, slow, fluid movement. Their eyes locked, their breathing matched. Finally, when he'd filled her, he kissed her again, urgent but tender. Rose reached up to grip his waist, and then lower until her hands cupped the firm cheeks of his butt. She pulled him to her, willing him to increase his speed, silently begging him to make her soar until she could crash into oblivion.

"Come with me, Rose," Jack commanded. "I can feel how close you are. Come with me. Now!"

His shouted his last word in release, one so strong it triggered her orgasm. There seemed to be no end to the pleasure, wave after wave washed over her in a heated rush. And just when she thought she couldn't take anymore, Jack's mouth latched on to that spot again, the one right below her ear, and she sailed just a little bit farther.

Jack smoothed his hand down Rose's arm and laced his fingers with hers, pulling back just enough to see her face. Ah, there it was. That look he craved, the one that said she had been thoroughly satisfied, and whether she knew it or not, thoroughly loved.

Jack lifted her into his arms and carried her into the bathroom.

"I can walk, Jack." Maybe. Given time. When he sat her on the marble counter, Rose gave in and relaxed. Why argue? He was responsible for her being in this condition; let him take care of it. She wondered quite vaguely if she should be embarrassed when he gently washed between her legs with a warm cloth. It felt *so* wonderful there was no room for anything but the soothing pleasure. "Thank you," she whispered, which earned her a smile and a light kiss.

"We can nap if you'd like." Jack carried her back into his office. She was so relaxed he thought she might have already fallen asleep. The idea of cuddling on his couch with her for a while was appealing.

"I'm not sleepy," Rose said languorously. "Just very, very mellow. I didn't know sex could do that. Does that happen all the time, Jack?"

"No, sweetheart, not all the time." Only with you.

ROSE COULDN'T SLEEP.

It was three in the morning; she'd had a busy day and the man in bed next to her had given her enough orgasms to put any woman into a blissfully comatose state. Instead, she stared at the slit of light peeking through the closed curtains of her bedroom window. For the last fifteen minutes, she'd waffled between getting up and adjusting the material, convinced that the little shard of light kept her awake. Or she could just turn over and forget it was there. Then there was the possibility that she was an idiot obsessing over a tiny bit of moonlight. She finally gave up. Sleep wasn't coming.

Careful not to wake Jack, Rose slipped out of bed. With a quick look at his sleeping form, she tiptoed out of the room. Naked. Right, she didn't sleep in the nude. But after she and Jack had officially had sex in her bed for the first time, and the second and the third, there hadn't seemed much point in putting on her usual nightgown. After all, Jack had reasoned with her that, in a few hours, she would be naked again. She might as well save herself the effort. Of course, he'd been right. Grinning with the sexy memory, Rose grabbed her robe and headed to her music room.

Edgar, asleep on the doggy bed that Jack had brought for him, raised his head at the sound of feet on the stairs. The slap of his tail signaled his approval of the intruder. He knew Rose, liked the way she smelled. He liked the sound of her voice, and the way she somehow knew his favorite spot to be scratched. He loved Jack with unwavering doggy devotion; Jack was his number one. But Rose was a close second. Jumping from his bed, Edgar rushed to greet her with wiggling enthusiasm.

"Hello." Rose bent down and scratched Edgar's muzzle, smiling at his whine of approval. "Do you need to go out, baby? Come on."

She waited while Edgar sniffed every inch of her backyard, the same one he'd explored when he and Jack first arrived. Rose didn't mind waiting. She sat on the steps and let her mind wander back to last evening.

After they'd dressed, Jack invited her to his place for dinner. Rose hesitated. She still felt a bit shaky. She didn't know what had happened between them, but it had been more than just sex. Something had shifted; it was subtle but unsettling. Spending the rest of the evening with Jack sounded right, natural. So maybe it would be better if she went home and gave herself some room to think. About what? She had no idea.

"I'd rather go to my place, Jack."

"That's fine. I'll go pick up Edgar and then stop for a pizza. I shouldn't be more than an hour behind you. Then over dinner, I can tell you about all the excitement we had here this morning."

Right, she'd completely forgotten the guard at the gate. At some point, she would have remembered and then it would have driven her crazy until she ended up calling Jack and getting the whole story. As Rose drove home, she reasoned that satisfying her curiosity was more important than being alone with her thoughts. Besides, those thoughts could be brutal when they wanted to be. Let them keep to themselves for a while. An evening of pizza, Jack and Edgar was much more appealing.

Jack arrived, dog and pizza in tow, and after they'd settled down at her dining room table, he gave her the scoop. It turned out the security problem was hysterical, at least from an outside perspective. That morning, without warning, women started arriving, lots of them. They wanted to meet the almost naked men from the video Jack had taken. The thing had been posted online almost a week ago and he and Drew had forgotten all about it. It never occurred to them that there would be a delayed mass pilgrimage, and while the women couldn't get into any of the buildings, they caused a traffic jam in the parking lot. There had never been any reason to lock the gates during business hours — until now.

Before the gates could be closed, they had to get the women out. Jack had taken pity on Drew and braved the frenzied throng.

Rose had called him on that description. *Frenzied? Really?*

Jack stuck by his words. Over two dozen women ready to charge the first naked man they laid eyes on? Frenzied seemed kind.

Rose conceded the point. Good thing he hadn't been naked. He hadn't, had he? Rose teased.

Jack assured her he'd had all of his clothes on.

It took him twenty minutes to make them understand that, as a rule, they didn't run around in their underwear and that none of the men in the video were even onsite anymore. He almost had them convinced when one of them called out for him to take his clothes off. It didn't take long for that to become a popular idea, and Jack soon ran for cover. He ended up amplifying the outside speakers to inform the women that if they didn't leave the premises now, and in an orderly fashion, he would be forced to call the police. That seemed to do the trick. After they had all cleared out, Jack posted men around the perimeter in case any of the women tried coming back. That was why idiot boy had stopped her at the gate.

It was a good story, Rose thought. But, to be honest, a little embarrassing for the female population. A good man might be hard to find, but come on ladies. Have some pride. Driving for hours on the off chance a guy you saw online would fall into your arms? Not cool.

The feel of a wet nose on her hand pulled her attention back to the present and a happy dog with an empty bladder. Deciding she could use the company, she invited him to join her down in her music room. Edgar only hesitated for a moment at the top of the unfamiliar stairs. He sniffed to get his bearings, gave Rose his best *ladies first* grin, and then trotted easily down behind her. Rose went into the nearby bathroom and filled a plastic bowl with water.

"There you are, Edgar." She set the bowl down away from anything that the dog could harm with his enthusiastic drinking style. "Make yourself at home. All I ask is that you don't pee on any of my instruments. Licking is allowed, within reason. And you can sniff to your heart's content."

Normally Rose would have picked up a guitar. It had always been her go-to instrument. Her mind became more fluid when she strummed the strings. Tonight, she gravitated to the keyboard on the far wall. She was a more than competent piano player. She used the electronic instrument mainly to provide a different sound when she composed. Sometimes it helped to shake things up.

Rose ran her fingers up and down the keys until they were warmed up and nimble. Then she just let them wander. There wasn't any real tune, not to start with. Just a series of discordant notes played repeatedly. The repetition settled her mind, cleared it of random thoughts. And as sometimes happened, the melody came. Her hands took over and played what her mind couldn't conceive. When the notes started making sense, Rose reached over and hit the record button on the console. She'd done the same thing so many times she wasn't even aware of doing it. Some part of her knew when it was time to preserve her ramblings. Later, she would refine and polish, but right now, she just needed to get the genesis of the song on tape.

That was how Jack found them. Rose, eyes closed, playing an achingly haunting melody, and Edgar, head resting on the bench beside her, a look of pure adoration on his face. Jack knew how he felt.

He had woken alone, his hand reaching for her warm body but finding nothing but empty bed and cold sheets. He stretched to his full length, which meant his feet hung off the bed by a good four inches. Rose might not have needed a bigger bed before, but she did now. He just had to figure out a way to convince her. He couldn't just have a new bed delivered. She wouldn't go for that. Jack bounced up and down, testing. If he broke it, it would be his responsibility to replace it. He'd think on it for a while. The solution would come to him. In the meantime, they would stay at his place.

Rose wasn't in the bathroom. Jack splashed some water on his face. Finding some mouthwash in the cupboard, he took a swig and then spit the liquid into the sink. It was time to let Edgar out. He pulled on his jeans and headed down. But there was no dog and no woman. They weren't in the backyard. While looking in the kitchen, Jack poured himself a glass of orange juice, drinking it in three gulps. He was about to check to see if Rose's car was in the garage when he heard the music. It was faint at first but grew louder as he walked towards the slightly ajar door. Music meant Rose. He felt his stomach as he started down the stairs. It had been crazy to worry. Did he really think she was going to disappear in the middle of the night taking Edgar with her? Of course not. Nevertheless, he felt better knowing she was safe — and near.

Rose let the last note linger before opening her eyes. Taking a deep breath, she rolled her neck, loosening the muscles. She suddenly noticed Edgar. He'd raised his head when she'd finished, his tail tapping his version of applause.

"Did you like that?" she asked, wrapping her arms around his neck and burying her face in the warm fur.

"It was amazing."

Rose jolted but stayed where she was. "Edgar, you've been holding out on me. Let's not tell Jack. He doesn't believe dogs can talk.

Jack laughed. They made quite the picture — the adoring dog and the beautiful woman. Walking over, he leaned down and gave Rose a kiss.

"Mm," Rose smacked her lips. "You taste like a minty orange. It's a surprisingly good combination."

Jack cupped her cheek and ran his thumb over her bottom lip. Soft, slightly damp, and irresistible, he leaned down and kissed her again, this time doing a much more thorough job. Tired of being ignored, Edgar butted his head up between them until they pulled apart. Jack gave in and greeted the dog with a vigorous tummy scratch.

"I meant what I said. That music was amazing." Jack raised his eyes to the piano. He hit a few notes with one finger. "How do you put all those notes in order and get what you were playing? I could learn how to play but what you do, it's magic, Rose."

"I know how to use my computer but I could never write a program for it, especially one as intricate and complicated as the ones you write."

"Not exactly the same thing."

"Technically, no." Rose patted the bench, inviting him to join her. After he had sat down, she played a simple pattern and motioned for him to repeat it.

"Every song starts the same. You have all the notes, the sharps, and the flats. All the variations are right in your head." She played the same notes again, but this time adding to its complexity. "Did you know that Irving Berlin couldn't read music?" Rose played the opening of her favorite Berlin song.

"Songs like *They Can't Take That Away From Me*? He would play the chords or sometimes just hum the melody, and a professional arranger would write it down." Rose sang a few lines then finished with a flourish. "I know. What does that have to do with anything? Nothing, really. Just a bit of music trivia to liven up your evening."

"Interesting," Jack conceded. "Is this your way of telling me you can't read music?"

"Nope. I, my friend, can do it all." She pounded out a little Scott

Joplin. Edgar yipped with approval. "Ah, a ragtime fan. Next time we watch a movie, we'll have to get *The Sting*. Edgar will be in heaven." She hit the keyboard's off button. "But to answer your original question, I write almost every day and some of it is good. Some of it's very good. But the magic, that's rare. The music you heard, I don't know where it came from. I've been trying to find just the right sound. Romantic but not sappy. Sensual, but not overtly sexy. Tonight I hit it. That, my friend, will be the love theme for *Wishes*."

Jack frowned. "*Wishes*? Why does that sound familiar?"

"Best seller? Currently being made into a movie?" Rose decided to cut Jack some slack. He wasn't exactly the target audience for an epic love story that spanned ten years and three continents.

"Your mother and sisters have probably read the book." Not wanting to be sexist she added, "And maybe your dad."

"I remember now." Jack eyes widened. "Rose, this is a big deal. You could win an Oscar." His gaze drifted to the shelves across the room. "To go with your three Grammys. Rose, you have three Grammys."

Amused, Rose watched as Jack rushed over to examine the awards. She was proud of them. She kept them down here where very few people ever came; her success was a private thing.

"You wrote *Grind*?" Jack turned towards her holding the double platinum record that she had been awarded a few months before.

She waited for one of the varied responses she always got. First, everyone wanted to know who the song was about. Second, they wanted her to know how they liked to play the song to seduce women or, like Principal Harriman, used it as a sexual aid.

"I play it every day when I run. Edgar's a big fan."

Well, Rose thought with delight, *that was a new one*.

"Don't you want to know my source of inspiration?"

Jack replaced the record, his mind still on the coincidence of Rose having written something he listened to every day. Then all of a sudden, it hit him what she asked.

"Are you crazy?" Jack shuddered at the thought. "Please, I'm begging you; keep it to yourself."

"But everyone wants to know." Rose hid her grin. She couldn't tell if Jack was slightly jealous or embarrassed. Either way she loved his response.

"I don't," he stated emphatically. "Now can we change the subject?"

Rose got up. She shut off the lights and closed the door behind them.

"What would you like to talk about?" she inquired as Jack and Edgar followed her up the stairs.

"You need a new bed."

Rose frowned. A new bed? The man could be so confusing. "If you're referring to the mattress, there is nothing wrong with it. I just got it last year."

Making sure Edgar was tucked in, with his bowls full, Jack took her hand and led her up to the bedroom. He stopped in front of the bed and made a sweeping gesture with his hand. "It's too short."

Rose paused to consider. Bigger mattress meant different bed frame and headboard. She liked the one she had, but she didn't love it. If she got rid of it, then she could redecorate the entire bedroom, design an entirely new layout, and color scheme.

"Okay."

Jack had been prepared to wheedle Rose into changing the bed. Pointing out the practicality without making it seem like he was invading her home. He didn't want to live here. When they moved in together, it would make more sense to use his house.

"No hesitation? No argument?"

"It's just common sense. When we spend the night together, we're bound to do it here from time to time. I want you to be comfortable. I like how roomy your bed is. In fact, I like everything about your bed. Give me the manufacturer and style, and I'll order it tomorrow. Now, if you think you'll be all right for the rest of the night, let's go to bed."

Rose took off her robe and tossed it on a chair. She liked how Jack's eyes lit up when she was naked. It felt good to know he desired her body as much as she desired his. Speaking of which, she quickly scrambled under the covers so she could enjoy the view.

"Aren't you going to take off your pants?" Then she added. "And get into bed?"

"I'm on it." Jack pulled off his jeans and hopped over her to the other side.

"I didn't mean for you to hurry." Rose stopped him from climbing under the covers. "I was hoping to spend some time admiring your splendid physique."

More than willing to play, Jack propped himself up on the pillows and put his hands behind his head. "Admire away."

Where to start? Deciding, Rose used one finger to trace his wonderfully defined abs.

"There wasn't a man."

Jack lifted one eyelid enquiringly. "Come again?"

"When I wrote *Grind*. There wasn't a man."

"Rose, sweetheart, as much as I appreciate you wanting to share? That is one subject I'd just as soon skip." Especially if she wanted to tell him about multiple partners doing sexually graphic things to her.

"No." Rose idly traced a circle on his chest. "I mean there weren't any men. None. I didn't write that song as some glowing tribute to a mind-blowing lover. I wrote it out of sexual frustration. *Grind* isn't about all the things I'd done. It's all about what I'd want to do — if I found the right man."

It sounded like a challenge to him, one he was thoroughly going to enjoy completing. "Look no further." Jack pulled her up until she straddled his body. "I believe the woman in the song had a list. Let's start with number one."

Chapter Sixteen

WORDS AND MUSIC. You can't have one without the other. Well, you can, but not if your producer is expecting both. Sam Laughton should have been happy that she'd made a breakthrough, half of the songs were written. But no, he'd spent the last ten minutes telling her to get her ass in gear.

"One month. That's all the time you have left to finish the songs for *Wishes*. And it might help if you stopped spending your valuable time judging rinky-dink high school talent shows."

"It wasn't rinky-dink. And, by the way, who the hell uses that term anymore? What are you, ninety?"

"I'm—"

"Why do you even know about that?" Sam was starting to get on her nerves. Not only was he constantly riding her about her work, but also he checked up on what she did in her free time?

"As—"

"It's kind of creepy, Sam. You need to get a life."

"Are you finished?"

Rose thought about it. "Yes, for now."

"First, I know about the talent show because it made a few of the gossip sites. According to my assistant, some of them considered it worthy of a mention."

"Must have been a slow news day," Rose quipped. Personally, she hated that kind of stuff but she was happy for the kids in the show. You never knew where even the smallest bit of publicity could lead and some of the contestants had been talented.

"And I do have a life," he continued. "Right now it involves making the best movie I possibly can, and if that means getting on your ass when you take time off for frivolous activities, then so be it. Believe me, there are a lot of ways I would rather be spending my time."

Rose stuck her tongue out at the phone. She didn't know Sam very well, but she was learning quickly. All producers wanted things done yesterday. Sam wanted them done two days before that.

"You wouldn't stop hounding me until I agreed to take this job. Now you won't stop hounding me about the work itself. Did you listen to the music? Is it not perfect? One encouraging word, Sam. Would that kill you?"

There was a pause on the other end of the line, and then she heard a deep, heartfelt sigh.

"The music *is* perfect, Rose." *Good boy*, Rose thought. Then he went and ruined their warm and fuzzy moment. "What I didn't realize was that you needed constant pats on the back to function. One of the reasons I was so keen to work with you was because of your reputation as a self-starter. If I'd known that I would need to heap praise on you every five minutes, I would have gotten someone less needy."

"It's a good thing you're not here right now, Sam, or you'd be walking funny for a week." Rose wasn't sure, but she thought she might have heard Sam chuckle. Maybe he had a sense of humor after all. "Now, if you'll leave me alone, I'll get back to work. It's your constant interruptions that are causing the delay."

"Fine, call me when you have something for me to hear. And make it soon, Rose."

Egotistical narcissist. Rose almost threw the phone across the room. But after calculating the odds of having to go through the trouble of getting a new one, not to mention the damage it might do to the wall, Rose carefully set it down on the hall table. Damn Sam Laughton. He had a way of re-knotting all the muscles that a night of great sex with Jack had so wonderfully loosened.

It was too nice of a day to lock herself away in her music room. Some sunshine and fresh air might be just what she needed to generate her creative juices. Her backyard wasn't huge, but it suited Rose's needs perfectly. Every spring, she hired a couple of neighborhood kids to do a general clean up. Rake leaves leftover from last fall, and pull any weeds that reared their ugly heads. Basically, get the yard as pristine as possible before she had the fun job of planting whatever flowers caught her fancy at the local nursery. At the moment, the beds were bursting with early spring flowers in shades of yellow, pink and red.

Rose was fixing herself a cup of tea to take into the back yard when the doorbell rang. For a brief moment, she considered ignoring it. She wasn't expecting anyone or any deliveries. Tyler and Dani would call if she didn't answer and Jack would just pound on the door until she let him in. She wanted whoever it was just to go away. The bell went off again. With a resigned sigh, she made her way to the front of the house.

"Yes?" Rose didn't recognize the man on her front steps. He was older, with brushed back gray hair. He wore a black suit, black tie, and crisp white shirt. He gave a slight bow and presented her with a white envelope. It was heavy for its size and made of expensive watermarked paper. Across the front, her name was neatly written in black ink.

"I am to await your answer."

Await her answer? Well, aren't we formal? Rose inspected the envelope again before opening the sealed flap. It wasn't every day she was hand delivered a letter.

"THE LONGER I live, the more convinced I am that the world is full of crazy people. And Regina Harper is their leader."

Tyler handed the embossed paper to Dani. As soon as the man had left, Rose had called her friends. They sat in Rose's living room passing around the invitation, or summons, depending on how you looked at it.

"Your name has been printed on the paper. Do you think she sent out to have just one invitation specially made?" Dani turned the paper over in her hands. "This is high-grade stuff. I can't quite picture old Reggie having an arts and crafts room. Martha Stewart she isn't."

Rose was invited for tea at Harper House on Wednesday afternoon. And for the life of her, she couldn't imagine why. In all the years she'd lived in Harper Falls, she had never met personally with Regina Harper. They lived in the same town but existed in different worlds.

"And having it hand delivered," Tyler scoffed. "What did you tell Lurch?"

"He didn't look like Lurch, more like Alfred from the old Batman TV show. And I said yes, of course. Wouldn't you have?"

"The day I'm invited anywhere near that place will be the beginning of the apocalypse. But damn right, I would have said yes, if only to spit in the grand lady's eye."

"I don't plan on doing any spitting, but I'll leave my options open," Rose promised. "I'm going out of curiosity. What does she want? What will she be wearing? I mean, how formal *is* afternoon tea? Pearls or diamonds?"

"Does she pour the tea herself or is there a person whose only job is to pour tea?" Dani asked. "And will she serve those little sandwiches with the crusts cut off?"

"I doubt Reggie has ever seen a crust in her life," Tyler sneered.

"Well, I guess I'm going to find out on Wednesday."

"We expect a full report," Dani told her. "How about dinner at my place that night, say around six-thirty?"

"And if you can," Tyler said, "get pictures."

ROSE FELT FOOLISH, which didn't make any sense. No one knew that she had spent an hour researching afternoon tea. In spite of it, she still wasn't sure what to expect. Almost every source she referenced agreed on one thing — afternoon tea is less formal than high tea. With that in mind, she had chosen a crisp cotton dress in the palest of yellow. The flared skirt hit her just above the knee and the belted waist was flattering to her figure. She wore heather gray sling back pumps, the four-inch heels giving her confidence. It was ridiculous to be nervous but as the butler — she would always think of him as Alfred — led her across the highly polished marble floors, Rose felt the distinct stirring of butterflies.

She had never been in this part of the house. During the Lilac Ball, access to anything but the ballroom and bathrooms was strictly enforced. Rose tried to take in all the details without looking like she was gawking. Elegant. Rose supposed this was what the rich aspired to one hundred years ago. Dark wood paneling on the walls, ornate sconces that at one time must have been powered by gas, and expensive little do-dads that had to be a pain in the ass to keep dusted. It was hard to imagine children running through these halls; they would be in constant worry of damaging something. No, the children raised here would have only two choices — either conform or rebel. Regina Harper's only child had rebelled — big time.

"Miss O'Brian, Madam."

"Thank you, Potts. I'll ring if we need anything else."

Potts? Well, that was disappointing.

"Miss O'Brian." As Regina Harper came forward to greet her, Rose was taken aback at how tiny the woman was. With her heels, Rose was close to a foot taller. Slender to the point of gauntness, the woman glided towards her in a subtle cloud of expensive perfume and breeding. There was nothing common about Regina Harper. The high cheekbones, perfect nose, and a thin, hard mouth that time, not genetics, had given her. Her eyes were a dark brown but completely devoid of warmth. Any nerves Rose had been feeling dissipated the moment she made contact with the other woman's cool, boney hand. Outer trappings aside, it was like looking at her aunt. Both women knew how to get what they wanted and had perfected their own forms of intimidation. Well, Rose didn't let anyone intimidate her, not anymore. Whatever Regina Harper wanted, she wasn't going to get it with an icy stare and superior attitude.

"I apologize for the early hour, but I have an appointment this evening that dictates a less than traditional hour for our tea."

Right, Rose remembered, four o'clock was the usual time for afternoon tea. That had seemed strange until she read that they didn't eat dinner until eight. How could you keep a schedule like that and not have bad digestive problems? Maybe that accounted for the pinched look on Regina's face.

"Do you take anything in your tea? Lemon, sugar, perhaps some cream?

"No, nothing. Thank you."

Regina went through the process of pouring them each a cup and then offered Rose an assortment of crustless sandwiches, *good call Dani*, and delicate little cookies. It was quite a show, smoothly executed, without a single spill or bobble. Rose realized that Regina, straight-backed and knees together, took her tea seriously.

"I'm sure you're wondering why I asked you here today."

Very Agatha Christie, but Rose was almost certain no murder had occured, so that couldn't be the reason. "I admit you have piqued my curiosity." Great, she'd been there less than thirty minutes and she used *piqued* in a sentence.

"This fall we will be celebrating the centennial of the founding of Harper Falls. Preparations have been ongoing for over a year. Now we are dealing with the final details and it was suggested that a piece of original music would lend a nice touch to the proceedings."

Was she asking Rose to write the music? Or perhaps was she needed for the name of a current classical composer? That seemed more like Regina's style. Since it appeared as though the woman wasn't going to elaborate, Rose decided to wing it.

"Music is always a lovely addition to any event. The idea of an original composition that the town will be able to use for years to come is brilliant."

"Yes." Regina seemed to think *brilliant* was overstating it a bit. "Several members of the committee thought it would be appropriate to have someone from the community do the composition. Your name came up."

"I'm flattered." Rose tried to think of another person in Harper Falls who had the qualifications for the job, but she drew a blank. Either way, Regina didn't seem terribly pleased. So why the one-on-one meeting? Why not have one of the faceless committee members contact her?

"We can pay you. I don't know what you're usual fee is for the little songs you write, but with all the prestige associated with the commission, we hope our little stipend will be enough."

Rose wondered if the woman was trying to be insulting or if it just came naturally.

"If I agree to the commission, Mrs. Harper, I would naturally donate my fee to charity. That said, I couldn't possibly agree until I had a better idea of what you and the committee wanted. The general tone of the piece, do you want words? Should it be rousing or reflective? I also need a timetable for when you would want the music. I would hate to accept and then find out that I couldn't finish in time because of my schedule."

"I see. We just assumed that you would make the time."

"Well, you know what they say about people who assume things." Hardly an original comeback but Rose was happy with it.

"No, what do they say?" Regina managed to raise one eyebrow and look down her nose at the same time.

Rose had never had anyone call her on that one, but what the hell. "If you assume, it makes an ass out of you and me." *Ball's in your court, bitch.*

"Ah." Again, Regina was not amused. "Then perhaps we should leave it for now. After I speak to my fellow committee members, we will get back to you. That is if we're still interested in your services."

Rose desperately wished Tyler was there. She was so good at putting people in their place, and the fact that it was Regina Harper would have been a nice bonus. Rose had peaked with the whole *assume* thing. Instead of verbally eviscerating her hostess, she set her cup on the coffee table and stood to leave.

"Before you go, I have a question for you."

Rose sat back with a sigh. She'd been so close. Two stiffly exchanged goodbyes and she would have been out the door to fresh air and freedom. Instead, she plastered a polite smile on her face and waited.

"Why did she come back?"

"I'm sorry. Who are you talking about?"

"Your friend. Tyler Jones." The name seemed to stick in Regina's throat.

That was it. Conversation over. Rose gathered her purse and stood again.

"I will not discuss Tyler with you, Mrs. Harper. If you want the answer, I suggest you go to the source. But if you do, I suggest wearing goggles." Before she left, Rose couldn't resist one last little twist of the knife. "Or you could always ask your son. Oh, that's right; he never speaks to you. So you could ask until you're blue in the face and you still wouldn't have your answer. I'll be looking forward to hearing from the committee."

Rose turned and walked out the door. From the stunned expression that she'd left on the woman's face, Rose imagined it had been a long time since anyone had had the last word with Regina Harper.

Chapter Seventeen

"IT WAS LIKE something out of a Bette Davis movie."

Rose snuggled up next to Jack. They were in his bed; her new one hadn't arrived yet.

"Which of you was Bette Davis?"

"Depends on the movie. The setting was definitely *Now Voyager*, but the dynamic was more like *Old Acquaintance*."

"I'll take your word for it." Jack loved how Rose's brain worked. He didn't feel the need to know all the references she made; it was just fun to hear her make them.

"I couldn't raise an ounce of sympathy for her, Jack. Her husband is dead; her son won't even be in the same room with her. And, don't get me started on living all alone in that museum. Shouldn't I have felt a teeny bit of sympathy for her?"

"I met her, once. We'd only been in town for a few weeks and I was coming out of the hardware store. Parked across the street was that ridiculously large Rolls Royce that she rides around in. I could see she was waiting for her driver so I thought I'd introduce myself." Jack shook his head at the memory. "I tapped on the window and waited while she looked me up and down."

"I know that look," Rose laughed.

"You only have to see it once for it to be burned into your brain." Jack pulled her in closer. No reason except that he liked her closer. "So, she finally rolls the window down. Before I can say boo, she tells me she knew who I was and considering my background was nothing to be particularly proud of, I had been wise to attach myself to her son. Window rolls up — end of conversation."

"Tyler calls her crazy. Not that that's *all* she calls her. But I think she's evil."

"Evil how?"

Rose thought for a moment. "Evil in the, *this is my world and if you don't live up to my standards I'll kick you out,* kind of way. She tried it with Tyler. She held on to Drew so tightly that he left her altogether. As I said, I should feel sorry for her, but…"

"But she makes it impossible."

"I thought about not telling Tyler that she was the real reason I'd been summoned to Harper House. That woman has already handed her too much crap and I hated being part of shoveling on another layer."

"But you *did* tell her." Jack understood wanting to protect someone she loved. Keeping things from them wasn't the way to do that. Besides, things had a way of coming out, and no matter how innocuous the omission, it was better to get it out in the open and deal with it right away.

"And she took it like I would have expected, with a sharp tongue and a shrug." Only Rose and Dani knew better. Inside that tough girl shell was a center of hurt and insecurity. Most things rolled off with little damage, but the Harpers were a wound that had never really healed.

"Do you think Regina realizes the main reason Drew moved back here was because of Tyler?

"He told you that?" Rose had always suspected; the timing was just too coincidental. But to have Jack state it as fact was something else altogether. Now she *knew.*

"Drew is pretty close-mouthed, and not just about Tyler. Now and then, when he's in a certain mood and has had a few drinks, he'll get talky. He's not over her, Rose, but something is keeping him from telling her."

"Fear of losing a vital organ?"

Jack laughed. "There is that. I just wish he'd do something. I would never have called Drew a merry old soul, but lately he's become even more reticent than usual." And it began soon after Jack had started seeing Rose, a fact he was not going to share with her. Seeing Jack so happy, with Tyler's friend, just magnified what Drew missed out on.

"I can't tell you how Tyler feels about Drew, she would never forgive me. And I promise not to tell her anything we've discussed tonight. If something is going to happen, it has to be up to them to do it."

"Agreed." Jack slid down until they were face-to-face.

"Such a pretty face."

"I beg your pardon?"

Loving the outrage in his voice, Rose cocked her head and studied him. "No, I stand by it. You, my friend, have a pretty face. I noticed it the night of the Lilac Ball. I was looking for someone with much longer hair, so at first I didn't recognize you. But when I did, the first thing I thought was how beautiful you were."

"Rose—" Jack wanted her to find him attractive, hot, and sexy. But *pretty? Beautiful?* Come on.

"Hear me out. I said beautiful, not feminine." Rose could tell Jack wasn't mollified by the distinction. "It was the short hair that did it," she continued. "And your amazing cheek bones." She leaned over and kissed each one. "And the bright blue of your eyes. I called them Paul Newman eyes."

"Great, another movie reference." Jack was about to rethink how much he liked the way her brain worked.

"But mostly? I found you so sexy I couldn't wait to get you alone and rip your clothes off."

"Now *that* I like the sound of. But I'm still growing my hair out." His blue, blue eyes held hers as he leaned in and claimed her mouth in a scorching hot kiss. "I need to let Edgar out. So it's either a quickie, or wait until I get back."

Rose slipped her hand between his legs to gauge his readiness. Making a happy hum, she squeezed his hardening length gently. "Why not both?"

Jack tumbled her back onto the bed. Why not, indeed?

JUNE WAS IN full bloom.

Rose could smell the sweet combination of flowers, their fragrance intensified by the hot afternoon sun. She had spent so much time working on the *Wishes* soundtrack that she'd almost forgotten what it felt like just to stand outside and take in all the sights, sounds, and smells of nature. Now that she had finished all but the final love song, she decided to break out of her self-imposed prison for the rest of the day and reconnect with the world. At least her part of it.

Rose had been using work as a way of avoiding Jack. And, to be honest, after almost a week, she had missed him. A lot. She missed him so much that she found herself calling him every night to ask how he and Edgar were doing. They would end up talking for an hour or more. She didn't mean to call. Or talk so long. If she was so busy, how could she spare the time? Why didn't Jack call her on it? If he had asked her to hang up the phone and come be in his bed, Rose knew she would have caved. However, he didn't ask. Her bed, the great big bed she'd ordered because he asked her to, sat in her newly painted bedroom, surrounded by her brand new bedroom furniture. The brand new ultra-soft sheets never having been slept on. Like an idiot, she slept downstairs on the couch — alone.

Why was she alone? She was a coward and Jack wanted to take her home to meet his parents. Not that he'd put it precisely like that. But that's what it amounted to.

On Friday, Jack was traveling to Oregon to help celebrate his parent's fortieth wedding anniversary. Seven children, eleven grandchildren, forty years waking up next to the same person every morning. He wanted her to go with him.

Rose had tried to get out of going by arguing that it was a family get together and she was *not* family. Jack had argued that everyone in the county was going to be at the huge event: neighbors, friends, and probably some drop-ins who just liked a good party. It wasn't going to be just family. The argument, though never heated, had gone back and forth until Rose threw up her hands and had told him she'd think about it.

She'd been thinking for a week. Even though he was leaving tomorrow, Jack hadn't tried to pressure her during their nightly talks. In fact, he hadn't even mentioned the trip again, which, as he probably knew, made her think about it constantly. Either he was sneaky as hell or he didn't care if she went with him. God, she had to stop or her brain would explode.

Tyler and Dani told her to go. It was one weekend, not a lifetime commitment. How could she pass up the chance to meet the woman who had named her son Jack Rabbit Run? Frank told her to go. She would be miserable the entire weekend if he went and she stayed home. Maybe she would be miserable in Oregon, but at least she'd be with Jack. Even Sam Laughton told her to go. If she needed inspiration to finish a love song where better to get it than at a fortieth wedding anniversary party?

Everyone thought she should go. And Rose? Damn it, she wanted to go. She looked at her phone but decided Jack had put up with enough phone calls, he deserved to hear her decision in person. He also deserved an award for the most understanding, patient man in the world. That and an apology just might start to make up for her idiocy. She hoped he thought so.

First, a quick shower, and a change of clothes. She had only ascended two stairs when there was a knock at the door. Groaning at the inconvenient timing, she changed direction. If this was another invitation from Regina Harper, poor Potts was going to get an earful.

"Look, I don't have time to…" Rose stopped in mid-sentence. It was the one person she had plenty of time for. "Jack."

"Should I go?"

"No!" She grabbed him and pulled him into the house before he could get away. "I was just coming to see you."

"Then I saved you a trip. Any particular reason you wanted to see me?"

"I'm sorry." Rose launched herself into Jack's strong arms and just held on. "If you've come here to tell me you've had enough of my nonsense, I don't blame you a bit. All I ask is that I can visit Edgar now and then and that you call me whenever you're, you know, in the mood."

Jack buried his face in her hair and breathed deeply, letting her scent wash over him. He'd grown accustomed to his daily fix of Rose. He had a week of deprivation to make up for and he planned on starting right now.

"Sweetheart, if you think you can get away with visiting Edgar *now and then*, you're out of your mind. I've had to look at his sad puppy face all week and it has gotten a bit old. I think he secretly blames me for your absence, but he's afraid I'll cut off his kibble, so he's kept quiet." Jack paused to kiss her senseless. "And I have no idea what nonsense you're talking about. As for calling you whenever I'm in the mood? For a while now, you've been the only woman to interest my mood so that one's a given."

Rose felt her mood lift and her libido kick in. Smiling knowingly, she pulled away from his embrace and slowly ascended the stairs. "There's a brand new bed in my room that needs christening. Do you think you're up for it?"

Jack started to follow her. "In about thirty seconds, I'm going to show you just how *up* for it I am. So unless you want those clothes ripped off right where you're standing, you'd better get your pretty ass up those stairs."

Twenty-five seconds later, they were both naked, limbs entwined, on the bed. They felt the urgency of a week without this, but neither was in a hurry for it to end. Jack took his time; he needed to taste every inch of her soft skin. Her breasts were of particular interest. He stopped to savor how they felt as he rubbed his cheek over her plump nipples and then pulled one into his mouth. Her gasp of pleasure shot through him, sending *his* arousal into overdrive. A man could die happy if his last moments were spent loving Rose.

"You know just where to touch me," Rose sighed. She reveled in the sensations that bombarded her as his hand slid between her legs. When he replaced his hand with his mouth, she wondered why her heart didn't burst from her chest. This was what she needed, what she craved. Jack was the only one who could give it to her.

"Tell me you've missed this — missed me." Jack moved over. Rose reached for him, her body begging him to fill her, to give her the release she craved more than air.

"Yes, Jack," she gasped at the feel of his teasing entry. "I've missed you, only you."

Hearing the words he craved, Jack entered Rose, driving them both closer and closer to the edge with every powerful thrust. When they toppled over, it was together, swallowing each other's cries of fulfillment with a long, soulful kiss.

Totally spent, Jack rolled to the side of the bed, bringing Rose with him. He tucked her into his arms; one hand gently stroking up and down her arm. She relaxed against his body with a sigh of pure contentment. Leaning back, he stared up at the ceiling. This was more like it. Jack was thrilled to know that Rose had been about to come to him, that she had missed him, needed him. Jack could be patient when necessary, but he wanted Rose so much it became more and more difficult to keep his feelings suppressed. Part of him knew he couldn't force her to love him. The primitive part of him wanted to beat his chest and keep her in bed until she admitted she couldn't live without him.

"Has this room been painted?" Jack's brain had been so busy running in the same circle it had been caught in all week that it took several minutes for him to register that he was looking at an entirely new color.

"It has." Rose was pleased he'd noticed. "Do you like it? It's a pale blue but in this light it looks a bit darker."

"It's great, really." He looked around the room. The furniture looked different and so did the curtains. "When did you do all this?"

"This last week. Though technically, I didn't do any of it. The painters finished two days ago and then the furniture and drapes came yesterday. I just opened the door and left them to it."

Jack shook his head in amazement. "I just asked you to get a new bed."

"Which I did, but then nothing matched." Rose looked around. Normally she would have done most of the work herself. She liked to paint — it was soothing. She'd wanted it done right away. Hiring professionals saved her time, which now was in short supply.

"You should see the little room off the front door. To be fair, I started that project a few weeks ago, but the half-bath looks amazing."

"Rose," Jack said softly.

"Now that the bedroom and bath are done, I was thinking about painting the whole house — inside and out. The guys who did in here gave me a great quote for the whole job."

"Rose." His voice was a bit firmer this time

"I know. I'm rambling." Her thoughts pinged off each other so quickly that her mouth couldn't catch up. She breathed in and steadied herself until what she wanted to say was in the right order.

"Thank you, Jack."

Jack laughed. "If you're talking about the mind-blowing sex, you're welcome."

"Thank you for not giving up on me."

"Rose." Jack took her face between his hands, his eyes an intense blue. "I will never give up on you — on us."

"You should." When he began to protest, Rose gently covered his mouth with her fingertips. "I should make you. I know if you honestly believed I wanted to end it, you would leave me alone."

"*If* I believed it."

"That's the problem, isn't it?" She trailed her fingers over his lips, across his cheekbones and then along his jaw. Touching him was addictive. She sighed. Right now, she didn't have the strength to give it up — to give *him* up.

"I know what you want, Jack. You haven't said it, and I'm grateful. I wish I could promise you that one day soon I'll be able to give you everything you need, everything you deserve. I don't know if I'm capable of that. God, I want to be. Maybe—"

This time Jack silenced *her*. "That seems like a good place to stop. Okay?"

Rose nodded. She kissed his fingers then pulled one into her mouth, so much better than any lollypop.

"Ready for another go, are we?" Jack groaned. He could feel the suction of her mouth down to his toes.

Rose nodded again, her eyes changing to a deep sherry color, warm and inviting.

"One more thing before I lose all ability to think. Oregon. Yes?"

"Oregon, definitely."

Chapter Eighteen

ROSE HAD PEPPERED Jack with seemingly endless questions about what kind of clothes she should pack. She knew he didn't understand, but she did appreciate his patience. However, once she started in on shoe choices, Jack finally reached his limit.

"Rose, I have no idea what my mother and sisters will be wearing. But if it's that important, I'll call Mom right now and you can ask her yourself."

Horrified at the thought, Rose snatched Jack's phone out of his hand.

"I'll figure it out for myself." They were leaving tomorrow and coming back on Monday. Not even three full days. Rose wanted to be prepared for any contingency. "There's plenty of room in your SUV. I'll bring a few extra things, just to be safe."

They had decided to go out for dinner. Rose, as usual had almost nothing in her refrigerator and Jack was in the mood for something more substantial than cold cereal. *On the Waterfront* had a great view of the river and eclectic cuisine. He looked at Rose over the top of his menu.

"We aren't driving, but there will still be plenty of room. Unless you plan on taking steamer trunks. The plane has lots of cargo space, but that would be pushing it."

"We're flying?" Rose didn't mind, but she *was* surprised.

"It usually takes less than an hour, so I like to fly when I visit my family." Jack smiled at the waitress as she walked up to take their order. Rose could almost hear the woman's wistful sigh. She understood completely. She'd felt the power of that smile the first time they'd met and it still got to her — every time. The crazy part was he wasn't even trying. He didn't do it consciously and he left a trail of breathless women in his wake. These days he reserved the deliberately sexy smile just for her. The poor waitress wouldn't have been able to function for the rest of her shift if she'd witnessed that one.

"Have you decided what you want, sweetheart?" The warmth in his voice sent a little shiver down her spine.

Oh, I know what I want, Rose thought. She was going to have to wait until they were alone to do anything about it

ROSE SLID OUT of Jack's SUV. Edgar bounced impatiently in the back seat, waiting for someone to let him out. It only diminished his enthusiasm slightly when Jack fastened a lead on his collar. Jack had decided to bring the dog with them so that he could visit the brother who still lived with Jack's parents. Rose knew the real reason. It might only be until Monday, but Jack would miss him. The private plane they planned to take was plenty big enough for all of them, so there was no reason not to bring him along. Taking control of the dog, Rose let him explore the exciting new territory while Jack unloaded their luggage.

"I can't believe after all that outfit anxiety, you only brought two suitcases."

"Dani talked me down and then helped me decide what to bring. Honestly, Jack, we're only going to gone a few days."

Rose gave him an innocent look, which Jack returned until they both burst out laughing. Shaking his head, he took the bags to the plane and loaded them in the cargo bay.

"Is the pilot already on board?" Rose turned away so Edgar could have some privacy.

"I'm the pilot."

Well, that was a surprise. Last night after dinner, Jack had told her that they would be taking H&W's private plane. He hadn't said anything about being a licensed pilot.

"Does that make you nervous?"

"Edgar and I trust you completely."

Jack wondered if she had any idea what hearing those casually delivered words did to him. Rose trusted him. He felt humbled that she had added him to a list that he knew to be very exclusive.

"I once knew a guy who tried to impress me by giving me a ride in his private plane."

"Really." Jack carried a clipboard with a list of things to check before they could take off.

"Of course," Rose said, bending down to pet Edgar, "once he'd given me a ride, he then expected *me* to give *him* a ride. If you know what I mean."

Finished with his pre-flight routine, Jack handed the clipboard to an airport employee. He then came over to Rose, pulling her into his arms.

"Oh, I know what you mean. Do you want me to track him down and beat him up?"

"Yes." She wrapped her arms around him. Tilting her head back, she met his sparkling eyes with her own. "But since he lives in Buenos Aires, and I doubt your mother would appreciate us being late, I say we let it go."

"Okay, but if you change your mind, just let me know."

Less than an hour later, they prepared to land at the airport located just a few miles from where Jack had grown up. He contacted the tower for instructions, giving the controller all the required information.

"Jack." The voice on the radio called enthusiastically. "Welcome back. We're all looking forward to seeing you at the big shindig tomorrow afternoon."

"Thanks, Jarvis. Tell everyone I'm looking forward to it too. How's Betty?"

"Sassy as always. Hey, I see your dad is just pulling up. Land safe."

"When Dad knows I'm flying in, he listens for the plane and drives over to meet me." Jack banked the plane and made his final approach.

The landing was as smooth as the rest of the trip had been. During the flight, Jack told Rose that both he and Drew had earned their pilot's licenses while in college. When they were able to afford it, they bought their first plane. Sometimes, when they flew a long distance, they hired a pilot. Otherwise, they liked to fly themselves.

Jack's dad waited for them at the hangar. Rose immediately saw the resemblance. Tall and still lean, Ned Winston's dark hair was peppered with gray. And though there were laugh lines around his eyes and mouth, he moved with the ease of a man half his age. His grin was so much like his son's. Rose could easily imagine how, as a younger man, he would have attracted women in droves. Probably still would if he gave them an ounce of encouragement.

"Welcome." Ned met Rose as she exited the plane, reaching out to help her down the steps. "You must be Rose. Jack's mother wanted to be here to greet you. If she'd come, the whole bunch of them would have tried to pile into the truck. One look at that group and you'd have jumped right back on the plane. Best we immerse you gradually."

"Dad." Jack hopped from the plane, Edgar right on his heels. He gave his father a fierce hug. It was obvious that both men were comfortable showing their affection for each other. When they'd finished their greeting, Jack's dad kept his arm around his son's shoulders.

"We've been listening to your music, Rose. Jack's sister Nina downloaded a whole mess of them and the girls have been playing them nonstop ever since they arrived yesterday. You have real talent, young lady."

"Thank you." Rose looked over at Jack. *Really?* Jack grinned.

"Don't worry," Ned added, winking. "We only play the PG stuff around the kids. The raunchier stuff is strictly adults only."

Rose broke out laughing and Jack's dad laughed right with her. What a charmer. *Yes, this man must still be beating them off with a stick.*

"Now, look who we have here. Edgar, your brother has been hopping around for days just waiting for you to get here." Ned gave the dog a pat. "What do you say we get that luggage into the truck and be on our way?"

The ride was a short one. Just as she had when they flew overhead, Rose noticed how rural the area was. Jack had told her he'd grown up on a farm. Until now, she hadn't been able to imagine him *as* a farm boy.

"Did you get up every morning before sunrise and milk the cows?" Rose teased. "And please tell me you had to walk twenty miles to school through ten feet of snow."

"As a matter of fact, I *did* milk *a* cow."

"But we let him sleep until dawn." Ned took his eyes off the road to send Rose a broad wink. "And it was only ten miles."

"Watch the flirting, *old man*, or I'll tell Mom on you."

"That's a good one, *boy*. There's no bigger flirt in the county than your mother. Why, just the other day, she had Ansell Waymart blushing so hard I thought the poor kid was going to expire on the spot."

Rose had never been around a father and son who teased like friends. The affection she'd witnessed when they greeted each other went beyond a filial bond. They liked each other. Rose could easily picture them hanging out — talking for hours. It gave her an odd sensation of warmth in her chest and she felt a tightening in her throat.

"Hey, you're awfully quiet." Jack put his arm around her shoulder and pulled her close.

"When would she be able to get a word in? Between the two of us, we've been yapping like there was no tomorrow." Ned pulled the truck to a stop. "Rose will get the hang of things soon enough. Around here, if you want to be heard, yell louder than everyone else."

The house was an odd hodgepodge of styles. Painted a pale green with white trim, Rose stood for a moment trying to decide what the architect had in mind with such an eclectic design. The porch was standard, but it wasn't in a straight line across the front. There was no straight line to follow. Now and then, the structure would jut out in an unexpected direction making her imagination go wild with anticipation to see the inside. She pictured interesting triangular corners and hallways that led to nowhere. Rose was charmed and hoped at some point during her stay she could get a detailed tour.

"What do you think of the old place?" Ned came up to stand next to her. He tilted his head as though he were looking for the first time too.

"Honestly? I've never seen anything like it in my entire life." She turned and grinned. "I absolutely love it."

"Beautiful *and* great taste. You're a rare one, Rose O'Brian."

"Dad built the place pretty much all by himself," Jack told her, the pride in his voice unmistakable. "As the family grew, so did the house. Solid as a rock too. That house will be here for generations to come."

Rose was about to ask Ned how he had managed it when the front door burst open. What seemed like an unending stream of women, all talking at once ran at them, making Rose wish she was still in the safety of the truck.

"Jackie."

Jack scooped up three of the women at once and twirled them in a circle. Kisses rained on cheeks, mixing with laughter and overlapping dialogue. Soon the next impatient wave pushed the first three to the side and they repeated the process. Rose knew that Jack had six sisters, but there had to be fifteen women of varying sizes and ages vying for his attention.

"Daughters and granddaughters." Ned looked on with indulgence. "Jack's the only boy among them."

"Your daughters have all had daughters?" Wow. That was amazing.

"And I wouldn't have it any other way. Course, there are six sons-in-law." Suddenly Ned's eyes took on a look of dreamy affection. "Ah, there she is."

She had to be Jack's mother. Standing on the porch, hands on hips, quietly waiting her turn. Rose thought she looked like a queen — a pagan queen.

Lorna Winston's short hair was the color of cotton candy and stuck up in artfully arranged tufts. An easy flowing top and long skirt gave her a look that the fashion magazines would have termed *boho* chic. Back in New York, Rose had known women who agonized for hours trying to look that effortlessly put together. Undoubtedly, this woman did it every day of her life without even thinking about it.

"Mom."

Just that single word, but spoken with absolute love. Jack gently peeled one of his nieces from his leg and quickly erased the distance between himself and his mother. She opened her arms and welcomed her only son, her baby.

Rose felt the tightening in her throat again. If this kept up, she was going to find it awfully hard to swallow anything this weekend.

"Now, let's see if you've been taking care of yourself." Holding Jack at arm's length, his mother looked him up and down. "You seem to be eating regularly. Good color in your cheeks. But what happened to all your beautiful hair?"

Jack just grinned and pulled his mother in for another hug.

"Now, why don't you bring your friend up here and introduce us. Girls, help bring those bags in and get back to supervising your men. I know Hal is a chef but the rest of them don't know a paring knife from a meat cleaver."

Waving as they went by, the group streamed back into the house. Ned gave her a quick hug and followed behind. Rose suddenly felt nervous. She'd met the rich and famous, worked with some of the biggest names in music. Meeting Jack's mother was much more intimidating.

"Mom, this is Rose O'Brian. Rose, my mother, Lorna Winston."

Rose didn't know what Jack expected, but he stood there as if they were going to do something highly entertaining.

"All right, you did your duty. Now go see if your father needs any help in the backyard. He's setting up tables and chairs, and Lord knows what else." When Jack hesitated, she simply raised an eyebrow. He gave Rose one last look and then headed into the house.

"He isn't worried that I'll scare you off," Lorna assured her. "He *is* worried that I'll tell you all kinds of embarrassing stories about him." She linked arms with Rose and started to stroll around the yard. "And believe me, I have plenty. For now, I just want to start the process of getting to know you. You've had an interesting career. Tell me how you got your start."

And just like that, Rose's nerves flew away. Lorna Winston put her so at ease that soon Rose felt as if she had known the woman for years. Lorna had a way about her that was genuine and welcoming. Oh, Rose suspected she could cut someone down in a heartbeat. She would be a fierce mother bear if anyone tried to hurt any of her cubs. But her nature was to gather people in, to accept them wholeheartedly. It didn't take Rose long to conclude that the world would be a better place if every child could be lucky enough to grow up with a mother like Lorna Winston.

"There you are." Jack joined them as they ended their walk at the back of the house. "Dad needs your supervision, Mom. He's afraid he might be putting something in the wrong place."

"Was it something in particular?" Lorna gave Rose an amused look.

"Nope. I think he's afraid he'll have to move everything if you don't give your approval first."

"That sounds about right." Just as her husband had done, Lorna hugged Rose. It was such a wonderfully natural gesture. "Now give your mother a kiss. Then take Rose and show her where she'll be staying."

Jack dutifully gave his mother's cheek a light peck and then taking Rose's hand, he led her into the house.

Knowing she would have time later to explore, Rose only gave the entry and living room a quick perusal. Color. That was her first impression. Happy bursts of color filled both areas with welcoming appeal. Jack pulled her along and up the staircase to the first landing. Pictures covered the walls. Seeing what looked like Jack as his younger self, Rose decided she would be coming back here, and soon. The next set of stairs led to a more open loft area that looked down on the living room. They moved across the room to a door on the far wall.

"With the whole gang here, we're all doubling up. You get to be my roomie." He opened the door, moving to the side so that she could enter first.

Rose was relieved to see that Jack's parents hadn't kept his room as some shrine to his youth. It looked like a comfortable guest room done in warm shades of blue and brown. The bed was huge; obviously, they knew their son well. The furniture wasn't a boring matchy-matchy. Instead, it complimented the style of the room.

"Just how many roomies have you had in here, Jack Rabbit?"

"Besides the ones I snuck in when I was in high school?" Jack grabbed her and tossed her onto the bed. Before she could scramble off, he landed on top of her, effectively trapping her under his hard as a rock body.

Rose refused to giggle. Giggling was undignified. Instead, she hid her grin in the crook of his neck. Then, just for the hell of it, gave him a big, wet raspberry.

"Hey," Jack pulled back. He met her grin with one of his own. "Okay, if you must know, you're the first." *And the last,* he added to himself.

"Good answer."

Then she kissed him. It wasn't a kiss that had anything to do with sex or the promise of it. It was just slow, warm, and friendly. When she pulled back, she looked him straight in the eye.

"There will be no sex while we're in your parents' home. Now get off me so I can unpack."

Jack rolled to the side. "You know they expect us to have sex."

"Don't get creepy, even if it is unintentional." Rose gave an exclamation of pleasure when she opened the closet door and found a full walk-in. And an attached bath. "Your dad is amazing. This is high-end work."

"When he was in college, he worked as a carpenter's apprentice. Rose," he rolled over so that she didn't appear to be upside down. "We're sharing a room, a room my parents willingly put us in — together.

"I know it doesn't make any sense. Even though your parents

assume we've been having sex, they don't *know* it." She turned. "Unless you…"

"Now who's being creepy? I don't discuss my love life with my parents. But it just doesn't make sense to deny ourselves."

Rose couldn't explain why she felt the way she did. Maybe it was because she'd just spent the better part of an hour with his mother. Maybe it was because she'd never gone with a man to meet his family and stayed in his childhood bedroom. All she knew was that it felt weird to think of having sex with him — here.

"And promise me you won't try anything in the middle of the night. You and I both know I won't be able to turn you down." She kept going, ignoring his smirk. "I'll expect you to be a gentleman. Oh, and don't come to bed naked."

"Do you think my sisters go without when they visit?"

"That's different, they're—"

Rose didn't finish; she didn't have to. Jack knew what she was going to say. *That's different; they're married.* She couldn't even say the word. He wasn't going to let it hang over them for the rest of the weekend like some crap bomb waiting to explode.

"What do you say we finish unpacking, and then I'll introduce you to the rest of the crowd? Don't worry about remembering everyone's names. We all answer to '*hey, you.*'"

"What will you give me if I *do* remember all the names and faces?"

"Well..." Jack looked toward the bed.

"Something non-sexual." Rose shook her head. "Swerve that mind to another track, Jackie. How about if I can do it, you detail my car when we get home, and if I can't, I'll do the same for your SUV."

"You're on." Jack knew it wasn't a bet she would make if she weren't sure she would win, but he was fine with losing this one. Besides, it would tickle his family to death if she were able to call them all by name after one introduction.

Dinner was a lively affair, which was to be expected when the twenty-seven occupants ranged in age from six months to sixty. There was no designated children's table or different meal times. Young and old ate together at a huge galley-style table made, of course, by Ned. While she helped to put out the silverware, Rose had marveled at the craftsmanship involved in taking one long piece of wood and making a piece of art. Art that they used and appreciated every day of the year.

"Technically, today is our anniversary, but Saturday is a better fit for a big celebration."

"Mom wanted to be a June bride," Nan, the oldest Winston child, informed Rose.

Shaking her head, Lorna laughed. "Mom wanted to get hitched before her water broke. You, my lovely Nan, were about ready to make your debut when Dad and I said 'I do.'"

Everyone joined in the laughter, especially Nan. "Well, I like my version. Telling people that my parents suddenly became traditional and decided to make me legitimate isn't nearly as romantic as the June bride story."

"They say when you marry in June, you're a bride all your life," Rose said without thinking. When she realized the table had quieted and she had become the center of attention, she cursed the songbook that constantly ran through her head.

"Sorry, I know that's a bit corny."

"I thought that it was lovely," Margie, the oldest granddaughter sighed. "Is it a poem?"

"Maybe." Rose had never thought about where it had originally come from. "But I was quoting a song from *Seven Brides for Seven Brothers*." She caught Jack's amused look. Remembering where she was, she caught herself just before she stuck her tongue out at him.

"I loved that movie," Nan exclaimed and then proceeded to fill everyone in on the plot. Rose thoroughly enjoyed the heated arguments over what happened when in the story. When someone insisted on getting their phone so they could look up who played the youngest brother, Ned put his foot down. There were no electronics at the dinner table.

"Fine," Anna, the middle child of the group huffed. "But it's going to drive me crazy until I know."

"You can stand to wait until we're done eating." Ned was easygoing about most things, but this was a 'no negotiations' rule.

Rose waited a few minutes until the conversation had moved on to a dozen or so other topics. Then, thinking no one was looking, she leaned down and carefully whispered in nine-year-old Stella's ear. She then sat back and continued eating the excellent fried chicken that was on her plate.

"Russ Tamblyn," Stella cried out. Rose silently applauded the little girl's perfect pronunciation.

"That's it," Anna cried out. "*That's* who played the youngest brother. You clever doll. How did you know that?"

Stella blushed at all the attention but, as instructed, refused to give up her source. When the little girl peeked up at her with adoring eyes, Rose took her hand under the table and gave it a squeeze. It was easy to get lost in a big group like this, no matter how loving. She'd noticed that Stella was quieter than her cousins, a little shyer. Rose remembered so well what it was like to be nine and unsure of yourself. Giving Stella the name of an actor wasn't much as gestures went, but for a little while, the girl had been the center of attention. A boost to her self-confidence, no matter how small, was a good thing.

After they cleared the table, the food put away and the kitchen put back in its usual order, everyone but the youngest children gathered in the living room. The huge stone fireplace, lit and roaring, lent a cozy layer of warmth. Lorna and Ned had taken their seats, center stage, so that their children could give them their anniversary presents tonight when it was just family.

"Thank you for what you did for Stella."

Rose looked up from the family photo album she'd been studying, surprised to see Janet, Stella's mother.

"You saw that?"

"No, Stella told me." Both women looked over at the girl who was snuggled in her father's lap, half-asleep. "She was worried because you told her not to tell anyone, but when I asked her how she knew, she just couldn't keep it to herself. She has a serious case of hero worship. So I wanted to thank you from both Stella *and* me." Janet gave her a hug then went to join her husband and daughter.

"So Stella told her mother." Jack sat down next to her. He put his arm around her shoulders and pulled her close.

"Does everybody know?" She'd thought she'd gotten away undetected.

"I'm the only one who saw you whispering to Stella. I imagine by tomorrow, word will have spread. Between that and winning our bet, you're going to be a legend around here." Jack laughed at Rose's disgruntled frown. "Secrets are nonexistent in the Winston clan. And when it involves a good deed? Forget about it."

Rose soon forgot to be annoyed when the anniversary couple started opening their gifts. They were mostly small things, sentimental and given with love. The last was one all seven children had gone in on together. When Lorna opened the plain, white envelope and read the contents, she burst into tears.

"A trip to Greece?" Ned said, shaking his head. He then grinned as Lorna's tears turned into an excited whoop. They spent the next ten minutes hugging and kissing children, grandchildren and sons-in-law. Rose sat back and enjoyed every minute.

When things had finally calmed down, and they were all settled comfortably in chairs or bundled together on one of the multiple sofas, Rose decided it was time for her to give Lorna and Ned her gift. She slipped away from Jack, telling him that she wanted a better look at the old piano he'd pointed out to her earlier that afternoon. The upright grand had been in the Winston family for generations. It had come to Ned and Lorna as a wedding present from his mother. Lorna played a little, as did a few of the girls. It was mostly a cherished piece of furniture that didn't get very much practical use.

Jack had mentioned the piano to Rose just in passing. When he told her about his parents' upcoming anniversary, she was inspired to write something for the couple. It had come easily, the irony of that not being lost on her. She could compose a song for two people she had never met but when it was more personal, like the love theme for *Wishes*, Rose couldn't even string together two words.

That was something to worry about on Monday. This weekend was about Jack's parents. She had planned on recording the song in her studio and sending the CD and sheet music with Jack. Now that she was here, she thought it might be nicer if she played it live.

She ran her hand over the well-polished wood. Rose felt a twinge of envy, which wasn't surprising. She tended to covet beautiful instruments like this one. The only thing that kept her from overindulging and buying every one that caught her eye was the size of her house. She just didn't have the room.

"Lovely, isn't it?"

Lorna had joined her, giving the piano a slightly wistful look. "I always hoped one of my children would catch the music bug. Nan and Paula play a bit, but that's it."

"Jack told me you play."

"Jack is being kind," Lorna laughed. "I can peck out a passable melody, but I wouldn't say I play."

"Do you mind if I—?" Rose glanced at the keyboard.

"Would you?" Lorna beamed, and then looked a little sheepish. "I've been trying to work up the nerve to ask you. But I didn't want you to think you had to sing for your supper."

"I would never think that." She ran her fingers up and down the keys, thrilled to find the piano was kept perfectly tuned. "I'll tell you a little secret. It was love at first sight. This is my equivalent of diamond jewelry. Of course, it's much harder to wear a piano around your neck."

She drifted into the melody of *A Love Song for Lorna and Edward*. Now that she'd met Jack's parents, Rose was certain she'd gotten the mood and feeling of the song right. Slightly dreamy, a strong touch of romance with a jazzy undertone. The lyrics were simple. She'd taken the bits that Jack had told her and woven a slightly sweet, slightly funny story. Their story.

Rose could see the surprise and then delight in Lorna's eyes when she realized what the song was about. The woman's eyes filled and she reached back, her hand grasping the air until her husband joined her.

Ned stood with his wife of forty years and listened to their story — and both of them wept.

When the final note faded, the room burst into applause and excited chatter, everyone crowding around the piano. Rose was thrilled by the enthusiastic response. She might not be a born performer, but she had enough ego that she was able to enjoy the warm approval of the Winston clan. Jack joined her on the piano bench, pulling her close. Leaning in, his voice thick with emotion, he whispered, "The hell with being a legend. After tonight, you're a full-fledged, fucking goddess."

Chapter Nineteen

ROSE COULDN'T IMAGINE where all the people had come from. Saturday had dawned bright and seasonably warm; in other words, a perfect day for an outdoor party. Last minute preparations kept everyone busy, including Rose. She helped wherever they needed her, including taking the restless children and pets to play in the nearby empty field. Edgar and his brother Digger acted as if they'd never been apart, running and exploring every gopher hole they could find. An hour later, they were all ready for some lunch and a nap. Rose opted out of the nap. After a night of sleeping in Jack's arms, she felt completely refreshed, her energy boundless. Jack had kept his word. He didn't try to seduce her; there was no *accidental* slipping of hands. They had gone to bed, turned off the lights, and fallen asleep. When she woke the next morning, her head was resting on Jack's shoulder, his arms holding her close. She felt warm and safe. It had been lovely. Now hours later, she still rode that wave of happy.

Guests were due to arrive at two o'clock but as with any party, there were early appearances. A lot of them. By four, Rose wondered if the rest of the county was deserted because everyone seemed to be in the Winston's backyard.

Trays of sandwiches and bowls of every imaginable kind of salad packed three large tables, a fourth reserved for plates, napkins and utensils. In the center was a huge four-tiered cake decorated with yellow and white swirls of frosting. Trays of cookies and homemade candy sat just to the side, giving people something sweet to snack on before they cut the cake.

As good as Rose was at remembering names, even she lost track after an endless round of introductions. She liked being anonymous but somehow in this crowd she was a celebrity. No one was rude or pushy. They just wanted to meet the famous songwriter. And take a few pictures. Rose was more than willing to oblige. However, she was grateful when Jack pulled her away so that she could get something to eat. She was ready for his rescue.

"I thought you could use a break." He handed her a plate already filled with food. She didn't bother to look at what he had gotten her. She'd seen the selection and it had all looked mouthwateringly good. They found two empty chairs and sat down to relax for the first time all day.

"Your family certainly knows how to throw a party." Rose took a bite of the best potato salad she'd ever eaten. "How long do these things usually last?"

"Most of the people will have cleared out by three or four." Jack offered her a bite of his beef stew.

"In the morning?" Rose asked after swallowing the tender piece of meat.

Jack chuckled. "This isn't any everyday occasion, so people like to make it last as long as possible. The children get tucked up in the house, sleepover style, and the grown-ups party until the wee hours."

In this case, the *wee hours* turned out to be four-thirty. That was when the last guest drove away, and everyone agreed to leave the cleanup for much later in the day. Rose could barely keep her eyes open long enough to brush her teeth and get undressed. She was asleep before Jack had finished in the bathroom and didn't wake when he joined her. When she stirred a few hours later, she was tucked in his arms. Smiling, she drifted back to sleep and didn't move again until late morning.

It was just before eleven and after a refreshing shower Rose hastily dressed in jeans and a cherry-colored t-shirt. She glanced out the bedroom window and saw several people gathering up debris and shoving it into oversized garbage bags. One of them was Jack. Hoping she wasn't the last one up, Rose quickly donned a pair of sneakers and made her way downstairs.

Nan was in the kitchen wiping the counter. Something smelled amazing and Rose realized that she was hungry. After all the food she'd consumed the night before, she hadn't thought she would need to eat for at least week.

"Don't look so panicked," Nan smiled. "Half the gang is still in bed. Nothing keeps Dad down much past dawn, but Mom is taking it easy this morning and having a lie in."

"Are those cinnamon rolls?" Rose almost floated over to the scent like a cartoon character.

"Help yourself. Mom made them up yesterday. She took them out of the fridge before she went to bed and then I stuck them in the oven about an hour ago. Your timing is perfect. Once the smell reaches the guys, there won't be anything left but a few crumbs." Nan poured them both a cup of coffee and joined Rose at the table. They relaxed, enjoying the rolls and a companionable silence.

"Where are the girls?" Rose asked after finishing off her second roll. She went to get more coffee, gesturing with the pot towards Nan's cup.

"I'm good," she said. "All of the kids, except the two babies, are outside somewhere. They're playing with the dogs and *helping* with the cleanup. Thank goodness the guys are so patient. I figure between nine little girls and three dogs, it should only take an hour longer than it would have without them."

"There you are." Jack came up behind Rose and kissed her neck. "Feel like going for a walk? I thought you might like to look around the farm."

"Jack, why don't you take Dad's truck? It looks like rain; the two of you might get soaked if you walk."

"We'll be fine, Nan." Jack smiled reassuringly. "But you might want to grab a jacket, Rose. It's a little chillier today."

"I'll be right back."

Jack grabbed a cinnamon roll and had it halfway to his mouth when he felt his sister's gaze.

"What, am I not allowed to have one?"

"I always wondered when you finally fell, what she would be like."

"And?" Jack didn't ask his sister what she was talking about. Every member of his family had to know how he felt about Rose. This was the first time he'd brought a woman home. And to do it on his parents' fortieth wedding anniversary? Jack would never do that unless his feelings were serious.

"And, I could never get a clear picture in my mind." Nan leaned her hip against the counter. It was unbelievable that her baby brother was a grown man and in love. She reached over and hugged him close. "What can I say, Jackie? She's smart, beautiful and has her own money, so you know she's not after anything but your body. She's perfect for you."

"I think so too. Now I just have to convince Rose."

"I take back the perfect part." Nan shifted into protective older sister mode. "How could she not want you?"

"Quiet, here she comes." Jack gave his sister a warning look.

"Ready when you are," Rose said, her eyes bright with anticipation.

"Great, let's go." Jack leaned over to give his sister a hug and whispered, "Not a word to anyone, Nan." Then he grabbed Rose's hand and headed out the door.

Jack wanted to show Rose all the places where he'd run and played and dreamed as a little boy. He was proud of his boyhood home, the place his parents had built from hard work and love. When Jack had made his first real money, he'd wanted nothing more than to share it with his parents. He wanted to pay off what they owed on the land, to make things easier for them. However, they wouldn't take a penny from him. At first he'd been hurt by their refusal, but he quickly realized it wasn't about him. Over the years, they had reduced their debt to almost nothing, something they were extremely proud of. They loved Jack for wanting to take care of them, and they were proud that he was in a position to do so. But when the day came and they made the last payment to the bank, they wanted to know that they had done it by themselves. Jack respected them even more, and he never offered again.

Jack and Rose took their time, strolling through his mother's raspberry patch, pausing to admire the two new foals that frolicked in the pasture. Everything was green and lush as if showing off for his girl. Jack took Rose by the hand and led her across a rocky patch of ground. They had come to his favorite place. It was secluded, hidden by a bank of oak trees and overlooking a long, shallow stream that, when he was a boy, he imagined that it ran on forever. He would sit under *his* tree and daydream of getting on a boat and sailing to faraway lands. It didn't matter that the stream at its deepest point was only two feet deep or that a mile down the road the water went into an underground well. This place was magic; the possibilities were endless.

"Oh, Jack," Rose breathed. "What a beautiful spot. It was yours, wasn't it? I can see you here, all floppy hair and long, skinny legs." Seeing Jack's questioning look, Rose grinned. "I've been looking at photo albums."

"I guess that's a pretty accurate description." He sat down under the old oak and patted the ground next to him, an invitation to Rose. He put his arm around her and settled them back against the sturdy, smooth-barked tree.

"I dreamed of so many fantastical things and my adventures were huge and far-reaching." He smiled when he felt Rose's chuckle. "I think I was about thirteen the last time I played here. I mean really *played*. I was just on the cusp of chasing girls instead of dragons and evil sorcerers."

"Did you stop coming?"

"No." His dreams became more solid, less fanciful. "My thoughts became more grown up. Was I going to make the football team? How could I find a way to sneak a girl here without my mom finding out?"

Now *that* Rose could easily imagine. "Your dad wouldn't have cared?"

"Sure he would have. But my mother has definite ideas about respecting women. From a very early age, she drilled it into my head that a woman was not just a plaything for my amusement. I should never do anything to my dates that I wouldn't want some guy doing to one of my sisters."

If Rose hadn't been crazy about Jack's mother before, this would have done it. "So how'd that work out for you?"

"I didn't lose my virginity until my first week of college." Jack gave her a slow smile. "And then I was off and running."

"So you never got a girl under this tree?"

"Nope. I was deprived of one of my biggest boyhood fantasies." He turned, slowly lowering them both to the ground. "Want to help me remedy that?"

"Well," Rose moaned when Jack lightly bit the spot right under her ear. "We aren't in your parents' house."

Jack unsnapped her jeans and lowered the zipper. "No one will ever know, I promise."

"Was that the line you planned on using back in high school?" He didn't need a line, not with those magic hands. He knew just where to touch, how to make her forget everything but his teasing between her legs, drawing the slick moisture from her body and using it to ease his way in. Two fingers and then three. Her hips shifted to meet him. She reached for more and sensing her needs, he gave it to her. Jack's thumb grazed her engorged tissue teasingly. *"Jack,"* she protested his light touch. His deep laugh sent shivers through her. Then he stroked her again, harder, with purpose. Sparks flew before her eyes as she spiraled towards the peak of her desire, hovered for one agonizing instant, then careened over in a glorious explosion. For a moment, she couldn't breathe. For a moment, she didn't care. Jack had taken her to a place that was becoming wonderfully familiar but always new.

Jack watched as Rose's breathing settled. Bringing her pleasure was becoming his addiction. He kissed her lightly. Her eyes slowly opened, slightly unfocused. She smiled and pulled him down for a longer kiss.

"Why is it I always want to thank you after you do that?"

"Modesty prevents me from stating all the endless reasons." Jack smoothed her hair back then reached his hand under her shirt, his hand enveloping her lace-covered breast. He pulled the cup of her bra down and teased the already hard nipple. "But I am willing to let you show your appreciation in a less verbal manner."

Rose reached between his legs, humming with appreciation. She caressed him through his jeans; his pulsing heat almost bursting through the material. Making quick work of the snap and zipper, she released him, her warm hand shielding him from the cool air.

"How about I show you my *oral* appreciation?" Rose nipped at his earlobe. Her mouth trailed across his jaw and down the exposed area of his neck. She hovered briefly, just long enough to meet his gaze. His blazing blue eyes were all the answer she needed. Licking her lips, she engulfed his erection with her warm, moist mouth. Minutes later, *he* was the one shouting his thanks.

THE NEXT MORNING Rose was packed and ready to leave. Well, she was packed. The last few days had been wonderful, and she hated to see them end. The Winstons had welcomed her without reservation, and she was going to miss them all.

She sat on the porch with Jack's mom, enjoying the sunny morning. Jack was out helping his dad repair some downed fence. They had no timetable, so they weren't rushing to get back to Harper Falls. Rose had said goodbye to everyone else when they left for their nearby homes. Jack was the only one of the Winston children that didn't live within fifty miles of their parents. Rose thought it was lovely that Lorna's daughters were close enough to visit any time they wanted.

"Stella wants to take piano lessons."

"Really?" Rose felt a burst of warmth. "It looks as though your piano is going to be getting a lot of use in the near future."

Lorna smiled at the thought. "I think she'll be the one to stick with it, to learn how to play."

"She's a determined little girl."

"She wants to be like you," Lorna patted her hand. "You're her hero."

"I—" Rose didn't know what to say. It was a new experience, one that held a host of responsibilities. She wasn't sure she was the right one for the job. "You've heard my songs, right?"

"You mean the ones about strong, empowered women?" Lorna asked. "Your women aren't victims, Rose. They stand up for themselves. As a mother and grandmother, that's exactly the message I want my girls to hear. You aren't just Stella's hero, you're mine too."

This time she *was* speechless. Lorna Winston, earth mother extraordinaire, had just given Rose the greatest compliment of her life and she had nothing to say in return.

Taking pity on her, Lorna changed the subject. "I used to worry about Jack. Oh, I didn't worry that anything bad would happen to him though I was never a fan of him playing football." She shuddered when she thought of all those oversized bodies jumping on her beautiful baby. "I worried about his unrelenting drive."

Rose frowned. "I don't understand."

"Perhaps worried is the wrong word." Lorna thought about it for a moment. "Confused is better. When he was a young boy, he used to run around with his sisters getting into mischief. I always thought he would be a farmer like his father."

"He loves it here."

"Yes," Lorna agreed. "But there came a time when it wasn't enough. He wanted something different, something more. Don't get me wrong. As much as I would have loved to have him near me like his sisters, the most important thing was for him to be happy. All of that focus on being the best and making money. I don't know where it came from. You can go back hundreds of years, on both sides of the family, and you'll never find anyone like Jack."

"Jack *is* unique." Rose imagined it would have been quite a shock to have your carefree baby suddenly turn into a driven business mogul. Rose wasn't confused; she knew exactly where he got his ambition — from his mother.

"Did I miss the joke?" Lorna asked when she heard Rose's chuckle.

"I'm sorry, I wasn't laughing at you," Rose assured her. "But I don't think you realize just how much it *does* run in your family." Rose looked directly at Lorna.

"With me? All I've ever wanted was my husband and family."

"Well, that seems pretty ambitious to me." For Rose, it seemed *beyond* ambitious. "For over forty years, you've loved one man and raised seven amazing children. Children who not just love you but respect you, want to spend time with you. They eagerly came together to celebrate the strong foundation you built for them. It's because you succeeded in *your* ambition, Lorna, that Jack was able to succeed in his."

"Oh, you sweet, sweet girl." Lorna pulled her close. "I hope Jack realizes how lucky he is to have found you."

Rose felt a surge of panic. "But we aren't, I mean I'm not—" How did she explain something to Lorna that she hadn't figured out herself? "I'm afraid I'll hurt him," she finally managed to sputter.

"But you don't want to."

"No," Rose exclaimed. "That's the last thing I want."

"Then the rest is a leap of faith." Lorna patted Rose's cheek, her smile understanding. "You can't promise not to hurt someone, Rose. But you can *try* not to hurt them on purpose. If you do that, then you have as much of a chance as anyone. Now, here come our men. Give me another hug and say you'll come back soon to visit."

"I'd like that." Before Rose pulled away, she whispered, "By the way, Jack is a terrific dancer. Thank you."

Chapter Twenty

ROSE GRIPPED THE phone in frustration. If she had been blessed with super powers, she would have used them to punch out the person on the other end of the line. Right now she would have to settle for punching him with words.

"Would you shut up for five seconds so I can get a word in?" She had been listening to Sam Laughton's rant for five minutes straight. He wasn't saying anything helpful. In fact, he wasn't saying anything new. Rose began to think he just liked the sound of his own voice.

"So speak."

Asshole. "I know the deadline is only a week away. I can't force the words. Why can't you record the songs you have?" Wasn't that reasonable? "Think how happy you'll be when I've finished. And I will finish. *If you get off my back.*"

There was a pause. Rose imagined Sam counting to ten or rubbing his temples. Or to make her happy, pounding his head on his desk.

"I thought you went on that trip last weekend to find inspiration." It sounded like Sam was gritting his teeth. "Seeing what forty years of love looks like should have made the words fly onto the paper. Obviously it didn't work. So what happened?"

"First, you were the one who thought the trip would inspire me." Even over the phone, she could tell he was going to interrupt her, so she hurried on. "Second, I don't know what happened. For some reason, I feel even more blocked than before."

Not that she would admit it to Sam, but Rose was more than a little a panicked. Partly because the song wasn't coming, she'd never had this kind of problem before. Even worse, she'd convinced herself that being able to finish this song would be a sign, a breakthrough. It would mean she was finally able to fall in love. And that meant she could love Jack the way he deserved to be loved.

"Come to Paris. And before you automatically say no, think about it as a change of scenery. If you fly over for a week or two, you might find the inspiration you're looking for."

"I've been to Paris." Just last year Sam had given her a personal tour of his studio. He'd made a pass, and she'd said no — absolutely not interested. He took the rejection well and the tour had continued. Undoubtedly, he would try again if she went to Paris. And be just as good-natured about it when she turned him down, again. "We both know my writer's block has nothing to do with location."

"Then just come for a few days. I might be able to push you gently in the right direction."

More like shove, Rose thought. Sam was not a man known for his warm and fuzzy approach.

"I promise to think about it." Rose could feel the beginning of a headache. She needed to take something for it. Even better, she needed to end this phone call. "Give me a few more days without any interruptions. Five days," she added quickly. "Please."

She heard Sam's sigh and knew she'd won, for now.

"Fine. I know you have it in you, Rose, but now I need it on paper."

Rose hung up and rubbed her temples. Who was she kidding? Not Sam, and certainly not herself. He might as well have given her five months instead of five days. Unless a miracle happened, that song was not going to get written. At least not by her. And wasn't that a frightening thought. Sam could give the job to someone else and she wouldn't have any right to stop him.

Rose filled a glass with water and swallowed a couple of aspirins. She was due to meet Jack in an hour. Movie night at his place with lots of buttery popcorn and a little necking followed by some hot sex. Earlier in the day, it had sounded like heaven but now she didn't know. Jack seemed tenser since they had returned from Oregon. Or maybe it was her, and she was projecting her doubts onto him. Either way the ease seemed to be slipping away from their relationship. She was letting her inability to write one song affect every aspect of her life and it pissed her off. She wanted to be with Jack. Everything else could wait for one more night.

JACK HAD NO idea what they were watching. It was a movie, obviously. A lot of things were getting blown up. And maybe somebody was about to betray someone. Hell, he didn't even care. He wasn't paying attention any more than Rose was. Her head was on his shoulder and she seemed to be watching but he knew if she'd had to, she couldn't have described the plot. Hell, Edgar probably knew more about it than either of them.

"I need some more to drink." Rose picked up her half-full glass and headed for the kitchen. "Can I get you anything?"

"I'm good."

When Rose returned — empty-handed — Jack gave up and turned off the TV. Rose sat back down without comment and neither of them spoke for several minutes. It was crazy. They always had something to say. It was the first time he could remember even a moment of awkward silence between them.

"What's wrong, Rose?"

"Nothing." She glanced at Jack. "Really. Other than that song I'm having problems with, I'm good." She waited another second before turning towards him. "Is there something you're not telling me about?"

Jack sighed. Fine, he'd go first.

"You've been tense the past couple of days. And it's not just because of work."

"I thought you were the tense one. I'm fine." Rose knew what she was doing. A little voice yelled for her to stop before it was too late. The rest of her wasn't listening.

"Me? Why do you think I have a problem?"

"Because you thought that by taking me to meet your family, I would suddenly be so dazzled by the warm family vibe that I would realize what I've been missing. You thought I would declare my undying love and beg you to marry me."

"Don't be ridiculous." Jack stood and began to pace. "I didn't think any of that. What's more, you don't believe I did."

"At least admit that, subconsciously, you were hoping something would happen."

"I wanted you to meet my family, Rose. End of story." Jack rounded on her. "And, by the way, I lied before. I do think this is all about your work. You've put so much importance on that stupid song that you've lost all perspective."

"Are you saying that my work is stupid?" God, could she hear herself? She spewed so much crap that she expected brown globs to start falling out of her mouth at any moment.

"You know that's not what I'm saying." Jack's patience was rapidly ending. "But admit it; you've equated not being able to write a love song with you not being able to love me."

What, now he could read her mind? True or not, she wasn't going to admit it to anyone, especially not Jack.

"It's just a song, Jack."

"Exactly, but you've built it up into some mammoth symbol of failure. The fact is, if you don't love me it has nothing to do with a song," Jack yelled.

"Damn it, Jack. You can't get angry when I warned you from the very beginning that this would happen."

"I'm not angry that you don't love me, Rose. I'm angry that you won't admit to yourself that you do."

"Sam Laughton wants me in Paris." Great segue. The man accuses you of being in love with him and you throw Paris in his face. "He thinks a change of scenery is what I need to get past my writer's block."

"Are you going?" All the heat had left his words. Now he just sounded incredibly tired.

Rose shrugged. "I told him I'd think about it." She wanted to scream she was sorry, to tell him that she didn't want to leave him for even a day. But the words wouldn't come out. Instead, she watched as his eyes turned a frigid blue.

"Go then."

"Jack—"

"Now, Rose." Jack picked up her purse and handed it to her. "Go home now. And go to Paris. I don't care anymore. If you think this thing between us is a game, then you're going to have to find a different playmate."

Again, she wanted to speak. She wanted to beg him to let her stay, just let her be with him. Instead, she walked out the door and didn't look back.

Chapter Twenty-One

"SO YOU PICKED a fight with him."

"That's not what I said."

Rose had decided to hunker down in her house and never come out. That resolve had lasted until about noon. It didn't take long for her to become sick of her depressingly dreary company and she dragged herself over to Dani's house. One look at her and Dani had called Tyler. After telling them everything that had happened, Rose expected sympathy. She wasn't getting any.

"You accused him of trying to manipulate you, even though you knew it wasn't true."

"I guess," Rose grumbled.

"And after he called you on it, you went and threw Paris *and* a hunky producer in his face."

"I never said anything about Sam being hunky." Great, her friends easily picked apart her arguments. It made it difficult for Rose to hold onto that little bit of righteous indignation that had kept her going for the last twelve hours.

"Admit it, Rose. You picked a fight with Jack hoping he would break up with you, hoping it would magically absolve you of any blame." Dani *was* sympathetic. She knew how difficult this was for Rose. Sympathy had to end somewhere, especially after knowing Rose as long as she had. Sometimes she needed to administer a swift kick in the ass. With love, of course. She looked at Tyler as if to say, *your turn.*

"This would be so much easier if you weren't in love with Jack." Tyler knew Rose would protest, so she simply sat back and let her get it out of her system.

"But that's the problem, I don't — I can't — love him. I want to. Jack is the only man in the world that I would love if I could." Rose felt panicky again. Heart pumping, short of breath. "I always thought something inside me was broken, but that's not it. I believed that because of my mother and Louise I was so damaged, loving someone just wasn't possible. I can't blame them anymore. I just don't have it in me. I never did. And you're right. I took the coward's way out and let Jack end it. God, I knew I was a mess but on top of everything, I'm a terrible person."

Dani and Tyler exchanged helpless looks. Okay, change of plan. She couldn't kick someone in the ass when she was already doing it to herself. Sitting closer, they gave Rose a group hug.

"It would help if you'd cry. Pressure reliever extraordinaire."

"Great," Rose whispered. "Something else to add to my list of things wrong with me. Number three hundred and six — Rose can't cry."

"There's nothing wrong with not crying every five minutes." Tyler leaned over and lightly slapped Dani on the side of the head. Her glare said she would have liked it to be a lot harder.

"I didn't mean it like that." Dani mouthed *sorry* to Tyler, hugging Rose harder. "I meant you need to find a way to let out all that tension. If you aren't relaxed, you can't think straight. You shouldn't make any plans when you're all tied up in knots."

"What I need to do is apologize to Jack." However, she couldn't face seeing that look of anger and defeat again. She could leave him a message, but that would be even worse. Apologies of this magnitude she couldn't give on voicemail.

"What we all need to do is hit the gym." Tyler stood and pulled Rose to her feet. "Dani's right about getting rid of all that tension. An hour or two working up a good sweat and you'll be thinking a lot clearer."

"Can't I just get in my pajamas and eat ice cream?" Rose let herself be pushed into Dani's car. "As my best friends, you're supposed to encourage me to sit around with messy hair and watch sad movies."

"I am burning all your rom-coms," Tyler proclaimed. "But I promise you can let your hair be as messy as you like while we're working out."

"Thanks a lot," Rose mumbled. Fine, she would go and sweat her ass off. But there was no way Tyler was going anywhere near her rom-coms.

"I WON'T GET any volunteers for you to beat up this time."

Jack didn't bother to look up. He was working and he didn't want to be interrupted. And he *definitely* didn't want Drew making any attempts to knock him out of his funk. Around four o'clock that morning, he had burrowed deep enough into his dark mood that he enjoyed its company. He was getting a perverse satisfaction out of brooding and he planned to keep it up for some time to come.

"If you aren't in here to tell me the building is on fire then get out."

"Maybe I want to talk business."

"Text me, email me. Hell, stand outside the door and tap out your message in Morse code. I don't care as long as it doesn't involve human interaction."

Ignoring him, Drew sat and put his feet up on Jack's desk. Not a move his friend appreciated when he was in the best of moods.

"This must have to do with Rose." Drew took Jack's growl as a yes. "So what did you do this time?"

"Me?" Jack shot out of his chair. "Why assume I'm to blame? You're my friend; you're supposed to tell me I'm better off without her — that I can do better. That all I have to do is snap my fingers and I can have a hundred women lined up to replace her.”

“Well, as much as I admire your oversized ego, let me tell you a few hard truths. First, I am your friend — your *best* friend. So you can trust me when I say you *aren't* better off without her, you *can't* do better and as for those hundred women? You could screw them all, but none of them would ever replace Rose.”

“Fuck you.”

“I don’t think either of us would enjoy that. But even if we tried I couldn’t replace her either.”

Jack sat back down with a thud. Drew was right, about everything. But how did him being right change anything? Rose didn’t want to be with him, and he was angry — out of his head angry.

“I can’t fix this, Drew. And *you* definitely can’t fix it.” Drew had spent ten years pining for the same woman. He needed to figure out his own love life before he started giving Jack advice.

“Fine.” Drew didn’t think his and Jack’s problems had anything in common. But Jack wasn’t going to listen, not now. If things didn’t work themselves out in the next week or so, then would be the time to put his two cents back into the pot.

“I assume you’re still going to Karen Poe’s movie premiere?”

“Nothing’s changed there. I’ll fly to Los Angeles in the morning.”

Drew nodded. “It will do you some good to get away for a bit. In fact, why don’t you stay down there for a few days? You can hook up with old friends, clear your head. There’s nothing pressing here so now’s a good time to take some personal time.”

“Clear my head. That’s what that producer said to Rose.” Jack had looked Sam Laughton up. Not that he would ever admit that to anyone. The guy had an impressive résumé and a string of female conquests that most men would have envied. Rose had once told him that Sam wasn’t her type, but until that night back in May, *Jack* hadn’t been her type. The thought of his Rose, in Paris, with a guy who had probably been hitting on her for years hadn’t done much to help his mood.

“I know I’m missing something, but never mind. Take my advice; get out of town for a few days. But tonight we’re going to Tom Tom’s.

We'll have a couple of beers, shoot some pool, and just hang out. We can talk sports, politics, religion, or that men should never wear unisex cologne. Hello, dude smells like a lady. But we will not be talking about women. Not women we know, or might know or may never know."

"I get it; no women."

After Drew had left, Jack swiveled his chair around and looked out at the town below. He liked it here. In a short time, Harper Falls had become home. The people were friendly and not too nosy. Last winter had been a skier's paradise with Canada to the north and Mt. Spokane to the south. His house was finally exactly how he wanted it, and Edgar had more trees to pee on than he could ask for. But would he be able to walk through town knowing Rose could be just around the corner? How would it feel to walk into the diner for lunch and see her sitting with another man? Even though it sounded like something out of an old movie, maybe it was true. Maybe Harper Falls wasn't big enough for both of them.

"I'M ALL FOR equality between the sexes but I'd be more than happy to sign away my right to sweat like a man."

Tyler's hour or two of working out had leaned heavily towards two and Rose was a dripping mess. She wiped her face with the towel she had draped around her neck then collapsed onto a nearby mat. Her only consolation was that Tyler and Dani looked like she felt — wrung out.

"Who decided an hour in the weight room should be followed by hot yoga?" One of them had made the brilliant suggestion, but her brain was too exhausted to remember which of them it had been.

"It was Dani." Tyler crawled next to Rose before sprawling in a sweaty heap. "Water, I need water."

Dani had used up the last of her energy to grab three bottles so she couldn't do more than roll a couple of them in the general direction of her friends. She gulped down half of her bottle then slumped backward.

"Someone told me it was a great class."

"They must hate you." Tyler sighed as the cool liquid slid down her throat. "And where did they find that instructor? I do yoga to relax. If I'm tempted to punch the guy who's yelling at me that my downward facing dog isn't up to his standards then what's the point?"

"He was a bit Sergeant Foley, wasn't he?"

"But Lou Gossett Jr. turned out to be one of the good guys. Yoga master Ted just wanted to kill us." Tyler grimaced as she rolled over, her sweaty shirt sticking to the mat.

Dani chuckled. "The way he looked at your butt, I'd say he was more interested in screwing you."

"Ugh, no thanks. He looks like he's on steroids, and you know what those things can do to a man's dick. Healthy jumbo dog to wizened cocktail weenie in ten easy injections. A really, really veiny cocktail weenie."

Both Rose and Dani shuddered.

"Can we change the subject? I'd like erase that image from my brain as quickly as possible."

After Tyler dropped her off and she slowly climbed the stairs to her bedroom, Rose had to admit she felt better. She was a sweaty, limp noodle who could barely drag off her clothes and climbed into a steaming hot shower, but her tension was a thing of the past. Her thoughts were still a mess, but she at least was able make a decision. She was going to talk to Jack, apologize, and see if they were really over.

Rose looked at the clock by her bed and was surprised to see how late it was. Nine o'clock wasn't too late to call Jack but what she had to say needed to be said in person. She would give them both until tomorrow to calm down.

Rose couldn't remember the last time she'd eaten, but the thought of food almost made her gag. Eating could wait until tomorrow too. Right now, all she wanted was an uninterrupted night of sleep. She crawled between the covers, pulled them up to her chin, and proceeded to stare at the clock, blinking whenever another minute went by. In order for her sleep to be uninterrupted, she was going to have to *fall* sleep. After the next minute had passed, Rose sighed and gave up. Maybe she'd have better luck curled up on the couch with the TV on.

At least the noise would be a distraction.

The sound of demented laughter jarred Rose from a fitful sleep. It took a moment for her eyesight to clear enough to see that she wasn't being attacked by a group of rabid clowns but that the crazy laugh came from the still on TV. If the reaction of the morning show's host was any indication, whatever story the annoyingly upbeat weatherman was telling must have been hilarious.

Rose raised her arms in a tentative stretch. No sore muscles. Well, that was good news. Switching off the set, she rolled off the couch and headed for the bathroom. Ten minutes later, dressed and finally feeling hungry, she opened her refrigerator and grabbed a container of yogurt. Mm, blueberry. She rooted around hoping to find some bread but wasn't surprised when she couldn't find any. Deciding that no matter how much she liked yogurt, this morning she needed something more substantial.

Rose picked up her phone on the way to the garage. Jack would have been up for a couple of hours already. She wanted to call him and ask if they could meet. Maybe he would let her buy him breakfast. She rubbed her sweaty palms on her jeans before hitting dial. Great, voicemail. He probably saw who it was and didn't want to talk. She contemplated her options before deciding to wait a few hours and then try again. If she had to, she would drive up to see him. There was no guarantee he would see her, but she at least had to try.

Rose took a deep breath. She could hear the siren call of the couch enticing her back to its nonjudgmental comfort. She could wrap herself in a blanket and wallow the day away. And hate herself for it. Pulling her car keys from her purse, she headed out the door determined to get some food and some fresh air. Jack would have to talk to her eventually. Right?

JACK WASN'T ANSWERING his phone.

Rose had tried three more times before getting in her car and driving to his office. Now she just had to make herself get out of the car. She'd been sitting in the parking lot for the last ten minutes; he had to know she was there. She could have rolled down her window and waved at the security camera — or flipped it off. Instead, she sat like an unmoving lump of indecision. She needed to either start the car and drive away or march up to the front door and hope that someone let her in.

Her hand was just reaching for the door when a knock on the window made her jump a foot. She looked over to see Drew tap again.

"Sorry," he said, raising his voice so she could hear him through the glass. "I didn't mean to startle you."

Rose hit the button and waited for the window to roll down. Drew bent over until they were at eye level. Had Jack sent Drew out to tell her to get lost?

"He's not here." Rose looked miserable. He would have loved to give her a hug. He wanted to tell her that everything was going to be all right. But even though she wasn't quite as antagonistic towards him as she used to be, he still wasn't her favorite person. And he didn't *know* if everything was going to be all right. It was an all-around screwed up situation.

"Would you even tell me if he were in there and just didn't want to see me?"

"Probably." Drew gave her a crooked smile. "But I promise you he isn't here. He's not even in the state. He left this morning for Los Angeles."

"Los Angeles? Was it some last minute business?" Or did he just want to get away from her?

"Old business. He's accompanying Karen Poe to her movie premiere tonight. I don't know if he ever mentioned Karen, but he still does the bodyguard thing for her. She seems to think he's her good luck charm."

"Right, he did mention that but I didn't realize it was tonight." She leaned back in her seat and sighed. Now, what? If she went home, it would mean another night on the couch and that was just miserable. She didn't want to call Tyler and Dani. They didn't need to hear any more of her whining and to be honest, she was sick of it herself. But, God, she didn't feel like being alone.

"Do you think Jack would mind if I went to his place and fed Edgar?"

"Edgar is here. Jack plans on being gone for a few days and so he decided to drop the dog off before he left."

Great, now she didn't even have Edgar's nonjudgmental shoulder to cry on.

"You have a key to Jack's place, right? And his security codes?"

"If he hasn't changed them."

"Rose, I don't know what happened between you and Jack, but I guarantee that his feelings are the same today as they were two days ago. Nothing has changed, including the security codes."

In spite of what Drew had told her, Rose couldn't help holding her breath as she punched in the numbers on the keypad by Jack's front door. She then entered the retinal scan override code that Jack had created just for her. To her relief, the alarm disengaged and Rose let herself and Edgar into the house. As usual, the place was immaculate. No dirty dishes in the sink or clothes thrown over a chair. The hardwood floors gleamed and the furniture dusted. She knew that once a week Jack had a woman from the town come in and clean but between those visits, he kept his house in order. Not that he was fussy, but Jack liked things organized and everything in its place.

"Are you ready for your dinner, Edgar?"

Rose patted the dog. No hard feelings from you, eh, boy? She looked into his big, brown adoring eyes and felt a little lighter. She fixed his bowl of kibble and dried kale with her usual grimace. Jack swore it was as good for Edgar as it was for humans. Maybe, Rose thought, but she was not a fan. Edgar ate his food with gusto, so she figured different strokes.

After taking care of Edgar's needs, Rose decided she felt a little hungry. Unlike at her place, Jack's refrigerator was always well stocked. She knew from experience that it wouldn't be difficult to find something that appealed to her. She opened the door and looked over the selection. Like the rest of his house, Jack's fridge was ruthlessly well organized. Everything in its assigned place, bottles and cartons in neat rows. She didn't feel like cooking, nothing new there, so she skipped over anything that required heat. Plenty of fresh vegetables — maybe a salad? Milk, eggs, yogurt. Wait, yogurt? She knew Jack was not a big fan. It was *her* favorite.

Rose removed one of the containers and stared at the label. The kind she ate. The kind that she could only get in one store in Spokane. She closed the refrigerator, leaned against one of the cabinets, and slid to the floor. Every little thing he'd ever done for her came rushing back. How she would get in her car and find that he'd filled it with gas or how he bought an electric kettle because he knew she liked tea in the morning instead of coffee. How he had automatically cleared a drawer in his dresser so that she would have some place to keep a few items. And on the night of the Lilac Ball, when he had tucked her dress in so it wouldn't get caught in the car door. So many times he showed her how he felt, little gestures filled with love. Love. Rose looked down at the carton of yogurt. Why else would someone drive miles out of his way to buy something he didn't even like? Blueberry, her favorite. She frowned when something dropped onto the carton. She wiped at it. Water? Where—?

Hand shaking, Rose lifted it and wiped at her cheek. Tears. She was crying. Amazed, Rose sat there not even attempting to stem the flow. Worried, Edgar butted her gently with his nose and she just wrapped her arms around his neck and sobbed. She cried for her mother, for the pain of never knowing her father. And she cried for herself. For that lost little girl and for the woman she became. A woman who would have thrown away the best thing that ever happened to her because she was afraid to open up her heart.

She didn't know how long she had sat there with the ever-patient dog but when she finally lifted her head, his fur was soaking wet. She wiped her cheeks and gave a watery laugh.

"Oh, my darling boy." She gave him another squeeze.

Sensing the storm had passed, Edgar wiggled excitedly and gave her still damp cheek a big swipe with his tongue.

"Yes, I'm done. I promise. At least for now." Rose got to her feet and poured herself a glass of water. She drank it all down, replenishing the liquid she'd just cried out. She washed the glass and put it away, just as Jack would have done. Jack. She looked down at Edgar and grinned, her emotions flipping from despair to elation in a matter of minutes.

"I know he should be the first one to hear this, but I have to tell someone. I love him, Edgar. I love Jack."

Edgar seemed unimpressed. He gave her a look that seemed to say, *Of course, you love him. I've known it all along.*

"Well, I didn't." Rose laughed again, twirling around and around. So this was what it felt like — effervescent and grounded all at once. And scary — really scary. But strong and bright. And unconditional.

Rose stopped. *Unconditional.* That was it. She grabbed her keys.

"Come on, Edgar. I have a song to finish."

Knowing what the jingle of keys meant, Edgar raced out to the car, prancing impatiently while Rose reset the alarm. She opened the door to the backseat and let the dog jump in. The trip passed in a happy haze as she hummed the tune that would accompany the words that were already forming in her head. She was so anxious to get to the studio while the inspiration was fresh that she almost didn't notice the strange car parked in her driveway. Since the sun had already set, the only light was from fixtures that bracketed the garage. Deciding to err on the side of caution, Rose parked by the curb instead up pulling alongside the car. The slightly tinted windows made it difficult for her to see the person sitting in the driver's seat, but something about the silhouette was eerily familiar. Telling Edgar to stay, she stepped out just as the other car's door opened. What she heard next sent a chill down her spine.

"Hello, Rose."

A voice she would never forget.

"Louise."

Chapter Twenty-Two

"**G**O HOME, JACK."

Jack sighed. There had to be something wrong with a man who had a beautiful woman on his arm and she did her best to get rid of him.

Karen Poe was a screen goddess. If ever there was a woman that men wanted to sleep with and women wanted to be, it was Karen. She was also funny, smart, and very observant.

"You did your duty; no one attacked me or even looked at me wrong. You even earned yourself a whole new group of female admirers. Not that you seem terribly interested." She flashed him her million-dollar smile. "Now get on that fancy plane of yours and *go home*."

Jack wanted nothing more. He had flown down to Los Angeles that morning. Karen hadn't needed to leave for the theater until that evening, so he did what Drew had suggested and called an old friend. Alan 'Buster' Loring had been one of the most feared linebackers in college football. Jack had always been grateful that they were on the same team. After four years of playing in the NFL, one too many concussions had ended his professional career and he was now making his first movie. Jack couldn't think of anyone better suited to the action film genre. He was a big man with an even bigger personality. Fans were going to love him.

"Looking good, my friend." Buster greeted him with a bone-crushing hug. His shooting schedule wouldn't let him get away for long so they were having lunch on the set. Wardrobe had Buster dressed in a torn t-shirt and dusty jeans, his muscles strategically smeared with blood and grease.

"You look like you lost a fight with a what, a time traveling cyborg?"

Buster laughed. "Close enough, except I didn't lose. Now tell me what brings you to L.A.?"

"I'm here for Karen Poe's movie premiere."

"Right, time to trot out the old bodyguard persona. Karen Poe, huh? Now there's a lovely lady. I don't suppose you'd introduce me?"

"Sure." Buster was one of the good guys and stopping to think about it, Jack thought he would be a good match for Karen. "But you do know that, movie star to movie star, it would be an easy thing for you to meet her anytime you want. You don't need me to play middle man."

"I thought it might be less creepy if the introduction came from a mutual friend. Someone we've both known for a while."

For all his swagger and tough talk, Buster was at heart a southern gentleman. He treated women with the utmost respect. Considering some of the bums Karen had been involved with, Jack was more than happy to play his small part in their potential romance.

Later that night, movie over, they were at the after party and Jack was not having a good time. Normally, he didn't mind dressing in a tuxedo. Tonight, the tie was close to strangling him and his shoes pinched. His skin felt too tight on his frame, almost as though something in the material of his suit had caused it to shrink. He felt miserable and if he could believe Karen, he looked even worse. By ten, he was past ready to leave. He was only still there because he was waiting until Buster arrived. Wrangling a last minute invitation for an up-and-coming movie star had been a breeze, so Jack thought tonight would be the perfect opportunity to introduce his two friends.

"If you aren't going to leave, at least stand someplace else. You're frightening everyone."

"I thought that was the point. Big, bad bodyguard equals look but don't touch."

"Do you want to tell me about her?" Karen squeezed his arm, her eyes full of sympathy. I figured that she would guess what his problem was, especially when the last thing he wanted to do was talk about it.

Even so, Jack almost caved. Karen was a friend and a woman. Maybe she would have some insight, some words of wisdom to help relieve the growing frustration that of late had become his constant companion. Jack was just about to spill his guts when he saw Buster waving at him from across the room. Just as well, Karen probably would have sided with Rose. Wouldn't that have added to his pissed off attitude?

"I appreciate the offer, Karen." She didn't look convinced. "I'll let you know if I change my mind. But right now there's someone I'd like you to meet."

As it turned out, Buster didn't need Jack at all. After a brief introduction, Karen and Buster drifted off as though he wasn't even there. In fact, they didn't seem to be aware of anyone else in the room. Jack watched for a minute. *They look good together*, he thought. *Right*. Was that how he looked when he was with Rose? Enthralled, besotted? A complete goner?

Jack glanced at his watch. Ten-thirty, it was a little late to fly home tonight. He'd be better off catching a few hours' sleep and then getting an early start in the morning. He looked at his friends again. Buster beamed and Karen stared up at him as if he was the only man on earth. And that's when he knew. He wasn't giving up. What he and Rose had was worth fighting for. It might take some time and patience, but he was going to do his damndest to make Rose believe it too.

Chapter Twenty-Three

"YOU'VE BEEN A very bad girl, Rose.

Those words, that voice. She used to hear both in her nightmares. It had been a long time since her subconscious had let Louise slip past the barriers Rose had erected. Just the whisper of that voice used to bring back the horrors associated with it, making her relive everything over and over again. Then when she awoke, it would all be fresh in her mind, as though the time between the past and the present had been days instead of years.

"I tried calling you but the number seems to have been disconnected." Rose almost gagged at the sugary sweet words. "Now why would you have done that?"

Rose could feel the familiar cold move over her body, telling her that even though she couldn't run, she *could* stop feeling. This time was different. She wouldn't let Louise win, not again. *Think of Jack,* her mind cried. *Jack is love. Love is warmth.* It was those thoughts that pulled her back. She wasn't a helpless child anymore. She knew how to fight.

For the first time, Rose looked at Louise, *really* looked at her. Over the years, she had built the woman into a larger-than-life villain but in reality, she was a head shorter than Rose was. In a fight, she would be able to snap her like a brittle twig. Feeling stronger, in control, Rose pulled her shoulders back and looked at Louise directly in the eye. It didn't matter why she was here; Rose was done playing her victim.

"Go back to whatever hole you crawled out of, Louise. There's nothing here for you."

Rose turned to let Edgar out and get them both into the house, but Louise wasn't giving up that easily.

"I was thinking how nice it would be if I moved to this quaint little town. Wouldn't it be wonderful if we could see each other every day?"

"Cut the crap, Louise." Rose's voice was strong and steady. "You don't want to live in Harper Falls. So tell me what this is about. And make it quick; my patience is wearing thin."

The surprise was obvious on Louise's face. She obviously hadn't expected any opposition.

"Very well, if you insist on skipping the niceties." Louise dragged out the last word. They both knew there had never been *anything* nice between them. "I'm a little down at the moment and since you wouldn't miss it, I want one hundred thousand dollars."

The amount didn't stagger her, but the woman's gall came close to doing so. Rose felt another burst of energizing heat surge through her body, clearing her mind, and sharpening her vision. Louise *did* look frayed around the edges. Her clothing was a bit wrinkled, her shoes more bargain basement than couture. It appeared her last fiancé had seen the light before she could get him down the aisle. If Rose had been meeting her for the first time, she might have felt some sympathy for her. A woman alone, few options left. But this was Louise. She was never alone for long and she always had a plan. Now, that plan appeared to be hitting Rose up for a hefty chunk of money.

"You do seem to need my help." Rose reached into her purse and took out a pen and her checkbook. The light from the nearby lamppost caught the satisfied, predatory gleam in Louise's eyes. Using the hood of her car for stability, Rose wrote quickly, she just wanted to put any end to this farce. She ripped the paper out and handed it to Louise.

"Now that wasn't so difficult, was it?" Louise was delighted. It was the easiest money she'd ever made. She practically quivered with excitement as she looked down at her salvation.

"What the hell is this?"

Rose imagined that three-octave shriek must have had the entire neighborhood looking out their windows.

"That is the name of a realtor in town who handles apartment rentals. He should be able to recommend some decent low-income housing, just until you get back on your feet."

Rose opened the car door and attached Edgar's lead. As always, he was as delighted to get out, as he had been to get in. Not bothering to put her car in the garage, Rose headed for her front door. She walked by Louise without a glance. She couldn't imagine that the woman would stay in Harper Falls, but if she did, Rose was finally past caring.

"I know where your father is."

She stopped, her head slumping forward. Louise had one final card to play. Up until that moment, Rose had been proud of the way she'd handled things. She'd gone from icy cold dread to hot indignation, and finally to an almost Zen-like acceptance. The bitch had finally done it; she'd unleashed angry Rose. Louise was not going to like her when she was angry.

She bent down and whispered to Edgar, "Stay here, baby. This will only take a minute."

"Did you hear what I said?"

"You stupid, crazy harpy." Rose rounded on her with such force that Louise stumbled back against her car. "The fact that you even have the nerve to show your face to me is bad enough. Then to ask me for money? Unbelievable. But to bring my father into this? Whatever sanity that you've been clinging to all these years must have finally completely deserted you."

Desperate to somehow salvage the situation, Louise drew herself up and gave Rose a look that at one time would have had her shaking with fear. Now it only added fuel to her fire. Louise ignored the warning signs and pushed on.

"Your mother never was woman enough for him." Louise ran a

bony hand down her side as if illustrating what men really wanted. Rose wondered if the woman had looked in the mirror lately. "He only married her because she got herself pregnant and he thought he should do the right thing. It didn't take much effort on my part to convince him that he'd made a mistake. We spent a glorious month in Aruba. I believe your mother pushed you out around that time."

Louise hoped her gouging words would open old wounds; she wanted to draw blood. Rose barely felt a twinge. The only reason she didn't walk away was morbid curiosity. How far would this woman go? How much lower could she sink?

"We still see each other from time to time. He's an amazing lover. I don't have to tell you about amazing lovers. Jack Winston would keep any woman satisfied. Did he tell you about my little visit?"

With that, Rose had her answer. Louise was *incapable* of hitting bottom; she just kept slithering down to new depths of awful.

"Enough." Rose cut the other woman off before she could continue. "These will be the last words I ever plan to say to you, so listen carefully. First, I don't know what kind of sick dynamic went on between my mother, father, and you. I do know that you all deserved each other. As for you knowing where I can find *dear old dad?* As far as I'm concerned, you can take that little secret to the grave. Don't you think if I'd wanted to find him I would have? The last thing I need is another narcissistic parasite in my life."

Rose watched Louise struggle to comprehend what was happening. It was all slipping away and this time there was no pulling it back. One more snip and Rose would be free for good.

"As for Jack? You never had a shot and the fact that you would insinuate otherwise amazes me. Jack wouldn't do that to me. I know loyalty is a foreign concept to you, but believe me, it does exist." Rose felt her anger draining away. Louise wasn't worth the energy. "But just for argument sake, let's say you'd met him before he knew me. Unlike so many women, you haven't gotten better with age. You reek of desperation. It rolls off you in sickening, unctuous waves. Jack wouldn't touch you; he could barely stand to be in the same room with you. As for me? Even out here, the stink of you is too much. It's over, Louise. *We-Are-Done.*" Rose picked up Edgar's lead; this time determined that nothing would stop her from getting into the house. She hadn't gone three steps when Louise let out an ear-splitting scream.

"Police! Someone, please. I've been viciously attacked. Someone call the police."

Rose didn't bother to look back. "I'll be happy to dial 911. But we've had an audience for the last half hour. You can try pressing your bogus charges, but I'm very friendly with my neighbors and they no doubt will be more than happy to testify on my behalf."

She put the key in the lock when she heard the slam of a car door. The motor protested once and then coughed to life. What followed was the sound of screeching tires. It signaled the end of Louise. That part of her life was finally over.

"No looking back, Edgar. My future is wide open, and I plan on living it with you and Jack."

Edgar followed her into the house. He didn't care about the drama that had just unfolded. He was with Rose, and she was happy. The only thing missing was Jack. Edgar knew he would be back soon. Jack never left for long. He made a circle in his bed and settled with a contented sigh. Rose and Jack, and Edgar — perfect.

ROSE WAITED FOR the crash. She had been up for almost twenty-four hours straight. In that time, she had fallen in love — or finally admitted it, had the long overdue confrontation with Louise, which by itself should have left her feeling like a wrung out dish rag. And to top it off, she had spent the last twelve hours pouring her heart and soul into the song she'd almost decided she couldn't write. When she picked up her guitar and played the first few notes, the words flowed out like the water from a gentle stream. Like Jack's favorite stream. The place where he'd shared his childhood dreams. Where they had made sweet love under the sheltering oak as a warm spring rain fell on them.

Twenty-four hours of emotional turmoil and she still rode an adrenaline high the likes of which she'd never known. She fed Edgar, and then let him out to run around and do his morning business. She then ran upstairs to take a quick shower. After she had dried off and put on a pair of leggings and a loose cotton pullover, she checked the clock. Eight-fifteen. More than anything, she wanted to call Jack and tell him everything. About the song, about Louise — about how much she loved him. But he wasn't due back from Los Angeles for a few more days and those were things that she needed to say to him in person. So instead, she called Paris.

"What!" Sam Laughton sounded out of breath and in pain. He grunted again and let out a whoosh of air. Whatever was going on sounded horrible.

"Sam, are you all right?"

"No," he grunted again. "My trainer is a sadist. Enough Monique; I think we've kept my flab at bay for another few days."

Monique? Of course, Sam *would* have a woman trainer.

"Sorry about that, Rose. My schedule has been so crazy that I have to fit my workouts in whenever I can. By the way, what time is it there?"

"Almost eight-thirty. You know, in the morning." All of a sudden, her nerves jangled around in her stomach and as usual, her mouth was overcompensating with inane comments.

"Since this is the first time you've initiated any contact with me in a few weeks can I assume that you have some good news?"

"It's done, Sam." She was glad he couldn't see her little happy dance. "When it finally came, it came in a rush. I had the words in less than an hour and then I polished a bit and recorded the background and vocals, and if you check your email, you can listen to the finished product."

"Impressive. Now, take a breath and relax. And no more caffeine.

"No caffeine here. I'm riding a natural high."

"Right," Sam sighed with exasperation. Artists, colossal pains in the ass, every one of them

Rose waited impatiently while Sam went to his office and opened the email attachment. She could hear the familiar opening chords. She paced back and forth for the next three minutes and forty-three seconds, now and then reminding herself to breathe. Then there was nothing but silence. Did he hate it? Love it? *Say something, damn it.*

"Where the hell did that come from?"

"Now see here, Sam. That is the best thing I've ever written — no contest. I thought you were supposed to know your stuff but obviously…"

"I meant," Sam's voice was barely below a yell, effectively cutting off Rose's rant. "Where have you been hiding this side of you? I'm familiar with all your work, Rose. I agree that not only is this the best thing you've ever written, it's also one of the best original songs I've heard in all the years I've been in the business. Congratulations, *Unconditional* is exactly the anchor the movie needs. You have yourself a standard; this song is going to be around for a long, long time."

Rose was floored. She knew it was good, but Sam's response was beyond anything she had expected. "It means a lot to hear you say that."

"Just don't get used to the hearts and flowers. I still need you here in Paris. When can I expect you?"

"You don't *need* me there, Sam." She had worked with some stubborn control freak producers in her time, but Sam Laughton put the others to shame. "But if I do come, it won't be until next week and I'll only be able to stay for a few days." She would have added that she wasn't coming alone, but she couldn't speak for Jack. She hoped he'd want to come with her for a mini-vacation but nothing was settled between them, and until it was, she didn't want to make any plans.

"I'll need you for more than a few days but we'll talk once you get here."

"I mean it, Sam, a few days at the most. Now if that's all, I have a dog who's probably wondering what happened to me."

"Wait, one more thing."

"Yes?"

"Your voice is amazing. Why the hell aren't you recording your songs? I want you to sign with me and—"

"No, Sam." Not in this lifetime or any other.

"With your looks and voice? Are you crazy?"

"Goodbye, Sam."

"Rose, don't hang up." Sam was incredulous. Nobody in her right mind turned down a chance like this. "At least think about it."

"No."

Rose ended the call before Sam could shoot out another offer. She had to admit it *had* been a killer demo. She had put everything into that vocal track. Her voice had contained a rich, vibrant, quality that had never been there before. What Sam didn't understand — and what she would never be able to explain — was that when she had recorded the song it had taken on a life of its own. For a few minutes only, she had been its willing vessel. She also knew without a doubt that she would never sound like that again. Some things you couldn't duplicate and, in this case, it was better not to try.

Rose scrubbed her hands over her face. There it was. She felt a heaviness to her movements. She was close to running on empty, but she still needed to do a few things before crawling into bed and shutting down for a few hours.

"Edgar." She called when he didn't come running. He was usually there the moment he heard the door open. The backyard wasn't a big enough area for the rapidly growing dog to get lost in or hide if he was so inclined. A little worried, Rose walked down the path to the little nook on the side of the house. The only place she couldn't see from the deck. Though it didn't seem likely Edgar would be over there, she went to look.

As she drew closer, she heard an odd noise. Not a whimper or a growl but a combination of the two. She hurried around the corner afraid that he might have somehow hurt himself. What she found stopped her in her tracks.

"Oh, Edgar."

There he was, his once clean brown and white fur now matted with mud. He had found an old bucket that Rose used when she gardened. During the last rain, it must have filled with water and Edgar had tipped it over into a recently tilled but unplanted flowerbed. After that, he was in puppy heaven. It looked like he'd dug himself a nice hole and then rolled around, covering himself from nose to tail in the wet dirt. He was a sight to see.

Edgar raised his head and sniffed the air; he knew that scent. He turned to Rose, grinning ear to ear. She had time to notice two quick things before the big, filthy dirtball smothered her. One, if his dark brown teeth were any indication, he must have eaten as much of the mud as he rolled in. And two, it was hard to be a stern disciplinarian with an adoring dog licking you.

Rose indulged Edgar and herself, rolling around with him for several minutes. By the time she finally called a halt to playtime, he had transferred at least half of the mud onto her

"We both need a bath." Edgar didn't look convinced. "Listen, fella, it will be my second of the day, so you're getting off lightly. First, I think we need to record this for posterity. Stay here."

Rose ran to get her phone then returned to find Edgar right where she'd left him.

"That's my good boy." She knelt down beside him. "Say *big juicy bone.*" Then she took their picture. Rose laughed as she showed it to Edgar, deciding to take his wagging tail as a sign of his approval. "We make a pretty photogenic pair. I think we need to share this one."

Rose typed a quick text, attached the picture, and hit send.

"That's done. No more procrastination, my friend. Bath time and you're first."

JACK WAS GLAD to be home. The flight from Los Angeles to Spokane had been smooth and uneventful, as had the landing and subsequent drive to Harper Falls. Normally he would have gone straight home but the idea of facing an empty house wasn't terribly appealing. He decided to stop at H&W first to check in with Drew and pick up Edgar. He didn't know if Rose had missed him, but he could count on his dog for an enthusiastic welcome.

As he pulled up in front of the office, Jack reached inside his jacket to get his phone and check his messages. He always turned it off when he flew, and since he'd jumped right in his SUV after landing, this was the first time he'd looked at it all morning. He scrolled through the list of missed calls and texts not seeing anything that was urgent. Then he saw that Rose had sent him a text about two hours ago. He got out and leaned back against the closed door. How bad could it be? Rose wouldn't end their relationship with a text. Bracing himself for the worst, he opened it.

Under a picture of Rose and Edgar, both grinning and both very muddy, it read, "See the trouble we get into when you're not around? Come home soon." It was simply signed Edgar.

Jack started to laugh. The heavy fog of doom and gloom that had surrounded him for the past two days lifted and he felt like he could breathe again. He looked at the picture again. What *had* they been up to? Feeling energized, Jack grabbed the door handle and swung it open. Checking in with Drew could wait, he decided suddenly. He had someplace a lot more important to be.

"Must be nice to have something to laugh about. Huh, Jack?"

His mind occupied with thoughts of getting to Rose, Jack hadn't heard Craig Lowe's approach. He'd let his guard down long enough for the man to get close — too close. But he *did* see the knife and felt it as it sliced into his flesh.

Chapter Twenty-Four

"WELL, I THINK you smell great. Tell him, Tyler."

Rose had finally gotten both herself and Edgar mud-free and it had been easier than she'd anticipated. The dog had taken being dowsed with water from the hose and soaped up with lavender-scented shampoo with amazing good grace. It was only now, after the fact that he seemed to be having second thoughts about how he smelled. Maybe she spent too much time with him, attributing him with assets he didn't possess, but Rose got the feeling that Edgar wasn't terribly thrilled with the less than manly fragrance. Tyler and Dani had arrived just in time to keep him company while she jumped in the shower for the second time that morning. She walked into the living room just as Dani was reassuring the dog.

"Edgar, unlike my friends here, I don't think you care one way or the other about smelling like flowers." Tyler grinned as the dog laid his head on her knee and stared at her with soulful eyes. "You're just missing the mud. You put in all that effort and then Rose goes and washes it off. *That's* the indignity."

"Was it just last week that you two were giving me a hard time about talking to Edgar? Now I find you carrying on a conversation with him. What gives?"

Dani took one of the cups of tea that Rose had brought with her. "He asked me a question. It would have been impolite not to answer."

"He asked you?" Handing Tyler a cup, Rose joined her on the sofa.

"With his eyes."

"Right. And what's your excuse?" she asked her other friend.

"I don't know what she's talking about, do you, Edgar?" Tyler leaned down until she was almost nose-to-nose with the dog.

"I wouldn't do that unless you want—"

Rose's warning was too late. Edgar considered Tyler's gesture to be an open invitation and he took full advantage by giving her face a big, wet swipe with his tongue.

Tyler sat back and grimaced. "And this is what I get for being on your side." She declined the tissue Rose offered. "That's not going to cut it. I need a trip to the bathroom and some anti-bacterial soap. And before you say anything," she addressed Edgar. "I know your mouth supposedly has fewer germs than those guys I let kiss me. But I'm not buying it."

Unconcerned, Edgar trotted over to his bed and settled in for a nap. After all, he'd had a very busy and exhausting morning.

"So, how are things going with you?" Spit-free, Tyler sat back down and turned to Rose.

"Great, never better." Rose grinned when she saw the look Tyler and Dani gave each other. "Okay, in order of importance, here is what has happened to me since the last time we spoke. I realized that I'm in love with Jack, I finished the song for *Wishes,* and I finally had my long overdue confrontation with Louise."

Before either Tyler or Dani could react to the information overload, Rose heard the ringtone she'd assigned to Jack. As she snatched up the phone, she said to her friends, "Hold those thoughts. I have to take this. Jack? I'm so happy you called."

"It's not Jack, Rose."

"Drew? Why are you calling me on Jack's phone?" Rose had a sudden sinking feeling. "What happened?" She asked the question as calmly as she could. Her heart raced and she wanted to scream but she held it together, waiting unti Drew answered.

"Jack's been stabbed." Rose couldn't make a sound; she just gripped the phone. She could tell that Drew was trying to keep the panic out of his voice. "I got him to the hospital as quickly as possible. He never lost consciousness; that's a good sign. They took him into one of the examining rooms as soon as we got here and then I called you."

"I'll be right there." Rose hung up and jumped to her feet. Her legs felt like rubber, but sheer will kept her upright. Rushing to grab her keys, there was only one thought in her head — get to Jack.

"Rose, what is it?" Dani had watched Rose's face turn an alarming stark white.

"Hospital, Jack." Her hand shook so badly that she couldn't open the door to the garage. Tyler and Dani had rushed after her as soon as they heard the word hospital.

Dani reached around her shaking friend and opened the door. She took the car keys from Rose and handed them to Tyler. "Drive her to the hospital. I'll make sure Edgar has enough food and water in case no one can get back for a while. Then I'll be right behind you."

Rose let Tyler take over. She sat in the car and watched the houses fly by, her mind running in a hundred different directions. What, how, where, when? When it came down to it, only one thing mattered — Jack had to be all right, not for her. She would walk away without a backward glance and never see him again, if it meant he would live a long and healthy life. Unfortunately, she knew that wasn't how it worked. No amount of self-sacrificing promises would guarantee Jack's well-being. She didn't waste her energy on such foolishness. *Jack was not going to die.* She wouldn't allow herself to think anything else.

Rose had the door open before Tyler could bring the car to a full stop. "Jesus, Rose, the last thing we need is for you to break a leg." But she was talking to air. Rose was already through the hospital doors and running towards the reception desk.

"Rose, over here."

She turned at the sound of her name. Drew was waiting and he took her arm, leading her down the hallway to their right.

"Have you heard anything yet?" She wondered if she looked as wild-eyed as Drew did. His white shirt had a large brownish stain on it. Was it blood? *Jack's* blood?

Drew was just about to answer when a voice boomed from a nearby room.

"Just give me a goddamned local and stitch the fucker up so I can get out of here."

"I guess we both heard *that*." He picked her up and swung her around. Relief washed over them and for a moment, they just clung to each other, no words necessary.

"You're smiling, so it must be good news."

Drew gently transferred Rose over to Tyler. He met her eyes and for once, they weren't filled with anger.

"If the strength of his voice is any indication, I'd say he's going to be fine." Rose gave a shaky laugh. "But just to be sure, let's wait and hear what the doctor has to say."

"Hey," Tyler lifted Rose's chin. "You're crying."

"Second time in two days." Rose wiped at her cheeks with both hands. "Dani was right; it does release a lot of pressure, but I hope I don't start making a habit of it."

They only had to wait a few more minutes for the doctor to come out and fill them in.

"Your friend was very lucky. Another inch to the right and the knife would have sliced into his kidney. Instead, he has a relatively minor wound that should heal with no complications. We would like to keep him awhile longer for observation, but he's insisting on being released. Perhaps one of you could try and convince him to stay." The doctor looked between the two women. "Rose?"

"That's me." Rose took a step forward.

"His biggest concern seems to be getting home to you. But since you're here, he might be willing to listen to reason."

"Not likely," Drew scoffed.

"I'll do my best, doctor."

Rose felt like she was floating. She would have sworn her feet never touched the ground on her way to Jack. Suddenly remembering the rush from her house to the hospital, she paused for a moment outside the door to smooth down her hair. Chiding herself for being ridiculous, she forgot about her appearance and entered the room.

Jack looked — well, he looked like Jack. A little haggard, a bit pale, but still bristling with an impatient energy. Rose suddenly felt a little shaky again, but this time with it was with relief. She'd heard him bellowing and the doctor confirmed that he would be fine. None of that had seemed quite real until now. Seeing him for herself finally put her fears to rest.

"You need to be a good boy and listen to your doctor or you won't be getting your lollypop."

"Rose." Jack sighed. When had just the sight of her become so important? He had been desperate to get to her, to let her know that he was fine; to tell her he was coming home. Now there was no more desperation. Rose was here — he *was* home.

Afraid of hurting him, Rose tamped down on her instinct that would have had her rushing into his arms and holding on for dear life. Instead, she let herself be satisfied with taking one of his strong hands in hers.

"You scared me."

Jack gave her hand a lingering kiss. "I'd like to be all manly and say it was no big deal but truthfully, I was pretty scared myself."

Rose brought his hand up to return his kiss. "Well, at least you'll have a nice manly scar." She tried to keep the catch out of her voice but failed miserably. Everything was still too fresh. She could make snappy quips, but it was impossible to ignore the large bandage that covered his side.

"Oh, sweetheart," Jack said gently. "All's good. Really."

The nurse came back in to do some clean-up. "If you're feeling up to it, the police would like to take your statement now, Mr. Winston."

"Should I go?"

"No." Jack kept hold of her hand. "I know you want to hear what happened. I'd prefer only to tell it once."

It wouldn't take long. The security cameras outside H&W headquarters had recorded the entire incident, so Jack only had to fill in a few of the details.

"I was in the parking lot just outside of our office checking the messages on my phone. I wasn't paying attention, so I didn't hear when Craig approached me. We had fired him a few weeks ago and apparently, he blames me for his life going to hell. I saw the knife and was able to turn sideways, but I wasn't able to knock it away before he stabbed me. He came at me again, but this time I blocked his arm and punched him in the face. He fell to the ground and that's when my partner, Drew Harper, arrived and made sure Craig stayed down." Actually Drew had beaten the crap out of Craig but since the police officer didn't correct him, Jack left that part out.

"Drew secured Craig with cable ties. Our assistant Pam had called 911, and since we could hear the sirens, we left Craig, and Drew got me into his car and brought me to the hospital. That's about all I can tell you, officer."

"You had an altercation with Craig Lowe at a local bar around the time you fired him, is that right?"

"No, that isn't right." Rose knew the man was only doing his job, but couldn't he see that Jack was running on fumes? "Couldn't the rest of your questions wait, officer? Jack needs to get some rest."

"And you are?"

"Rose O'Brian." She leaned over and watched him write her name. "No, Brian is spelled *ia* not *ie*, and you should capitalize the b." It didn't really matter, but the police officer pissed her off.

Jack hid his grin. He was all for Rose standing up for him, but what he wanted was to finish and get out of here.

"I'm fine. Rose is right, officer. There wasn't any altercation. In fact, neither Drew nor I even talked to Craig that night. He'd had too much to drink, which is a problem for him, and pretty much fell on his face. One of the men who works security for H&W saw that he got home safely. That was it. The last time I saw him was the day we fired him."

"And how did that go?"

"He seemed to take it well." Which was the truth. Craig hadn't even raised his voice. "I never thought there would be any trouble. Today came out of the blue."

"Well, that should do it." The police officer closed his notebook and put it away. "Lowe is in custody and we have the security tapes. We shouldn't have any more questions but if we do, we'll call you."

"I always hate when witnesses get snippy with the police on TV shows but from now on I'm going to be a lot more sympathetic."

"Would it do any good if I pointed out the obvious?"

Rose knew what he was going to say. "He may be doing his job, and he may be very good at it. But you were stabbed, and you've lost a lot of blood, and all I want to do is get you home and take care of you. He was stopping me."

"Delaying," Jack pointed out. But what she wanted sounded like heaven. "I asked the nurse to have Drew get the paperwork going for my discharge so it shouldn't take much longer."

"The doctor says you should stay awhile for observation." Rose did want to get Jack home, but his health was the most important thing.

"There is no way in hell I'm staying in this hospital any longer than necessary. Especially if you meant it when you said you wanted to take me home."

"And take care of you." Rose planned on tucking him up in that great big bed of hers and keeping him all to herself for as long as possible. "I sort of stole your dog while you were away. If you want to see him, you'll *have* to come home with me."

"That's right. I got Edgar's text. He looked like he was having so much fun I don't know if he'll ever want to leave."

The text. Jack had said he'd been checking his phone when Craig attacked him. Had the text distracted him so much that the psycho had been able to sneak up and stab him?

"No," Jack said firmly.

"You don't know what I was thinking."

"You're blaming yourself for distracting me."

Rose sighed. He didn't have to look so smug. "I thought we'd established that Edgar sent the text."

"Well, it isn't Edgar's fault either. The mistake is that it's too easy for just anybody to drive up to the office. After that whole female invasion debacle, Drew and I should have changed the system. From now on, all unauthorized visitors will have to stop at the gate. Craig never should have been there. Add to the fact that he was half-drunk and had a huge chip on his shoulder. Sweetheart, it was a shit storm just waiting to happen."

"You think it's your fault that he was drunk?" Rose was ready to argue that point.

"No." Jack frowned. "I meant I should have been able to handle him better in the first place. I'm bigger and stronger, and my brain isn't permanently pickled."

"But he had the knife." Rose wasn't going to forget that fact anytime soon.

Jack just looked at her. They both knew how lucky he was to be there; even the doctor had said so. There was no argument for that.

"Look at you." Drew came in the room with what Rose assumed were the discharge papers. "I'm starting to wonder what all the fuss was about. I came in here expecting to see you all weak and helpless. Instead, you're lounging around flirting with a beautiful woman."

Rose left the men alone and went out to the waiting area. Tyler and Dani looked up as she approached.

"He's going to be all right?" Dani had arrived about thirty minutes behind them. By that time, Rose was in with Jack and all the drama was thankfully over.

"Yes. Jack is insisting on being discharged. As soon as the doctor gives the final okay, he should be able to leave." She hugged her friends, grateful for their support.

"But what I want to know is," Dani said slyly, "how did Tyler get along with Drew while you were in with Jack?"

Rose and Dani both crossed their arms and waited for an answer.

"Rose cried." Tyler threw that little nugget onto the field hoping to turn the focus away from her. It worked, temporarily.

"What?" Dani exclaimed. "When did this happen?"

"When we found out Jack was going to be okay. So yes, it appears the flood gates have opened and I will now be crying at every greeting card commercial. Have your tissues at the ready. Enough about me. Tyler hasn't answered your question. Drew wasn't limping when he came into Jack's room so it couldn't have been too bad."

"He's ready to go now, Rose."

Tyler gave a sigh of relief. For the first time in ten years, Tyler was glad to see Drew walk into a room.

"Don't think you're getting out of it that easily," Rose whispered as she passed. "Something happened between you and Drew and I plan on finding out what it was. The next time we all meet at the coffee shop, be prepared to spill."

Drew moved aside so that Rose could push Jack's wheelchair towards the exit. He reached back and grasped her hand.

"Take me home, sweetheart."

Chapter Twenty-Five

"**A**RE YOU COMFORTABLE? Maybe you should be up in bed instead of down here on the couch. Are you hungry? The doctor's instructions say you should eat something when you take the pain medication, but you said you didn't need any yet. Are you going to let me keep on rambling or are you going to answer one of my questions?"

"I was waiting for you to wind down," Jack teased.

Other than lifting his arms to let her remove his shirt, and stepping out of his pants as she lowered them to the floor, Rose hadn't let him move a muscle since they'd gotten to her house. Not that he had any complaints. Sitting in nothing but his underwear and having a beautiful woman fuss over him was no hardship. He enjoyed the attention and she needed an outlet for her lingering anxiety. She'd already tucked in his blanket and fluffed his pillows half a dozen times. Enough was enough. They both needed to settle, preferably here and now, and together.

"Rose." Jack let her set down the cup of tea he didn't want, but she'd insisted on making. "Rose, sweetheart. Sit by me." He patted the cushion next to him. "Edgar and I are getting dizzy watching you."

Actually, after his initial excitement over Jack's return, Edgar had fallen asleep and was peacefully snoring in his corner.

"I don't want to disturb your wound."

"That's why I want you to sit on this side." He gave the seat another brief pat.

"Okay, but only if you promise to tell me if you're in any pain."

Rose carefully lowered herself so that she was perched on the very edge of the couch. Jack would have laughed at how silly she looked, but he didn't think Rose was currently finding much humor in the situation.

"If I have to pull you down next to me, I just *might* hurt myself. Now slide back and put your head right here." He indicated his right shoulder.

She eased into his embrace, inhaling the scent of antiseptic and warm man. Rose laid her hand on his chest and felt the steady beat of his heart. With a grateful sigh, she fully relaxed for the first time since she'd received Drew's phone call. Jack lifted the blanket so that it covered them both, and before they knew it, they had drifted off to sleep in each other's arms.

Rose moaned. In her dream, Jack's mouth teased that spot just below her ear, the one that only he could find, the one that drove her from interested to fully aroused in record time. She moved her head to the side so that he could have better access. Then he bit down. She'd never climaxed while dreaming, but this time she was close. Just a little harder, she urged silently, and she would topple like a row of dominoes.

"Can I make you come just by biting your neck?"

Rose's eyes popped open. As much as she would have loved to have him continue, now wasn't the time to find out just how talented his mouth was.

"No, Jack."

"No? Are you sure? Because I'm willing to wager pretty big that I can do it."

"I'm sure you can and at some future date, I'd be happy to let you show me." Rose slowly pulled back, away from temptation. "But right now, you need to keep still and stop trying to seduce me."

"Sweetheart." Jack tried to pull her back, but Rose just slapped his hand away.

"I mean it, Jack. You are in no condition for anything as strenuous as sex. Do you want to have to tell the doctor at the emergency room that your wound opened up because you couldn't keep your *you know what* in your pants?"

"First of all, I don't think I'd have to say *you know what* in front of the doctor." Jack took advantage of her reluctance to hurt him and brought her back into his arms. "And second, you saying the word penis won't make it magically jump out of my pants."

"I just want you to be a good boy and keep still." Being in his arms felt so good Rose didn't want to move so she snuggled closer. "If you don't, I'll have to move and I don't want to do that."

"Then I'll just sit here and let you do all the work."

"Are you crazy?" You had to give the guy points for perseverance.

"I'm not going to get any rest in this condition." His erection was killing him and he needed relief, immediately.

"Then let me give you a helping hand."

"It *is* crazy, Rose, but right now I need to celebrate life. With you. *Inside* of you."

"You can't do any moving, Jack." Rose knew this was a bad idea, but she couldn't say no to him, she didn't want to say no. She slowly eased his shorts over his hips. "Swear to me, or I'm stopping right now."

With her straddling him, his penis brushing her wet, slick center? He would have promised her anything.

"Don't make me beg, Rose."

His fingers dug into her hips as she lowered herself inch by agonizing inch. Finally, when she had taken all he had to give, she held herself completely still. Rose looked deeply in Jack's eyes willing him to see what she'd yet to say out loud. How could he not? It was all there. The way she *wanted* him. The way she *needed* him. The way she *loved* him.

Rose's eyes glowed, becoming molten amber right in front of him. However, there was something more. Something was in the depths that Jack had caught a fleeting glimpse of before but had never quite been able to hold onto it. This time every emotion shined bright and clear — every bit of it just for him.

"That's right, Jack." Rose moved ever so slightly, tightening her inner muscles around his pulsing length. "Look at me. Everything I have is yours. Take it, take *me*."

Jack groaned; her words having as much effect as her exquisite body. Yes, everything was his. Rose moved in a slow, steady rhythm. It all felt so close — his release — Rose. His eyes stayed locked with hers — as clear and blue as the ocean. But his mind became fuzzy and all he could think about was how perfectly she fit him. How when she moved, it was like nothing he'd ever known. He was there, at the edge, and he could tell that Rose was with him. As they tumbled over together, he called out two words. "Rose! Everything!"

Rose leaned her forehead against Jack's and fought back the tears. Lord, she was becoming a weepy mess. Now wasn't the time. She needed to say the words. She needed to let Jack know with more than just her body that he wasn't alone. *He* was *her* everything.

Feeling Jack gingerly shift his body, Rose carefully eased herself away and then slid to her knees.

"Raise your arm, love." She felt Jack stiffen. Damn it, she never should have let him seduce her. She gently lifted the bandage to peak beneath. She couldn't see any blood, so that was good. It looked like they had been lucky, but she wasn't going to chance it again.

"Everything seems fine." She met his eyes, but the look in them made her frown. "Is something wrong? You look a little dazed. I knew making love was a bad idea. I hope you enjoyed it because that was the last time until your doctor tells us you're fit for strenuous activity. Now, let's get you upstairs and in bed for the night." She helped him to his feet. "Can you make it on your own? Jack nodded. "Good. You go ahead. I'll get Edgar settled for the night. Oh, my God. Edgar. Jack, we just made love in front of that poor, sweet puppy. I don't know whether to be embarrassed or horrified." She noticed that Jack hadn't moved. "Do you need some help after all? Let me get around to your good side and you can lean on me."

"No," Jack shook his head. "I can make it." He started up the stairs but only got halfway before he turned back. "Rose?"

"Yes?"

You said love three times. He looked down at her beautiful, smiling face and wanted desperately to ask her what it meant. But he couldn't do it, the words wouldn't come out.

"I'll see you upstairs."

"Okay. I'll only be a few minutes."

Jack's body moved slowly, but his mind raced. Rose *never* used the word love. They always had *sex*. Tonight she had called him love. *Raise your arm, love.* He'd been so stunned by her casual use of the word that she'd thought he was in pain. On top of that, she said *made love*. Not sex — love.

Jack went into the bathroom. He badly wanted a shower but that was out, so he ran the water until it was steaming and cleaned himself as well he could with soap and a washcloth. After brushing his teeth and giving his stiches a quick glance, he climbed under the covers and waited for Rose. He'd come back from California ready to fight for her, but nothing would make him happier than to skip the fighting and go straight to the loving. Did Rose love him? Had it just been a few slips of the tongue from the emotional events of the day?

"I'm pretty sure I was worried for nothing. Unless he was faking for my benefit, I think Edgar slept right though and didn't see what we were up to on the couch." Rose bent over and kissed his cheek. "You look nice and comfy." She set a glass of water and his pain pills next to him on the nightstand. "I know you're being all he-man and insisting you don't need those, but I brought them up just in case."

"Rose, I—"

"Do you want a pill?"

"No, you go ahead and get ready for bed."

Rose looked at him for a moment. Something was wrong, but she honestly had no idea what it was. When she came out several minutes later, Jack's eyes were closed, his breathing deep and even. Asleep. Rose shook her head with a smile. She'd known exactly what she was going to say. Why she loved him and how she wanted to spend the rest of her life showing him. All that could wait until tomorrow. Jack was here and safe. Right now, that was all that mattered.

She eased into bed trying hard not to disturb him. She adjusted the bedding, leaning over him to pull the blanket up over his shoulders. His face was inches from hers, so handsome and dear. *I love you, Jack.*

Jack's eyes slowly opened. "I love you, Rose."

Rose looked back at him, surprise written on her face. That was supposed to be her line. It didn't matter that he had beaten her to it. Jack loved her. Now it was her turn.

"Marry me, Jack."

This time Jack was the surprised one. He'd hoped that she would tell him she loved him too. He knew what a big step that was for Rose. Then his plan had been to make himself so indispensable that getting married would become a natural extension. It might have been a silly, outdated rhyme, but Jack had it in his head that "first came love, and then came marriage." Rose had it backward.

"Sweetheart, I know you got quite a scare today but I promise I'm not going anywhere. There's nothing I want more than to spend the rest of my life with you, but I don't want you to think you have to do this when you're not ready for it."

Rose smiled. She didn't blame him for questioning her motives; he had no way of knowing how her feelings had changed. "Do you remember the last time we talked about marriage? When I told you that there was only one reason I would ever marry you?"

Jack tried to swallow over the lump that had formed in his throat. He couldn't speak, so he just nodded.

"I said the only reason I would ever marry you was if I loved you. I do, Jack," she kissed him gently. "I love you with everything I am."

Jack felt as if his heart would fly out of his chest. He pulled her to him and kissed the tears from her cheeks. His Rose was crying. Their lips met again, sweet and loving. Taking her in his arms, he held on, never wanting to let go. It was all so new that he needed a minute to let everything sink in. The lump in his throat had vanished along with all his worries and doubts. Rose loved him.

"I have so much to tell you. Between the yogurt and the song and Louise, I don't know where to start."

Jack listened, throwing in a comment now and then.

"Yogurt? If I'd have known it would have that kind of effect on you, I would have stocked the entire fridge with the stuff weeks ago."

A few minutes later, "Damn straight I'm going with you to Paris. I trust you completely, but that Laughton guy is another matter altogether."

Finally, when she told him about Louise showing up here at the house, Jack was speechless. But not for long.

"Tell me you hit the crazy bitch."

"Nope." Rose snuggled closer. She felt so happy it almost didn't seem real. "But she left limping. I wish I'd had it out with her years ago."

"You weren't ready." Jack hated that Rose had gone through the confrontation with her aunt alone, but he also knew she was stronger for it.

"*You* gave me the strength, Jack." She stopped him when he would have protested. "It's true. When I first saw her, I felt that terrible familiar cold start to invade my body. All I wanted to do was shut down. Then I thought of you. Knowing I was able to love you sent a deep warmth radiating through me. Then I got angry, and it felt good. I had let that woman have too much power over me for too long."

She quickly told him the rest, wanting to put it all behind them so they would never have to mention that woman again. Rose hoped they'd seen the last of Louise. However, even if she came back, it wouldn't mean anything, not anymore. Happily, that chapter was over, once and for all.

"You never answered my question," Rose reminded him, many kisses later.

"Did you ask me a question?" Jack asked innocently. "I don't remember."

Smartass. Well, Rose decided, two could play at that game.

"You know I think you're right. I didn't ask you anything." She started to slide out of bed. "I don't know about you, but suddenly I'm starving. Can I get you anything?"

Rose expected Jack to stop her. Her steps slowed and she was almost out the door before Jack finally spoke up.

"I would love a pizza. It's not too late to get one delivered from *Mamma Joan's*. Oh," he added enjoying Rose's obvious frustration. "And get one of their house salads too. They make the best dressing."

"No problem." Rose turned away in a huff. That hadn't turned out the way she hoped.

"And Rose?"

What now? Bread sticks? Extra cheese?

"Will you marry me?"

Rose turned back, her smile beaming. Sitting next to him, she took his hands; her answer was simple and from the heart.

"Yes, Jack. I will marry you."

"Why?" He knew, but he wanted to hear it again.

"Because I love you."

Epilogue

PARIS WITH JACK had been amazing. They had stayed a week — Jack insisted. After all, he reasoned, even though they had both been there separately, how many times do you go to Paris for the *first time* with the one you love? Therefore, it made sense that once she had finished her work with Sam Laughton, they decided to stay a few extra days and enjoy the city.

Rose had always scoffed at the idea that Paris was any more magical if you were in love. Well, it was. The lights seemed brighter. The food was even more amazing, and everywhere they went, everything overflowed with romance. And the sex? Well, she'd never had sex in Paris before, but now that she and Jack were making love, it was better no matter where they did it.

However fantastic it had been, Rose was glad to be home. And home was now at Jack's house, or as he kept reminding her, *their* house. She loved her little cottage, but it made more sense for them to live up on Crossfire Hill. Jack's family would never fit in her old place and she wanted them to visit often. Then there was Edgar. He was still growing and needed all the space he could get.

Jack took her hand and led her up the steps to the front door. Rose stood by while he took care of disengaging the alarms. When she would have entered, Jack stopped her.

"I know that technically we're not married yet..." he swept her up and carried her across the threshold. Laughing, Rose put her arms around his neck, her blue diamond engagement ring sparkling like Jack's eyes whenever he kissed her.

"I'm fine with keeping the romance going. In fact, I've decided you should carry me through every doorway, no matter where we are."

"Close your eyes."

"Why?"

"Because I asked you to."

"Fair enough," Rose conceded. "But if you would just kiss me, I'd automatically close my eyes."

"You've been known to keep your eyes open." Jack loved their verbal sparring but right now, he needed her to do what he'd asked. "Promise not to peek?"

Rose's lips hovered next to his. "Promise."

Jack's kisses always made her head spin; this time was no exception. She was so lost in the feelings he aroused that she hadn't realized he'd moved from the doorway until he sat her down on a hard, wooden surface.

"Eyes closed," he reminded her.

Rose didn't have to look to know what Jack's surprise was. She'd spent too many hours sitting on benches just like this one not to recognize what it was. Unable to stay still, she bounced with excitement. Jack had bought her a piano.

"Ready? Okay, open up."

Rose's eyes popped open, her fingers already reaching for the keys. What she saw made her freeze.

"Jack," she breathed. It couldn't be. "I don't understand."

It was his mother's piano. So beautiful and dear that Rose couldn't bring herself to touch it for fear it would melt away like in a dream.

Jack sat beside her, pulling her close. Seeing the stunned look on her face, he explained. "The family voted, unanimously, by the way.

Everyone agreed the piano belonged with the person who would appreciate it the most. They all thought it would be a nice surprise to have it waiting when we got back."

Rose carefully ran her hand over the smooth surface. "But your mother loves it so much, she should wait and give it to Stella or another member of the—"

"Family?" Jack finished for her. He gently wiped away the tears that ran freely down her cheeks.

Rose laid her head on Jack's shoulder and knew that she was home.

TURN THE PAGE FOR AN
EXCLUSIVE PREVIEW OF
BOOK TWO IN THE
HARPER FALLS SAGA

If Tomorrow Never Comes

Chapter One

FOURTH OF JULY in Harper Falls was much like it was in cities and towns all over the United States. A large crowd gathered every year at Riverside Park for picnics and games. People came and went throughout the day, but everyone made sure they were there when the annual fireworks display was set off. Even though the bursting lights could be seen for miles around, most people preferred to pack together and watch them with their friends and neighbors.

Dani could remember coming here as a little girl and impatiently feeling like it would never get dark. The one time during summer vacation that she wished the sun wound go down early. Eventually, the time would arrive and her father would hoist her onto his shoulders so that she could be just a little bit closer to the colorful lights. Then her mother and brother would gather close so that they could enjoy the display together. She eventually grew too old to sit on her father's shoulders. And though she and her brother would spend all day running around with their friends, when it grew dark, they always found their way back to their parents so they could watch the fireworks as a family.

One of the things she'd missed most when she left for college and a career away from Harper Falls was this — coming to the park with her mother and father. She'd even missed her annoying brother Caleb though she had to admit he was much easier to get along with now that they didn't have to share a bathroom.

As Dani searched the crowd, it didn't take her long to find her father. As usual, he manned one of the propane barbeques that the city set up every year. For a few dollars, anyone could buy a huge plate of food. It consisted of tender pork ribs, potato salad, and corn on the cob dripping with butter. And a piece of chocolate sheet cake personally made by Dani's mother and topped with a thick layer of her famous caramel frosting. People bought tickets weeks in advance for the dessert alone.

When she and her friends returned home almost two years ago, Dani wondered if the Fourth of July celebration would possibly be able to live up to her memories. She shouldn't have worried. There were minor changes but nothing worth mentioning. Familiar faces mingled happily with newcomers. Her family still gathered when it got dark. Now the family included Caleb's wife and two children. Changes, but good ones.

Changes affected her little circle as well. Oh, Rose and Tyler were still the best friends she could ever hope for. But Rose was now madly in love and engaged to be married. Dani was thrilled and she couldn't have picked a better man than Jack Winston. It was obvious to anyone who looked at them that he adored her. And that meant Dani and Tyler were more than happy to expand their circle to fit another member.

Deciding to give her skin a break from the afternoon sun, Dani found a relatively deserted place under one of the park's many shade trees. She leaned back and closed her eyes, concentrating on muting the noises around her. As a result, she was able to bring the din of the crowd down to a gentle roar. Then suddenly the rumbling of a motorcycle pulling into the nearby parking lot broke the spell. Nothing was gentle about that noise.

Dani lifted one eyelid to get a peek at the new arrival. Motorcycles weren't unheard of at the picnic, but most people tended to come in groups of friends and family. There were trucks, mini-vans, and even a few RVs. The mode of transportation wasn't unusual, yet that the driver had arrived alone was.

From where she sat, the rider looked to be tall and well built. A helmet covered his head, but as he removed his leather jacket, she could see that under his black t-shirt were well-muscled arms and a flat stomach. Nice butt too. His faded jeans showed off long legs that Dani imagined were as muscled as the rest of him. As he unbuckled the strap under his chin, she sat up a little straighter. If his face was even a fraction as good as the rest of him, Dani was ready to be a welcoming party of one.

The man removed his helmet revealing thick, longish dark hair, slightly damp with sweat and having a tendency to curl. Better and better, she smiled. Then as he turned towards her, Dani froze, certain her eyes were playing tricks on her. Five years later and covered in a shaggy beard, that face was still as familiar to her as if she had seen it yesterday. She felt a burst of joy overtake her body. She jumped to her feet, ready to welcome him with open arms. Before she could move, someone beat her to it.

"Alex!" A curvy brunette burst from the crowd and threw herself at the man. He laughed and caught her in his arms with ease, as though he'd done it a hundred times before.

Dani felt as if her heart was being ripped from her chest. He hadn't come for her. The ridiculous fantasy that she had held onto all these years was just that — ridiculous. As she watched Alex look down at the woman in his arms with what any fool could see was love, she felt the last bit of hope slip away forever.

About the Author

MARY J. WILLIAMS lives in Eastern Washington just like the characters in her books. Harper Falls is fictitious, but many of the aspects of small town life mirror her hometown. *If I Loved You* is the culmination of a longtime dream and now that it has become a reality, she plans on writing many more. Please visit Mary's website at maryjwilliams.net. If you would like to ask a question or just say hello you can contact her at mary@maryjwilliams.net.